The Schönbuch Forest

R.J. Goddard

Bright Pen

Visit us online at www.authorsonline.co.uk

A Bright Pen Book

ISBN 0 7552 1045 X

Authors OnLine Ltd
19 The Cinques
Gamlingay, Sandy
Bedfordshire SG19 3NU
England

This book is also available in e-book format, details of
which are available at www.authorsonline.co.uk

I would like to gratefully thank Hans Mayer for his kind permission to use information contained in his book, "Das Soldatengrab im Schönbuch." It was, in part, this book which inspired me to write the novel.

This book is dedicated to my wife, Martina Goddard, who encouraged me to write the story in the first place. Like so many people, Tina can not always see the wood for the trees. The book is also dedicated to Martina's maternal grandfather, Josef Felbinger, reported missing somewhere in Russia in 1943.

Author's note

This book is a work of fiction. However, the towns of Herrenberg and Hildrizhausen, the Schönbuch Forest and the soldier's grave exist. Furthermore, I was initially inspired to write the book by events which happened in the forest in 1945 and which are recorded in, "Das Soldatengrab im Schönbuch," by Hans Mayer.

Woher die Dinge ihre Enstehung haben, dahin müssen sie auch zugrunde gehen, nach der Notwendigkeit.

According to necessity, where things come into being, so they must also go to earth.

Document 1

My dearest Bub

Today I received two letters from you. Unfortunately you did not get your birthday parcel. Mathilde packed it especially for you, but it must have got lost. With all this bombing around us, I am not surprised. What a pity this is. There were so many good things in the parcel. I would love to send it to you again, but it is probably lost forever. Did you receive the ration card?

Today your aunt and your sister sent letters to you. I hope they arrive, and you will see that we are all thinking about you. Any day now Bub, you will be a father too. Mathilde is well, and we are all prepared. Perhaps when the child is born, we will be at peace once again. Let us pray that it is all over soon. May God look after you, my son, and may He protect your child from harm.

Unfortunately you do not get any leave, and we would love to visit you, but it is too dangerous. Frau Wenck tells us that Nordheim was very badly bombed, and the railway there is all but destroyed. I can easily believe that repairing this is very hard work. How I wish you were at home. I am sure that a couple of days with us all would do you the world of good. I would make you so many good things to eat. Let us hope that you come home soon. Don't forget to write, but don't worry about us. We get a lot of day workers for work on the farm.

Emil has written to you today, and Paul wants to write to you with his new address. I think he posted a letter today. So my beloved Bub - I hope you get the parcel. Do try to eat well, and may God always be with you to love and protect you.

With all my love

Mum.

Chapter 1

Berkshire, England. November 1999

My mother admired the English and loved their sense of humour even though she guessed it was a shield for unacceptable emotions. Sitting in the doctor's surgery, I wondered whether I was the victim of black humour or a practical joke. This was one of a series of thoughts that passed in rapid succession through my head when he told me the news. I opened my mouth to protest but managed only a string of sounds before articulating, "I don't understand."

The doctor was a small round man in a tweed jacket and sensible brown shoes. It was easy to imagine his fleshy face vibrating with laughter over a pint in one of the local country pubs. That morning, his face remained impassive, and the eyes that looked into mine had not a hint of humour in them.

"It was quite sudden," he said, "but not unexpected."

I felt myself backing away from him as if from a swinging fist.

"No," I said.

My voice sounded strange. Its tone was unfamiliar and appeared to come from a great distance. I rubbed at my eyes and forehead to ensure I was connected to the world. Leaning heavily against the chair back, I repeated what I had said before. This time, I almost shouted the word. It was a useless attempt to drown out the note of doubt that had crept into my tone.

"No."

I wanted to correct the doctor's foolishness. I wanted to tell him that a mistake had been made. Relentlessly, he carried on with his task.

"It was a heart condition," he said.

My right leg twitched, and beads of moisture pricked at my skin. Then I went cold.

"Condition?"

The doctor's eyes studied mine. The shadow of some emotion of his own touched his face. The surgery was charged with feeling.

"That's right," he said, "a heart condition. She had suffered from it for ten years."

I stared at the elbow patches on the doctor's tweed jacket while rebellion and rejection bounced around inside me like a pinball.

"How could she do that?" I said, perhaps more loudly than I had intended.

The doctor flinched though he did not turn his eyes from mine.

"Do what?"

I leaned forward and breathed deeply. Bringing my hand to my mouth, I pressed at my lips with my knuckles. I swallowed, closed my eyes for a second, and then relaxed. The doctor chose this time to jump in with a reassuring tone.

"It could have happened at any time," he said. "She was living with a time bomb."

He was searching my face for a reaction. My lips formed words while I tried to articulate what I was thinking.

"But why ...?"

Before the question was out, I knew the answer. My mother may have been ill for ten years but, as with all things unacceptable, she managed to file the illness away, and in a very real sense, it ceased to exist for her. The doctor leaned back in his chair and, lowering his chin onto his chest, he raised his eyes to mine.

"Why didn't she tell you? Is this what you want to know?"

I started as the telephone squealed. I felt resentment that a unique time should be interrupted like this. The outside world had no right to interfere with its trivia. The doctor's jacket stretched alarmingly over his shoulders as he leaned forward to pick up the phone. He muttered rapidly into the mouthpiece and replaced the handset. Glancing at his watch, he rubbed his forehead and sighed.

"Your mother was a strong and brave woman," he said. "She wanted to keep you from worrying. It was enough that she had to live with it. She felt she had no right to burden others with her problems."

I stared back at him, wondering how long he had given me. Five minutes? Ten? I caught sight of the eye-test card behind his head. It was then that I realised my eyes were filled with tears.

"But I was her son," I shouted, looking vainly around the room for support.

The doctor said nothing while I tried to come to terms with my mother's secret. I was mouthing silently while tears rolled down my cheeks. All my emotions seemed to distil into one of rejection and betrayal. This distillation was like a blow to the stomach. How could she have lived with death and told this doctor without telling me? Bending forward, I put my elbows on my knees and let my head fall into waiting hands. A tear rolled off my chin and dropped to the floor.

"It's so unfair," I muttered.

The doctor remained silent. Then his chair creaked, and a few seconds later his sensible brown shoes appeared at my feet and crushed my tears into the carpet. I felt the pressure of his hand on my shoulder blade. I turned my head towards his. I had a need to ask him a question to which I was sure he would not know the answer. This was my secret.

"Did she ever tell you," I said, "that she was German?"

*

Over the following weeks, I came to recognise two levels of reaction to mother's death. The first was an inner layer, a core of feeling with a wound so strong that I was unable to confront it. The outer layer was a protective scab, a cushion which convinced me the loss was only temporary. For longer than I realised, I lived suspended between these two levels while the inner wound healed.

When I started rummaging through mother's belongings, I expected her to turn up at the front door to explain where she had been and why she had not told me about her illness. It was when I flicked through her photograph albums that I wondered what other aspects of her life she had kept in the dark. What struck me was that her existence had started in 1945, which in a sense it had, because that was when she was born. But most of us have some kind of past before that. Not mother. Before 1945 there was nothing. There were no photos of uncles, aunts, sisters, brothers, or grandparents. There were simply empty pages, a deep black hole.

I had always assumed that it was the holocaust and shame that forced my mother to reject her German roots. The curtness of the comments she made on her German parentage discouraged further enquiry, especially when I was busy growing up. Fortune had smiled upon her, she once said, the day she was brought to live in England. I simply accepted events as she told them. Her death was, therefore, a trigger - a release. It was a release from restraint, and I was free to peer into that deep black hole and find the hidden German half of my self.

My father disappeared from our life before I was old enough to associate people and faces with times or places. I was unable to remember him, and mother was able to file him away. The father issue became a forbidden area. I had to wait until I was eighteen before mother told me in her tight-lipped way that father had eloped with a neighbour when I was four. She thought he and his lover had gone to Australia.

The crucial point for me was that father's disappearance freed mother from all balances, and she created me in her own image. I never really questioned the life she had planned out for me. There was a framed photo on her bedroom wall. It showed my school rugby team for 1987. I was the stretched adolescent standing in the back row. It was only the second fifteen, but it was enough for my mother. She was proud that her son should be involved in this example of Anglo-Saxon values. Nothing distinguished me from the other fourteen team members. We were all staring with steely glint in eye straight at the camera. In my case, the glint had been compensation for my delicate frame, while the full-face shot was my attempt to hide my long and pointed nose.

Nor did anything distinguish me from the people who had taught me. They did such a good job, that when I fulfilled my mother's ambitions and became a history master at my old school, I simply filled my ex-teachers' shoes. The only thing which had changed was my nickname. Word had got around that I still lived at home, and I was forced once again to put the steely glint in my eye and turn my back on the giggles and whispers of "mother's boy" that followed me whenever I appeared in the school corridors.

My mother was delighted that I would carry on a tradition and teach all the right things, that is, the things that had moulded her. According to my mother and me, the peaks of human progress were Anglo-Saxon democracy, the rule of law and the tradition of the Magna Carta. The hallmarks of the free world were the Market Economy and Capitalism. The Second World War was, for us both, a struggle between good and evil. Those who opposed Fascism were worthy of unreserved respect. This meant that the Serbs and the Czechs were brave, friendly and democratic. The Slovaks, Croats and Baltic nations, who we thought to have collaborated with the Fascists, were somehow flawed.

It never occurred to me to question mother's opinion until extreme forms of nationalism came out of Serbia, and the Baltic States started to develop as truly European nations. By the time my mother died, I was seriously questioning what I was doing in the classroom.

The really important discovery came several hours before the funeral when I stumbled on the letters. I was not expecting to find anything when I stepped onto the ladder and pushed at the hatchway that led into the attic. The hatchway was resistant, and I had to push hard to break several layers of paint that sealed it. With one final effort, it cracked open. An explosion of dust forced me to lower my head, and flaky white paint settled like snow on my hands and arms. Taking a step further up the ladder, I poked my head through the hatchway. A needle-thin ray of sunlight pierced the roof.

I waited for my eyes to accustom themselves to the darkness, and my nostrils twitched at the odour. It was the musty old smell that often comes from the yellow and airless pages of books which have lain unopened for years. And with the odour, the shape of a trunk gradually emerged as a shadow in the darkness. The trunk lay like a mummy's tomb in the centre of the attic. I clambered down the ladder and ran into the kitchen to collect a pencil-torch. With the torch held tightly between clenched teeth, I pulled myself back up the ladder. Feeling like a pirate intent on plundering a treasure chest, I peered again through the hatchway. A cloud must have passed across the sun, for the needle of sunlight had gone, and the shadow of the trunk seemed to have been swallowed up in the darkness. But its odour of oldness still seeped out as a reminder of the unseen presence of time past.

I hauled myself into the attic. At first, I stumbled in the blackness, and the hand that held the torch was trembling. I found the torch switch with the flesh of my thumb, and a beam of light flared and shone out like a burning crucifix as it struck a metallic catch. The trunk was within an arm's reach, but my feet were rooted to the floor and reluctant to move. I took a hesitant step forward and, dropping to my knees, I positioned myself in readiness to slam the trunk shut in case some evil genie should jump out. I gingerly flicked back the catches and slowly opened the trunk.

My fears were groundless. The trunk contained nothing but one old photograph and a bundle of letters tied up with a ribbon. The photograph showed my mother as a young woman. There was no mistaking the blonde and curling hair, the softly delicate skin and, despite the faded black and white of the photo, there was no mistaking the bright and fiercely determined eyes. The photo also showed a young man. I knew at once that it was my father. As a very young child I must have looked up into his face countless times. I could not say that I recalled the face, but it sharply brought to mind an emotional response to some place or incident in the past. Although the places or the events were forgotten, the feelings they had evoked were still there, wandering like a ghost in the memory.

The couple sat hand in hand and smiled at the camera. Love and happiness shone from their eyes, through the light of the torch, and touched my heart. There was something about them that suggested the couple would have a bright future. It saddened me when I thought that their bright future should end here in the darkness of an attic.

The letters could only have been mother's. Nobody else I knew would have folded them so neatly that not one edge of paper was out of place. This reminder of her character was so strong that I was already closing the trunk when I realised that the letters were mine. It was with great respect for my mother's memory that I carefully unfolded the top letter and scanned it with my torch. The letter was dated November 1965, and under the date was the name of a place that could have been German, Hildrizhausen. Still on my knees, I placed the letter on the floor to read it.

Dear Mrs Slater

Thank you for your letter and your enquiry regarding Martin Spohr. Let me say at once that although you have written to Father Paul Fischer, I must inform you that I, his son, opened the letter because my father passed away last year. Let me please apologise for my poor English. We do not often have the opportunity to speak English here in the parish of Hildrizhausen. I will do my best.

So, I have put three documents concerning Martin Spohr in this envelope. You may find them interesting. Once again, I have tried to translate them into English as best as I am able. The first document, Document 1, was a letter found in 1945. We believe it was the last letter written to Martin Spohr by his mother and was received by him shortly before his death.

The second document is more difficult to explain. It seems that on 25 April 1945, seven dead soldiers were brought to the parish church of Hildrizhausen. The priest at that time was my father, Paul Fischer (1884-1964). He reported the event first to the authorities and later in his unpublished "Hildrizhausen and the Nazi Times."

It would seem that two of the soldiers had embraced each other and died wrapped in the arms of the other. Near them, a coat and an identity card (soldbuch) were found. In the soldbuch we found the letter (Document 1). The coat and the soldbuch belonged to a Martin Spohr. However, it soon became unclear whether either of the dead men was, in fact, Martin Spohr. The following (Document 2) is a translation of extracts from my father's 1945 report and the later history.

Document 3 is simply a letter written to my father in the fifties. I have enclosed it because it will show you how important Martin Spohr has become for us in this community and in Germany as a whole. He has given much comfort to so many different people.

Please do contact me again if you have any further

questions. There are more letters and documents relating to Martin Spohr but they are all written in German.

I remain, yours sincerely

Hugo Fischer.

I looked again at the date and made a quick calculation. My mother must have been twenty when she received it. Thank you for your letter, the priest had written. My mother had obviously not cut herself off from her German past as completely as she had wanted me to believe. And who was Martin Spohr? I passed the torch beam across my watch and started. Time was moving on. I could not be late for my own mother's funeral. I slipped the letters back into the trunk and dropped my feet through the hatchway to the ladder below. A good deal of dust came down with me and it rose in a breeze that came up through an open downstairs window.

*

The vicar, a few friends and I buried my mother in Barnfield Parish church that morning of 11 November 1999. She would have approved of the Saxon church with its long-since forgotten but well-tended graves. The anonymity of the place and its historical tradition would have appealed to her. During the service, I was hoping and half-expecting to see some new faces, faces from her past, faces from the other half of me. I hoped in vain. My mother had made no room for them in the life she had created for herself. There were only her friends from the Bridge Club. Certainly my mother would have approved of their presence. They were all so frightfully sorry to ask and they hoped I did not mind them asking but did she suffer? Nobody cried. Stiff upper lips were the order of the day. My mother would have loved it.

Ashes to ashes. As the coffin was lowered, and I gazed at the mourners, it slowly dawned on me that we were all just mirrors in which my mother saw her self reflected back at her. She had ruthlessly created her own identity, and we at the funeral merely confirmed her success.

And dust to dust. The first handfuls of earth fell on the coffin lid, and I was unable to suppress another and stronger burst of resentment. I felt guilt too, guilt that this resentment should come on the day of her burial. But guilt or no guilt, I had to recognise and accept the stirrings of rebellion. My mother had created me in her image in the same way that Doctor Frankenstein had created his monster. My purpose had been to mirror and to confirm her identity. My head span with increasing resentment and guilt, and feeling trapped and claustrophobic, I took several deep breaths and tried to persuade myself that it was not me who was being interred.

After the service, I told everyone that I wanted to be alone. I had the strange sensation of wanting to be anywhere but where I was. I just had to escape from my own skin. I ran back to the house with the devil himself behind me. It may have been my imagination, but I was sure I heard a shout from behind. I did not look back. I kept on running, but I could not run fast enough. My legs felt the heaviness of a bad dream. I did not turn until I reached the front gate. I stopped to catch my breath and with feelings of dread I glanced behind me. There was no sign of any pursuer.

Breathing heavily I let myself into the house. I had not planned it, but I went immediately to the attic. I pushed at the hatchway, and there was no pressure this time. It opened easily and invited me to look inside. I knelt down in the darkness and dreamed for a while in the emptiness. I sat on my haunches with the hum of silence in my ears and with the growing realisation that this dark and dusty attic was the place in which my mother had filed away the unacceptable.

I took a deep breath and threw the trunk open. I was not thinking of evil genies when I put my hand inside. I simply removed the bundle of letters and took them downstairs so that I could read them in the light of day.

Document 2

Parish of Hildrizhausen, 02.05.1945

On 25 April 1945, towards 8 o'clock in the evening, seven bodies were brought in. Along with one of the bodies was an Iron Cross and a wound medal. Was this soldier called Altner? On his ring was inscribed H.A. and the number 327. He also had three pens, a pair of clean socks, a knife and fork, and a photo of a woman and children. The body had a wound in the stomach and was found together with a friend. Both had probably been wounded on 19 April, and between four and six in the afternoon when the French came into the wood. We can only speculate but they must have helped and comforted each other, and waited to die. On Altner's face was a smile. The exact time of death was not really known.

On the 26 April two more dead soldiers were brought in, and we buried all of the dead together in a communal grave. We left Altner and his friend as they were found – each in the arms of the other. We read from Apostles 1: 13.

We tried to inform Altner's relatives in the usual way. On Wednesday 2 May, the father, Peter Altner, came to Hildrizhausen to identify his son. Johann Altner had been a bricklayer in civilian life, and his wife was called Helen. They lived in Reutlingen. Of Peter's three sons, one was already missing, and the other was known to be in a prisoner of war camp somewhere in Russia.

We still did not know who the other dead man was. He also had a bayonet wound to the stomach, and his tunic was heavily soaked in blood. In addition, he had a severe grenade wound to the buttock. All we knew was that Martin Spohr's identity book (soldbuch) and greatcoat were next to him. From the soldbuch we learned that Martin Spohr was, until recently, a schoolboy. He was a Catholic, and he was born on 13 February 1926. His eyes were said to be brown, and his hair dark brown. His face was described as round, and his height as 1, 78. We knew he was from Ostheim, that his father's name was Andreas, and his mother was Rosa nee Bauer. In Martin's soldbuch was a letter from his mother, and from this, we learned the address of the parents.

However, it did not seem that Johann Altner's friend was, in fact, Martin Spohr. The identity number on the dead man's disk was 1524, whereas the identity number in Spohr's soldbuch was given as 3333. Furthermore, the photograph in the soldbuch did not look like the soldier embraced by Johann Altner. Moreover, the wound stripe and the Iron Cross were not mentioned in Martin's soldbuch. It was one year later that the dead man was finally identified as Walter Kleine. So, the problem remained - who was Martin Spohr, and what had happened to him?

Chapter 2

The luggage trolley and I were helped through the swing doors of Terminal 2 by a blast of cold winter air that contained the force and the bellow of an enraged bull. Welcome to Heathrow the sign read. Welcome to the timeless zone I muttered.

I struggled with the trolley down the grey plastic tube that finally ejected me at departures. Surrendering my belongings at the check-in desk, I felt a familiar numbness settling on my consciousness. I knew this to be the first of a series of symptoms which might later develop into fully-blown lifelessness and apathy. It was a condition that often afflicted me on becoming a creature in transit.

I replied to the routine questions like an automaton. Yes, I had packed the bags myself and no, nobody had given me anything to take. Even as I answered, a residual awareness seemed to whisper in my ear: *There was nobody else to pack the bags for you. Nobody knows where you are or where you are going, right?*

The feeling of being disconnected was reinforced in the overheated departure lounge. In the fake pub, I was served by young people of uncertain origin who could easily have been stateless refugees forced to work in this nowhere zone. I drank my coffee and watched the other waiting passengers. I wondered if they felt as disassociated as I did. They had all temporarily given up secure connections with home and they had yet to arrive at those places where they could unpack their belongings and stake out a piece of territory for themselves. Neither in one place nor another, they were suspended in space. They left a trail of nervous anticipation behind them.

By the time I approached the departure gate, I was moving mechanically. There was a little boy some way in front of me. When he reached the gate, the boy turned and briefly looked at me. Then he ran into the sloping corridor that led into the plane.

Where the child had vanished, a woman appeared. Upright and proud, she was walking with the measured steps of a queen. She never looked my way, but I recognised her immediately in the beating of my heart. I shook my head, and as my brain flashed temporarily back to life, the woman disappeared like an airy vision.

I knew then that I still had not come to terms with the permanence of my mother's death. At the airport I must have dropped my defences, but that protective scab, the cushion that convinced me her loss was only temporary, was still operating. I was constantly expecting her to turn up, and there she was at the departure gate to see me off.

*

From the moment we took off, it was clear that on the short trip to Stuttgart we were going to experience turbulence. We bumped and shook in and out of dark, billowing clouds that dumped enormous quantities of water on the wings. Most of my fellow passengers appeared unnaturally relaxed. Some had severely strained faces. My travelling companion, a German of about my own age, was taking in gulps of air and blowing out noisily through his mouth. He sounded as though he was preparing for a hundred metre sprint. His agitation soon made him talkative. In a rapid and high-pitched voice, he asked me where I was going. When I told him, he seemed puzzled.

"Why Herrenberg?"

"I've got an appointment with the priest in a village nearby - Hildrizhausen - know it?"

A look of alarm spread itself across his features. Perhaps the association of priests with death was too much for him.

"The priest?"

"Yes," I said. "He has some information about my family. My mother was German. She came to England soon after the war."

At the mention of the war, a glazed look appeared in my companion's eyes. The plane bumped and shook, and my friend's hands gripped at his arm rest. His fear of death somehow highlighted the indifference I felt towards my own fate. I knew this indifference was connected to my mother's passing. I had no family, no wife and no girl friend. I was absolutely alone. In the event of my death, there was nobody who would grieve for me. I was not unduly worried about this. What saddened me was the thought that there was nobody to whom I would have to apologise for dying. My companion evidently had someone waiting for him at home. He was breathing noisily again.

"I'm hoping to do some skiing in the south," I said.

"Ah, skiing" he said, and then started a monologue on the best resorts and the merits of each. I was content to let him talk without interruption and I politely listened for half an hour until the engine note changed. The plane banked and then dropped through the storm clouds.

Far below, and shrouded under a soft mist, a forest stretched upwards as though it would touch us. Still, dark and ever green, the forest reached out its tentacles and held villages and towns in its grip. From our height, the roads were shoe laces that wound away from the edges of the towns and trailed away into the trees. Here and there, the light glinted on the foaming water of streams that rushed and tumbled and plunged silently into the undergrowth. I turned to my companion.

"That forest," I said, "down there. Is it the Black Forest?"

He leaned over, smiled a strained smile, and pointed over his shoulder.

"The Black Forest is in another direction."

"So …?

"This must be the Schönbuch. Yes, the Schönbuch Forest."

At that moment the plane lurched. The pilot's voice came over the intercom. The tone was calm and soothing.

"Ladies and gentlemen, in about ten minutes we shall be landing at Stuttgart. We'll try to avoid the black fluffy stuff you can see outside, but at some stage we have to point the plane at the runway. Since you may experience some turbulence, we recommend that you return to your seats and keep your safety belts securely fastened."

I smiled at my companion, pulled my belt even tighter, and waited for a bumpy landing.

Document 2

After the war, (1947), a soldier's grave was found in Goldbachtal in the Schönbuch. It was about one kilometre from Neuebrücke. The name Martin Spohr was inscribed on the cross. The inscription was fast disappearing because of the weather. In fact, the site itself had become so overgrown that it was only by luck that it was found at all. We can only speculate but it seems that Martin and his friends were in the forest when Martin was wounded. He probably threw away or dropped his soldbuch and greatcoat before he died. His companions, among whom were Walter Kleine and Johann Altner, buried him before hurrying away. They must have taken Martin's coat and soldbuch with them.

I wrote to Martin's family in December 1945, and in January 1946 Martin's uncle came to look at the soldbuch. He told us that since 1942, Martin's father had been reported missing somewhere in Russia. We also learned that Martin's young wife and mother had been killed. Apparently they used to stand outside the house every day in the hope that they would see Martin returning from the war. They were waiting there and killed one day by refusing to go into the shelter when the bombers came. All the other members of Martin's family had fled before the advancing Russians, and he did not know where they were. Martin's young daughter was in the care of British Army authorities.

The uncle was extremely persistent. He told us that he was not investigating for himself. He was doing it for Martin Spohr's child. One day, he said, she would want to know what had happened to her father. In August 1947, the uncle tracked down the original report about the two embraced soldiers. More information was hard to get, but he started looking for a grave in the Schönbuch Forest because Martin's last letter came from that area. In November 1947, a forester told him about a soldier's grave in Goldbachtal. In January 1948 the uncle went into the wood and found a cross and a helmet. The name Spohr was written inside it along with the number, 3333. This was the number that was written in Martin Spohr's soldbuch. We never saw Martin's uncle again.

Chapter 3

Herrenberg. 22 December 1999. Afternoon

The tightly spiralling staircase was lightless and claustrophobic, and I took the steps two at a time. I guessed the narrow confines were even darker for those who were descending. With their vision temporarily impaired by the glare on the church tower's balcony, these people were unable to see clearly and they brushed roughly past. To me they were as unattractive as muttering strangers glimpsed at night along a lonely street. Occasionally, I turned to follow their vague shapes as they stepped nervously downwards. Nobody apologised for walking into me, and I wondered what I had done to irritate them.

There was another visitor ahead. The even and decisive footsteps sounded loudly in the church tower, and they were undoubtedly masculine. I expected to see his heels on the stone steps in front of me, but he was always several twists of the staircase out of sight. At the top of the steps, I stopped to catch my breath before pushing through a doorway and entering the bell tower. It was a chaos of dust-coated beams. They rose from the floor and criss-crossed beneath the ceiling. Hanging below the beams, a bewildering variety of bells bore witness both to the medieval origins of the church and its role in time present. For hundreds of years these bells had rung out the old and rung in the new. For the time being, they were hanging in breathless anticipation.

I was looking for any obvious way through the chaos to the balcony when the echo of the other man's footsteps reached out to me as they pounded over the wooden floorboards. Only when I caught a glimpse of him, reflected and distorted in the surface of a new bell, did I hurry on in pursuit. I ducked and wove my way forward, and by luck, I saw his feet disappearing up some wooden steps.

He pushed at the balcony door and stood on the threshold, and I was at last able to settle my eyes upon him. Having emerged from the semi-darkness of the bell tower, he appeared as a shimmering silhouette against the light of the setting sun. The silhouette was of medium height and lean, but when the sun sank and its rays were snuffed out, the man emerged. He was about seventy, and elegant in an old-fashioned way. He wore a brown jacket with double pleats, and the hands, held tightly but butterfly-fashion behind his back, suggested a military background.

His head flicked sideways like the head of an animal catching scent of the hunter. He slowly twisted from the waist and, turning to face me, he pulled back his shoulders and thrust out his chest. The hair was cut and combed with extreme precision, but it was so fine that it looked like a film of cobwebs through which his scalp was visible. His face was thin and dominated by a pointed nose. He lifted his chin and closing one eye, he aimed the other along his nose in such a way that suggested he was looking at me down the sights of a rifle. Embarrassed by this intrusive eye, I shifted my attention to my feet. They seemed to have developed a life of their own, and I gazed at them in surprise. While they shuffled in discomfort, I heard the crackle of the man's shoes swivelling on concrete before he took a pace forward. He must have moved quickly, for when I looked up, he had disappeared from view.

A few steps later, I was myself at the door and on the threshold of an exposed and narrow balcony that skirted the church tower. From the corner of my eye, I saw the old man, his double pleats now flapping in the breeze. What really grabbed for my attention was the snapshot of life far below me in the marketplace. People were shutting windows, chattering in the square, hurrying home with shopping baskets, or riding down the main street on bicycles. It was a picture of transient busyness in an enchanted place, a topsy-turvy world of beamed walls, crooked roofs and chimney pots. I had entered a world charged with the magic of childhood stories, and it would have been no surprise to see witches flying about as the stuff of everyday life.

Beyond the ruins of the town walls, the main road to Stuttgart and Tübingen was clearly visible as a paper chain of red and white car lamps. On the edge of the old town was a large area, almost as big as Herrenberg, which I took to be a car dealership. Models of many different colours stood in rows and glinted in the light of the Mercedes star which shone proudly over them.

The military man had raised his hand to shield his eyes. Scanning the hills towards Tübingen, he was nodding to himself, and I heard him muttering and mumbling as if carrying on a conversation with someone at his side. Then, turning his face in profile, he aimed his nose at the Schlossberg. Beyond the crenellated walls of this ruined hilltop castle, an avenue of beech marked the entrance to the Schönbuch Forest.

My face was touched by a light wind that gusted away into the trees. There was a flutter of movement, and a sound, deep and distant, like the echo of faraway thunder. I turned my eyes to the forest. In my entranced state, I was half expecting to see elves and pixies dancing and playing to the light of the rising moon. The trees in the forest heaved and creaked as they caught a stronger gust of wind, and looking upwards, I saw buzzards circling in pairs. I must have closed my eyes for a second. When I opened them again, the light had faded still further, and the scene below had altered.

The cyclists had gone, the windows were cleaned and the conversations finished. I leaned against the balcony rail and held myself quiet so that I could listen to that distant echo of thunder. I caught only a murmuring silence. I had not heard any other movement so I was surprised to see that the old man had gone. I gingerly peered over the balcony to the paving below. I wondered whether there had been some undertone of sadness in the man's mutterings or whether there had been something desperate and haunted in his eyes that suggested he would take his own life. I shook my head. I had not come to Germany to get involved with the sadness of an old man.

The breeze, that was picking up from the west, suggested an advancing storm. I pulled my coat close about me. Angry clouds were packed down on the horizon, and the sun had left a dull red glow between them. Below, the Christmas lights sparkled under the eaves of the crooked houses that flanked the market square. The lights cast an eerie and unearthly glow on the old snow that had been neatly swept and packed in the corners of the marketplace. But I saw no witches.

I clattered down the twisting staircase and out into the vestibule. Stopping to enjoy the sweet smell of old stone, I closed my eyes to the damp coolness that radiated from the walls and touched my cheeks. I was heading for the exit when curiosity stopped me dead in my tracks. It was not the church's medieval architecture but the sound of shuffling feet that reached out like a hand and placed itself on my chest.

I peered along the aisle to the place where the altar rose dark against the darkness. To one side of it, shadows flickered and danced to the light of candles. In front of them, stood the old man. His hands were folded over his stomach, and his head was lowered in prayer. Perhaps it had been the meeting of our eyes on the bell tower steps, but this man and I had forged a relationship. It was respect for this bond, and his prayers, that prompted me to push gently at the heavy doors and to tiptoe through them into the gathering darkness of mid-winter.

My hotel, Haus Kirchgasse, nestled at the foot of the long flight of steps, which fell away in front of me. Lamps were burning low in the hotel windows, and shadows arched over the ceiling of the interior. I shivered as a gust of wind cut through my coat. The hotel was suddenly inviting. I was half-way down the steps when I felt self-conscious, aware that someone was watching me. I span round. The church tower grew naturally from the top step as if both had been hewn from the same block of stone. The tower rose majestically heavenwards, and balanced on the top of it was a golden and almost oriental dome that looked like an onion and seemed to retain the glow of the setting sun.

I let my gaze fall from the dome, to the balcony, to the bricked-in windows, to the gargoyles, and then to the old man framed in the church doorway. He stood still, but his head was angled upwards and swivelling slowly like the head of a hunting dog sniffing at the air. In a movement that reminded me of a clockwork toy, he threw one arm forward and marched down the steps behind me. I walked on in front of him, but the sound of his feet clicking on the marble was an out of place and out of time echo of my own steps, and I found it unsettling.

Then, I heard low and murmuring voices. Their suggestion of sweet tobacco and idle fireside talk on a winter afternoon encouraged me to hurry down to the hotel. Rushing through the entrance, I collected my room key and made my way up the stairs to my room.

It was four-thirty. The day was dying, and the evening had yet to begin. In that dreary interval, morbid thoughts appeared uninvited in my head. I walked around the room for a while, trying to keep one step ahead of thoughts about my mother. Eventually, I switched on the television, sat on the bed and flicked through innumerable channels. I stopped at a local channel on which an interview was taking place. It was the appearance of the interviewee that struck me. He was a man of about seventy years of age with long and white hair. Swept back from the forehead and temples, the hair lay thick, rich and curling like a lion's mane over the nape of the neck. His face carried with pride an aquiline nose, which competed with a strong and aggressive chin for my attention. Tufts of hair sprouted like grasses from his ears and nostrils, and the skin of his face appeared to be stained with brown ink. Occasionally, he would cock his head to one side. This movement interrupted his flow of eloquence as his mind and his words turned in another direction. Despite his advanced age, the eyes were piercing and they burned a single and irresistible passion.

When the interview was over, I lay down on the bed and, staring at the ceiling, I half-heartedly fought off a wave of tiredness. Below, the front door slammed, and then I drifted into a light sleep and dreamed a dream.

I was floating just above the mattress and I saw my mother standing in the market square with a cap that disguised her features. I wanted to ask her something and I walked forward trying to approach her, but the square was filled with people, and I could not reach her or make her hear me. I was uncomfortably aware that although I knew what I wanted to ask, I did not have the words to express it.

I awoke breathless and panicky. It was pitch dark, and I had no idea where I was. Fumbling for a light switch, I heard a mumble from the rooms downstairs. There was a strangled cry, and it was followed by the practised calm of the proprietor's voice. In the silence that followed, I walked to the window and put my head out. The church and the Schlossberg behind it now brooded against the night sky. I was drifting away with the beauty of the scene when there was another shout from below. I tensed as a fist crashed down, and there was a screech of chair legs scraping on the stone floor. I looked at my watch. Six-thirty. The overt expression of anger had disturbed me, but it was time for dinner, and I was hungry.

This discomfort pursued me down the stairs but faded when I entered the lobby. It seemed to breathe the air of Christmas and its winter smells of chestnuts and mulled wine. I closed my eyes to enjoy this evocative smell and pushed blindly through the dining room door. At first, I thought I had walked into my own shadow. I was nose to nose with the proprietor. We both stepped backwards and mumbled apologies, he in German and me in English, but both of us in embarrassment. Smiling, he took a step sideways and walked out through the door.

I was alone and feeling conspicuous in the middle of the dining room while conversation lulled around me. Most of the tables were full, but I spotted an empty chair at a table in one corner. The table's sole occupant was the old man I had seen in the church. He was sitting sideways and avoiding eye contact with the other people in the room. His hands were clamped between his thighs, and one shoulder was hunched and raised in a way that effectively negated the presence of everyone and everything except his own thoughts. His head was held upwards, and his nose was aimed at the windowpane in front of him. A half-empty wine glass stood amongst the remains of a bread roll that lay scattered on the tablecloth.

Walking over to his table, I muttered good evening. The old man removed his hand from between his legs and carelessly motioned with his palm that I should sit. He let the palm rest on the table and leaned against it. His face was pale, and beads of sweat had formed on the scalp and collected on his forehead and temples. Whispered half-words came from between his lips but if he was conversing with someone, it had to be with some inner voice of his own creation. Following the direction of his gaze, I saw he was looking through the window at an empty courtyard. His eyes were red and stricken by some terrible thought or memory.

Conversations around the room continued in the subdued tones of those who dared not raise a voice for fear of rekindling the anger and emotion that hung like cigarette smoke in the room. The sound of cutlery against china was unnaturally loud, and I found myself whispering my order for something called Swabian Ravioli while I picked nervously at a piece of bread. Unwilling to face my table companion or his mood, I scanned the other tables. One table by the door seemed to radiate the most influence. Its occupants were two children, their attentive mother, and a man with a walrus moustache, who dominated the table like Christ at the last supper. He was long and thin, and his sudden and nervous movements suggested a pool of suppressed energy.

"American are you?"

I looked around for the owner of the voice. It was so deep and resonant that I was surprised to see the frail old man looking expectantly at me.

"English," I said.

The old man slowly nodded and looked through the window again. After a few seconds he twisted round and looked reflectively at me.

"Tell me," he said, "how would you feel if you renewed the acquaintance of people over whom you once had the power of life and death?"

A gust of wind came through the door. It brought with it the tolling of church bells, the smell of percolating coffee, and snatches of secretive whispering from somewhere near at hand. Then I heard a door slam. The proprietor's wife materialised at my elbow. She was carrying a plate with my Swabian Ravioli. My companion was looking intently at the woman and slowly shaking his head.

"And more to the point," he said, "how should these people feel on meeting the person who saved them? You would expect some reaction, wouldn't you? You would expect them to at least show some interest. But these people? Pah ... nobody will even listen."

I shuffled uncomfortably. The man was causing a fuss, and my mother had always disapproved of people who made a fuss. I hacked at the ravioli as if it were made of rubber.

"I'm sorry," I said, "but you've lost me."

The old man fixed me with detached and speculative eyes. Gesturing to the window, he mouthed soundlessly before saying out loud:

"There, in that courtyard, in the last days of the war, was a half-track. But we had to go on. We had no petrol, you see? I should have destroyed it ... but I did what I thought was right."

His tone was forceful to the point of desperation.

"You know, if I had blown it up, the explosion would have taken this building with it. It would have taken the people inside it too."

He shook his head in what seemed to be a desperate attempt to shake the words from his mouth, but when they came, the words were almost inaudible.

"And there were people inside it, the current owner's father for example. And I could have prevented them all from existing."

He shrugged and breathed deeply. His eyes scanned my face while he struggled to maintain strength and control.

"A second's hesitation, a whim, a judgement made on the wing. It could have gone one way or another. But the owner would have been killed, and his son, that imbecile proprietor, would never have been given the chance to exist."

Staring once more through the window, the old man paused before continuing in hushed tones.

"These people," he said, "they have chosen to forget the war. And if they have chosen to forget, then they have chosen to forget our suffering."

He turned to look at me. His eyes were weary, but they contained a dying surge of savagery that shocked me.

"So why did we do it? Why did we suffer if future generation choose to forget us, the survivors?"

His breathing was irregular and heavy, and he clenched

and unclenched his fists. The muscles in his jaw tensed and knotted while he attempted to fight off the waves of emotions that threatened to engulf him.

I closed my eyes and tried to collect my thoughts. My old school had been dedicated to the memory of those who had died in the two World Wars. Every morning, the first thing I saw when I approached the school was a large stone cross which bore the names of former pupils who had died in the struggle against tyranny. Below these names, in bold capitals, there was the legend, LEST WE FORGET. I had never seriously questioned whether or not these pupils had given their lives for the freedom of the world, or whether their sacrifice had been worthwhile. I had unquestioningly accepted my mother's version of history. Those boys had died to protect freedom and Britain's constitutional liberty. There was no question of forgetting those who were morally right. But then, I mused, are not the winners always morally right? It had never occurred to me to ask how the losers, the condemned and eternally punished, dealt with their war dead.

Silence fell on the room. The silence had a breathless quality of expectation about it that prompted me to open my eyes. I saw immediately that a young woman had entered the room. Everyone seemed to be staring at her, and I stared along with them while my stomach tightened and my hands went clammy.

What had come through the door was as fresh as the wind itself. It still touched her cheeks and brightened her eyes. Even her unremarkable clothes, jeans and ski jacket, seemed to billow outwards like a summer tree full of breeze. Her brown hair was short at the neck but long on the top. Thrown carelessly over the ears, strands of hair constantly threatened to fall over the forehead and drop like a veil over the crackling blue of her eyes. There was something timeless about her, about her clothes, her freshness, and the all-consuming vigour of youth. She looked around the room and when she saw me staring at her, she put her head a little on one side. Her eyes met mine and then slid away.

My mind was in turmoil. We seemed to have recognised each other and yet we had surely never met. Or had there been, perhaps, some sense of immediate acceptance of mutual worth?

I looked in dismay as she came towards me with her mouth slightly open. She appeared to be on the verge of saying something. Perhaps she was going to greet me like an old friend. I wondered where I could possibly have met her before. Her head was still slightly cocked to one side, and she unflinchingly held my gaze while a smile flickered across her lips.

I was disturbed by a scraping of chair legs. The old man had risen to his feet and stood hunched and tense over the table. All conversation ceased as he raised his head and looked around the room.

"So tell me," he hissed in English, "what was the point of it all?"

And with that, he brushed roughly past the young woman and strode out of the room leaving bread crumbs on the table, and a red wine stain slowly spreading on the tablecloth where he had been sitting.

Document 3

Letter from Eugen Mayer to Paul Fischer.

19.04.1955

It has always been a great pleasure for me to look after the grave. With the passing of the years, I have put up a new iron cross, I have repaired the old bench, and I have built a new one. On this day, the anniversary of Martin Spohr's death, I have been to the site and cleaned and tidied everything. The grave is now as good as new, and it looks well cared for.

You may well ask why it is that I take so much trouble over the grave. Well, like many others, I lost a brother in the last war. Unfortunately, I do not know where he fell and so, because I am unable to visit the place where he died, I come here to pay my respects and to let my brother know that someone is still thinking about him. Also, the anniversary of Martin's death happens to be my birthday. I walk here from Herrenberg every year on this day, and on any other day when I feel low or in need of peace and quiet and a place to think.

This forest hideaway brings me such a wonderful peace of mind. I must have spent many hours sitting on the bench in this still place. My soul finds peace here. It is really a holy spot. To be with God and his wonderful natural creation brings such joy to me. It is love that I have again found here. It is comforting to see the beautiful flowers on the grave, and it is uplifting to see the walkers and cyclists stopping for a moment to pay their respects. All this gives me hope for the future and brightens the past. It makes me see that the sacrifices made by this boy and the hundreds of thousands of others like him were not completely in vain.

Chapter 4

When I arrived at the door of the priest's house for the first time, I saw myself as an innocent bystander and the curious observer of events that had happened before my birth. There were a few questions to ask of a churchman with whom my mother had corresponded in the sixties. I was confident that his answers would leave me free to disappear to the mountains and enjoy a week of skiing.

This guiltless young man parked the hire car, knocked at the priest's door and waited with his head buried in the upturned collar of his jacket. It was around one o'clock when the door swung open, and a gangling and stooping man in a baggy pullover and jeans stood on the threshold. He scratched at his beard and peered down at me, his eyes sparkling through thin-rimmed glasses. I was inclined to take a liking to this ageing hippy, but I was also aware that my mother would never have approved of a priest who let his hair grow long and curl over the shoulders.

I was feeling off-balance when he ushered me into his house. I stepped in, and the door clicked shut behind me. I was about to comment on the weather when the priest spoke first.

"Your shoes."

I looked down at my shoes and then at him. He was pointing to a doormat on which house slippers lay.

"If you don't mind," he said, "but forests are not clean

35

places. If you lived in the middle of one, you would insist on this too. We do try to keep it out of our houses."

I bent down to unlace my shoes, but the priest did not move. I found myself kneeling at his feet like a sinner begging forgiveness.

"It's good of you to see me," I said, rising to my feet and looking up into his glasses.

The priest's face betrayed not a glimmer of emotion. It was impossible to tell what he was feeling, but I construed the absence of expression as displeasure. I felt like a man who has intruded on a private dinner party and who has tried and failed to join the conversation. The priest slowly raised his arm and, pointing to some inner room, he managed to make his invitation sound like a command.

"Please," he said, "this way."

The silence that fell between us was broken by the ticking of several clocks which competed with one another for prominence. Standing guard by the front door was an ornate grandfather clock and, walking into the lounge, I caught sight of what appeared to be a station clock between the windows. A similar clock was ticking in my ear.

The priest took several steps past me and took up a position between the windows. He swung round to face me and clasped his hands in front of him. With an irritable twitch of the shoulder, he lifted the sleeve of his pullover and glanced at his watch.

"I do appreciate your agreeing to see me," I began. "I thought I could combine business with pleasure so I decided ..."

"So?"

"I was going through my mother's belongings and I found ..."

The priest made another sudden and irritable twitch of the shoulders. He took a short and sharp intake of breath and glanced again at his watch. It was then that I noticed his ears. Partly hidden in the bushy and greying hair, the ears were large and fleshy and seemed to be rapidly changing colour - white to pink to red.

"What exactly," he said, "do you want from me?"

I was feeling off-balance again, and tension quivered between us. With one eye on his ears, I said:

"I found a letter in my mother's belongings. The letter was written by you in 1965. The letter contained some very ..."

"Yes, yes, I know what the letter contained. It was my translation of three documents that I have here. What exactly do you want?"

I was shocked into silence by the man's rudeness. He turned his head and glanced quickly through the window. In a more conciliatory tone, he said:

"I don't want to hurry you, but this is not a good time. I've got another appointment. Perhaps you can tell me what I can do for you?"

I took a deep breath and scratched at my hairline. I focused my eyes to the right of his head and looked through the window. A dark cloud gave a false impression of early evening.

"Why did my mother write to you?" I said.

The priest stretched his cheeks in what looked like a smile and he wagged his finger between his eyebrows.

"To my father to be exact," he said, pushing at his glasses.

Trapped between the urge to respond to the priest's bluntness, and the need to make something of my visit, I made excuses for what I saw as his discourteous behaviour. I guessed that the priest's character had been moulded by endless meditations on philosophy or the existence of God. Having discovered eternal truths and laws, he liked nothing more than to pass them on to others. I supposed that over time, he accepted nothing less than the immutable truth in return.

"Who was Martin Spohr?"

"Martin Spohr was a soldier," the priest said with a shrug. "He was killed just before the end of the war."

"And why was my mother interested in him?"

The priest glanced at his watch and then turned the palm

of his hand outwards. He appeared to study it with the concentrated gaze of the academic who was handling some highly-prized volume. I wondered if he had heard my question for he turned his back to me and peered through the window. Indistinct words reached me through the sound of ticking clocks. It was some seconds before I realised he was talking to me. He swung round, and his hair flew in a wide and ragged arc before settling again on his shoulders.

"Many people are interested in him. Or perhaps, I should say that they are interested in his grave. Tell me. What do you know about the grave?"

I shook my head, but it was less of an attempt to respond negatively than an effort to shake away the feeling of unreality that was taking hold of me.

"Nothing," I said.

"Ah, there we have it at last. You've come to find out about the grave, is that it?"

I rubbed my thumb and forefinger together. They were slippery with perspiration.

"Well, not exactly," I said. "I was more interested in Martin Spohr."

But the priest refused to be corrected. He may have been puzzled by my insistence or maybe he was genuinely relieved that at last he knew what it was I expected of him. In any case, his mood seemed to change at this point, and our conversation briefly took on a more relaxed and chatty tone. He removed his glasses with a flourish and folded them neatly in front of him. He blinked rapidly at me.

"You know," he said, "Martin Spohr's grave has come to symbolise for many, the resting places for all those sons, brothers and fathers who never came back from the war. You have read my documents? Then I suggest the following procedure. First, I tell you more about the grave. Second, you visit the grave for yourself. It's not so very far from here. Third, come back, and I'll tell you what I can. How does that sound?"

I uttered some words, perhaps in a rather half-hearted

way, to the effect that I agreed. Silence fell between us again. Time ticked slowly past in my ear, and I mused on the fragile assumptions we make about others. We assume that priests are honest, they tell the truth. I wondered where these assumptions originated. Were they the collective wisdom of centuries handed down from generation to generation until we inherited them from our parents? I could not ignore the vague but troubling doubts that began as a mere puff of wind and quickly spread to fill the air between me and the priest. I was unable to provide evidence, but instinct told me that this priest was hiding something. Experience told me that hiding something was as good as lying.

"Before you tell me about the grave," I said, "can you tell me why my mother wrote to your father in the first place? And why did the correspondence finish?"

The priest lowered his chin almost to his breast bone. He lifted the glasses to his nose and slipped his face expertly into them. To me, he appeared to be putting on a mask. I noticed his ears had turned pink again. I realised then that the ears changed colour according to the priest's state of mind. White signalled calm. Red meant anger or frustration.

"Did I say the correspondence finished?"

Instinctively, my arms crossed over my chest. The quick intake of breath I heard was my own. My fragile constructions were crumbling fast. Whoever said that the one person you can trust in life is your mother?

"You mean she wrote back? She replied to your letter and the documents you sent?"

The priest looked confused. He took a step towards me, his face becoming visibly strained.

"That's correct," he said. "She wrote to thank me. She wrote something I shall never forget. She said that some things are bigger than us. And she never wrote again. Maybe she was right. Some things are bigger than us."

I flinched. These were my mother's words. She used

them often - to me. It was unsettling to hear them in the mouth of a stranger. It was a kind of betrayal.

"But she never wrote after that."

"No, she never wrote again."

"Do you know why not?"

The priest turned his gaze downwards and studied the floor. After some consideration he shook his head.

"My guess is that she wanted to finish with the past."

He studied the palm of his hand for a while before taking another step closer to me.

"But perhaps," he said, "the past is not finished with us."

I raised my hand to my forehead and rubbed hard at my skin. I studied my fingertips for signs of blood or dirt, but my hands were clean. The priest glanced at his watch again and pushed nervously at his glasses.

"Listen," he said, "we've agreed on a procedure, and I have five minutes to give you. Let me tell you first about the grave."

He unhooked the glasses from his ears and gazed at me. His eyes were wide open and staring, his chin had dropped, and his lips were slightly apart.

"Some of the story you know already," he began. "We first came to know about it all in 1947 when Martin Spohr's uncle was told about the grave by a forester. A helmet was balanced on the cross, and a name had been roughly scratched on the wood. The inscription was just legible. It read Martin Spohr."

As he warmed to his story, his words came faster but the voice behind the words was edged with impatience and irritation.

"The document I sent your mother makes it clear Spohr and his comrades were in the wood in 1945. It isn't so clear what exactly happened. It seems that Spohr was killed, his comrades buried him, and they took away his soldbuch and his coat."

His ears turned bright red and he spluttered out the words with difficulty.

"But these are not facts," he said. "We can only guess. It is, you understand, only speculation."

After several seconds he calmed down and looked at me apologetically, appealing for my patience and understanding.

"Spohr could never have known what would happen after his death. When the grave was discovered, many people looked after it. This is fact. At first, there was only the small cross that the forester found. Then, stones were put round the grave, and an iron cross replaced the old wooden one. Perhaps it was a local from one of the villages. A local who lost someone? This is also speculation. What we know for sure is that people took care of the grave."

As time progressed further, his voice got fainter and fainter like a fading hope. He kept his eyes fixed on the wall behind me, and I had the uncomfortable feeling that he had forgotten my presence and was speaking to the wall as though practising an important sermon.

"And we don't know who put the vase with flowers there, and the name and birth date of Martin Spohr. I do know that in 1949, my father held a service at the grave. And I do know that in 1953, a certain Eugen Mayer from Herrenberg put up another iron cross and two benches there. From the late sixties, more and more people visited the grave - not only local people, but people from all over Germany. Nobody ever intended it, but this spot has become a focal point for sadness and memories."

He lowered his face and slipped it into the waiting glasses. He seemed on the verge of tears. Then he cleared his throat and scratched at his beard.

"The grave slowly came to symbolise, for many people, the last resting place of a loved one who never returned. Nobody expected it and nobody questioned it. And in the same way, we have never had need to ask people to look after the grave. First there was Anna Bieber, whose only son had been killed in 1945. When she died in 1982, the grave was looked after by Greta Brücher. Her brother had also died in the war. Greta took care of the grave until her death in 1995, and since then, the Forestry Commission has looked after it."

I took a deep breath and verbalised the assumption that had been forming in my head.

"So, it's become a sort of unknown soldier."

The priest frowned.

"A what?"

"The grave to the unknown soldier," I said, "in Westminster Cathedral. It officially represents and symbolises the fallen from all wars. Buried among kings. Very symbolic."

The priest enthusiastically nodded.

"And ours," he said, "is unofficially buried among the trees."

"Aren't there other graves like this one?"

The priest's eyes twinkled. There was now friendliness in them, and an eagerness to please.

"There were," he said. "And the local people had to fight to keep this one. The authorities wanted to put everything into one mass grave. With regard to Martin Spohr, so many people resisted that eventually the authorities agreed to let the grave stand as it is."

"So," I said, mindful of the priest's preference for direct communication, "I would still like to know why my mother wrote to your father about the grave."

"She did not know about the grave," he said. "She wanted to know about Martin Spohr. I decided that the least I could do would be to send her a translation of my father's report and the translations you have read. Since receiving your recent letter, I've been making further inquiries."

He lifted his arm and pre-empted my objections with an upturned palm.

"No, please," he said. "This afternoon, soon, I am to meet someone. Please follow the procedure. Now go and visit the grave. Then come back, and I'll try and tell you everything I know."

The atmosphere between us had undergone a change that seemed to place the two of us in some other place or time. The world around us became strangely still as the clocks ticked away their seconds. The priest's expression slowly changed to one that I found difficult to accept - priests were not supposed to show it - but this priest was afraid. I let my arms fall to my sides, glanced at the clock between the windows and said:

"Four-thirty then?"

The priest nodded, and the firm set of the jaw suggested he had nothing more to say about the grave or about Martin Spohr. Reaching over to a bookcase, he picked up a sheaf of papers and held them towards me.

"You might want to look at some of this," he said. "It's my translation of a book written about the grave. In German the book is called, "Ein Soldatengrab in einem Wald." That translates as, "A Soldier's Grave in a Forest." It was written in 1995. Read it while you are away. Take the Introduction and Chapter 1. They might give you some idea about what it is you are asking."

Nodding my thanks, I absent-mindedly took the papers from his hand and slipped them into the inside pocket of my jacket. I turned into the hall, the clocks ticking like heart beats in my head. The priest stood impatiently over me as I hurriedly got into my shoes. When the door eventually shut behind me, I realised that my shoe laces were still untied and my thoughts were in complete disarray.

Setting off into the depths of the forest, dark thoughts shifted in my consciousness, and I glimpsed the birth of attitudes which, until my mother's death, had been alien to me. The feelings were vague stirrings, but I could not deny a developing suspicion and mistrust of those in authority.

Until her death, my mother had dominated my life, and I had happily lived in her shadow, accepting everything and questioning nothing. I had become all the things she had ever wanted me to be. The discovery of the letters, and the information that she had hidden from me, had somehow destroyed the image of perfect motherhood. I saw now that she was just a human being. I could not blame her for being imperfect but it was easier to rebel against the imperfections of authority.

Feeling comfortable with this, I took the sheaf of papers from my inside pocket with the intention of scanning through them while I walked to the grave.

Book Extract

Ein Soldatengrab in einem Wald. Introduction

The soldier's grave is well known to many of those who live in the Schönbuch area and beyond. It lies at a lonely spot in the middle of the forest, but despite this, the grave remains, for many, much more significant than the official war monuments. So it is that walkers and bikers know the place as a geographical reference point on their maps. Sooner or later, these walkers and bikers find themselves here. School children are also brought into the forest in the early summer.

They come to learn about the flora and fauna, but they bring lively and inquisitive minds with them and of course they ask questions about the grave and the man who died there. It is not only the children who ask these questions. The grave has become well known and yet, memories are short, and very few people know any details about the dead soldier. The local press knew about the grave of course, but they had no idea how the soldier came to die, and what he was doing in that part of the forest at that time.

19 April 1995 was the fiftieth anniversary of the death of Martin Spohr. We thought perhaps it was time to discover the story behind the 19 year-old. After all, his grave had a significant meaning for the post-war populations, not only of the local villages, but also for people in many other parts of Germany. These people do not live forever, and it did not seem right that the story

behind the grave should pass from their memory and into obscurity. I would like to say that without the help and the often painful memories of the bereaved, this little book could never have been written.

We are writing of a time shortly before the end. It was just a few weeks before the final surrender, and the war was already lost. The German armies were retreating almost everywhere. The last reserves had been called up. Old and invalid men, and children of school age, were called upon to do their duty. These children and young men had, since their earliest years, been subjected to the most powerful and insidious propaganda. Can we blame them if, brainwashed and filled with ideals, they willingly went to faraway places like Stalingrad and North Africa to leave their bodies there for the German Reich? In April 1945 the young ones never had a real chance against the hardened adversary, but they nevertheless fought to the end. So it was that right up to the last days of the war, these youngsters were to die a useless and pointless death.

The soldier's grave in the Schönbuch is, for many, a memory of that time. It is the only monument to these young warriors and loved ones who never returned. It is a real consolation for those whose sons, brothers, fathers and friends were never found but who are still listed as missing.

It is to these unburied ones and to those who were, and are, obliged to live with painful memories, that the grave and this little book are dedicated.

Chapter 5

The forest. 23 December. Afternoon

On either side of me, brilliant, blinding and flashing knives of sunlight sliced through the darkness of the forest. Its shadows lay as deep black pools at my feet, and the path plunged in and out of them as it took me to the grave. The way seemed much longer than the priest had suggested, and I had already finished the pages of the book he had given me. I now had plenty of time to reflect. I supposed I should have been excited by the prospect of seeing the grave or perhaps concerned at the reticence of the priest. In reality, I had revisited the previous evening and I was replaying my meeting with the young woman and wondering what I could have done better.

The old man's dramatic departure from the hotel had temporarily stunned the dining room into silence. The young woman stood over me with her head still cocked to one side, and with an enigmatic smile playing around her lips. There was a questioning expression around her eyes that seemed to ask, "Who was that?"

She sat down at my table, and we watched each other for a long time before starting to speak. Her name was Barbara, and her English was almost faultless. She told me she had spent three years studying at a British university. It had been at the suggestion of her father, a great Anglophile, she said. These were not the initial topics of our conversation, but her opening line had been one that no amount of mental rinsing would ever wash away.

"You look afraid. Have you been sitting with a ghost?"

While she fumbled at the fasteners of her jacket, I got a good look at her. Her nose was straight and high-bridged, the lips pursed, and the chin firm but with an uplifted hint of arrogance. A sharp scent seemed to emanate from her. It was a natural scent, like that of cut young grass, and it was intoxicating. She brushed the bread crumbs off the table with a suggestion of irritability, and placed a mobile phone in front of her.

From the corner of my eye I caught sight of the closing of a door and the fleeting vision of a walrus moustache. There was a faint stirring in the air where this powerful and vital presence had passed through, and he was followed by a woman and children. With their departure, the centre of attention seemed to shift to us.

There was a familiar voice in the air around me.

"Not a ghost, perhaps only the spirit of the past."

I looked up to see who had uttered the words. Then, I realised it was my own voice I had heard, but its tone had been more constricted and high-pitched than I was used to. What was more, my heart was thumping, and I was slightly short of breath. I had made my comment as a mild joke. I had wanted to make her smile, but her face remained without expression, and her eyes blinked in confusion. This was not a good start.

"He's just an embarrassment," she said, with a dismissive upward tilt of the chin, "not the spirit of the past, just a relic."

Silence fell between us. I was struggling to find something to say that would entertain her. My mind went blank. I consoled myself with what my mother had always said. Germans did not have a sense of humour.

"Is this your first trip to Herrenberg?" she asked.

"Yes," I said.

This was only a half-truth. In the previous two weeks I

48

had been a frequent visitor in my dreams and on the Herrenberg web-site. In many ways, I had been expecting the town to be waiting for me, and in a sense it was. But life did not stop because a foreign individual came to make inquiries about some mysterious letters he had found in an attic.

"So," she said brightly, "why are you visiting us?"

A light mantel of tiredness came upon me. I looked back at her, unable to prevent the growing sensation that I had somehow managed to step outside my body and I was seeing myself as she saw me. The church clock struck eight and reminded me that I had already been up for sixteen hours.

"I'm going to Kleinwalsertal," I said, "for Christmas skiing. I decided to stay for two days in this area before driving down."

She looked at me reflectively. Her silence invited me to say something, but I had nothing to say. I did not want to mention the real reason for being there. It was the war, always the war, and it might lie between us like the Berlin Wall.

Outside, the wind was gusting. It touched a lamp that hung outside the window and then, the wind blew down the street towards the market square. The lamp squeaked and swung to and fro as if at the push of a hand, and the wind picked up the leaves and tossed them lightly into the air. The lamp caught the leaves in its light, and they hung undecided; long skeletal shapes of dead things, for a brief moment transparent, and then swallowed by the darkness.

"There's a storm coming," she said.

The waitress appeared and hovered at Barbara's shoulder like a bird of prey. Barbara muttered something in German, and the waitress scurried away. Barbara leaned forward, picked up the phone and spoke into the mouthpiece. The sudden switch to a language I barely understood came as a shock. In a breath, she was a different person. Her life, her power and the very essence of her humanity were snatched away. The sounds she was using taunted and frightened me because they told me something that I had not consciously considered. She could never belong to me.

From the corner of my eye, I watched the waitress sweeping back to our table. The thump of the beer glass on the table top roughly shook me away from my thoughts. I looked up and found Barbara's eyes looking into mine. With an effort of will, I managed to compose myself. I was about to respond to her comment about the weather, when she said:

"While you are here, would you like to meet some young Germans?"

I frowned back at her while I tried to interpret her meaning. It never occurred to me that the question was as simple and as direct as it seemed. I gave a short nervous laugh.

"I'm not really so concerned about the past," I said.

The look of confusion returned to her eyes. She placed her hands on the table and looked at me quizzically.

"Would you or would you not like to meet some young Germans?"

"Well," I began, "I don't want to interfere ..."

"And do you or do you not like cinema? Yes or no?"

"Yes," I had said.

*

I wheeled round in alarm. Something had startled me. A footfall perhaps, or was it an animal? I saw only droplets of water, thousands upon thousands of them, disturbed by the breeze and now filtering through the twigs and branches of the Schönbuch Forest. Brilliant slashes of light still cut through the trees and bathed the earth, now covered in layers of fallen leaves from autumns past.

The Goldbach stream trickled beside me and its sound seemed almost indistinguishable from the wind that danced and played on its surface, picked up the water, and deposited it like undecided rain drops on my skin. It was a beautiful spot, and I would have enjoyed it more had I not sensed that I was being followed. I repeatedly turned sharply. I was expecting to see someone standing close behind me, but there was nobody and nothing except the sound of the earth crackling under my feet.

About twenty metres from the grave, the stream turned away and plunged downwards, a trickling murmur fading away to silence amongst the trees. I stopped and pricked up my ears. In the depths of this endless stillness, I took in my surroundings. The evergreens were swaying gently. The bare deciduous trees jutted aggressively skywards, and the path disappeared into the stunted grass of Goldbachtal. Nothing else moved. I was alone.

The grave lay in the shade and the shelter of a great evergreen tree. Its trunk rose as straight as a ship's mast into the sky. A question appeared in my head and it threw my thoughts into disarray. Was it me standing in the heart of this forest? Was it me who had come here, or was it my mother's imagination? Had she, in her mind's eye, seen the iron cross placed there by a local villager? Had she known something of the heartbreak that prompted the flowers and the name, so lovingly carved, in dear memory of an irreplaceable son or brother? Had she known, or had she imagined, that here in the middle of the Schönbuch Forest was a cross with the legend, Martin Spohr 1926 - 1945?

I suddenly felt self-conscious. I looked around me, sure that I was being watched from the shadows by a crowd of onlookers. I was vulnerable, and in that lonely place I imagined that those shadowy spaces between the trees harboured the souls of the dead, and that they were patiently waiting for me to join them. I shook my head free of this image and overlaid it with warmer recollections of the previous evening. I had been with Barbara on our way up to the open-air cinema.

"Look," Barbara had said, indicating the top of the steps.

The church was now below us, and a blue moonlight glow had wrapped itself around the Schlossberg. Barbara led, pausing occasionally to hold the torch above her head so that I could find my footing. In the artificial light, I saw her face, the high-bridged nose, and the chin with its hint of arrogance. Her skin seemed pale, and I wondered whether she was ill, but when I slipped and grabbed at her outstretched hand, the grip on my elbow was firm and strong.

Above and to my right, dark against the darkness, the Schönbuch Forest rose. On that chill December evening, and in my state of tiredness, I saw an eternal world, a cruel and forbidding place where past and present lived side by side, and the dead rustled through the undergrowth with the living. I thought I heard rolls of thunder from an approaching storm, but I soon realised it was the sound of car engines reverberating round the hill's top. Furthermore, the blue tinge I had imagined as moonlight was actually the lighting from the outdoor cinema we had come to visit on the Schlossberg.

Despite Barbara's assurances that the Christmas outdoor film festival was always well attended, I was surprised to see crowds of people in the crisp winter air. Some were talking excitedly, others wandered hunched against the cold, but all were shrouded in the clouds of water vapour which gathered over their plastic cups of mulled wine. Below us, and in the artificial light, I could just distinguish the marketplace, its edges still packed with old snow. I noticed that a screen had been put up against the castle wall, and I was still trying to take in this extraordinary scene when the air was suddenly filled with music. A hush fell on the gathering. I felt a hand on my elbow, and Barbara's breath was warm against my cheek. I hardly listened to the words she said. It was her tone that impressed me, and the vision of another of my mother's prejudices dying before me. Germans have no sense of humour, she used to say.

"It's 'The English Patient'," Barbara had said. Then she had whooped with laughter and added, "I'm afraid he's speaking German tonight."

*

So accustomed had I become to my imagined pursuer that it took me some time to accept the fact that I really was not alone. I looked up from the grave and, scanning the wide expanse and the stunted grass of the valley floor, I examined the trees on the other side. Here and there, patches of the forest floor were covered under layers of old snow. But it was the changing shapes and flashes of light from the gaps between the trees that held my gaze. I stared at these shapes until I realised that somebody was skulking in the undergrowth.

A man was moving slowly from tree to tree, and between sunlight and shadow. I made out a long coat ruffling against his ankles. Slowly turning his head from side to side, he hesitated, changed direction and came towards me with a purposeful stride. A scarf swirled from around his neck, and above the scarf, his head was balanced proudly. As the distance between us closed, at first came a suggestion of old-fashioned elegance, then a long and pointed nose, and at last the fine hair, neatly combed over the scalp.

Initially, I thought the old man was drunk because he was swaying towards me. I soon noticed that the swaying was not as erratic as drinking suggested. It occurred to me that he might be playing silly games. The rapidly building clouds stained the valley floor with icy, ink-blue shadows. The shadow patterns swelled and shifted with every whim of the breeze, but it was the ground between the patterns that seemed to frighten the old man for he swayed around these spots of sunlight. They could have been bottomless hollows that threatened to swallow him up.

He stopped and raised his hand in greeting. Then he looked wildly about him in such a way that convinced me he too believed he was being followed. I wondered how many other graves like this there were in the forest. Were we both being pursued by ghosts? He stopped about five metres from the grave, but his voice reached out to me, deep and resonant like a death knell.

"An old soldier's trick," he said. "Always keep to the shadows, especially when the enemy is around."

With his hands clasped behind him, he stood squarely before me and looked questioningly into my eyes while a light wind blew between us. Behind his head, the bare trees were splayed against the sky.

"Well …," I began.

"There's no enemy around now. Is this what you want to say? The war is finished? Maybe it is. Actually, I thought you were someone else."

He was still looking around him with slow but deliberate turns of the head. Before I could utter a word, the old soldier raised an eyebrow, half-closed his eyes, and looked at me thoughtfully.

"No, you are not who I thought you were. But the enemy? They are always around."

He hissed out the words with an anger that shocked me. Then he smiled, thrust out his chest, and took a few paces towards me, his coat-tails flapping in the wind.

"Tell me," he began, in a tone that suggested he had retained his balance, "do you believe all those formulas that have been invented to cover the truth, or do you sacrifice yourself and simply pretend you believe?"

If he had started his questions with a balanced mind, he finished off with a bitter and ironic tone. What struck me again was that he seemed to be continuing a conversation from some other place, and with another person.

"I'm not sure what you mean," I began, "I ..."

He looked at me sharply. There was some emotion expressed in his eyes. It could have been fear or resentment at my presence. Perhaps he had been rehearsing the words he wanted to use with the person he had been expecting to see. I certainly had the impression that I was intruding on a private conversation.

"Ah, you don't know what I mean? You think this grave represents something noble? You have come here to give yourself the satisfaction of relieving your conscience. This is true, isn't it?"

I looked down at the man's thin and dry face. In a flash, I saw him for what he was – a once proud man now in terminal decay.

"Now look," I said, "I don't have a conscience about anything here. I am simply curious to know about this man, to understand why his death is significant for the local people."

My companion snorted.

"Your curiosity runs after emptiness, my friend. You want to understand things that are based on nothing - at least, nothing but conventional words. And you know, these local people wouldn't understand the words even if they examined them. And they never have examined them. It's simply a fact that one day they made up their minds to accept them and decided to understand what they wanted to understand. By doing this, they have effectively silenced me."

What he did next contradicted the dignified personality I had created in my mind for this old man. He stepped forward and coughed. He hesitated. Then, he spat, and his spittle landed on the cross and hung there for a second before slowly stretching out and dropping to the ground. I took a step backwards in order to disengage myself from this violation of sacred ground. I was speechless for several seconds before saying out loud:

"How dare you? How dare you do that to other people's memories, to other people's dreams?"

I shrugged, and my words faded away while tiredness gathered behind my eyes. There was stillness between us until the old man took a shuddering and deep breath. It was so deep it seemed to fill his whole body. Between the collar of his coat and the scarf, I saw his bones pressing against his shirt.

"How dare I?" he whispered. "I have spat on your dreams? Is this what you think? Is it? Well, let me tell you about mine."

Despite his murmuring, the fall force of his being was behind the words. He had drawn back his thin, colourless lips, and his breath was now coming in the short, sharp gasps of the dying. I was fully expecting to hear his bones rattling. In front of me was a depth of emotion that trivialised my own. His anger was the anger of the soul. He was touched by something that came from inside, and it rocked and shook his whole being. It was almost insane.

"For fifty years I have lived with my dreams," he said. "Let me tell you what happens when you want to clutch at something and you reach out and almost touch it because you want to change the dream. But the dream slips away again beyond your reach. And from a distance it mocks you and challenges you to come again the next night. How would you feel? What would you do? I tell you, I have been silenced."

I stared at him while my mind tried to keep up with his words, but he had lost me. I supposed he was referring to an awful memory from the war.

"Tell me," he said, "when you recall some past event, do you recall the moving picture or do you simply remember the frozen frame - just one image or perhaps a sound that symbolises the rest?"

I considered his question, but it hung there between us, unanswered. The old man raised his chin and stared past me into empty space.

"I have this one picture," he said, "and it symbolises something terrible for me, something inhuman, a horror that I shall never be able to forget."

There was a silence while he seemed to gather himself to go on. His lips were pursed, and the dry skin on his face vibrated with the power of his feelings. His eyes were perfectly still. They were staring, not at emptiness as I had thought, but at the grave behind me.

"I see the pieces of flesh and blood that spatter the church walls. In the corner is a dead man propped up under an image of Christ. From the dead man's mouth a cigarette butt dangles, and on his head is a large and perfectly formed piece of shit. I should have felt outrage and horror at this desecration. But the horror I am forced to confront is worse than this desecration. This horror is myself. Confronted with this beastliness, I was filled with content, and I wanted to laugh - yes, laugh."

A strong gust of wind momentarily howled through the trees of the Schönbuch Forest and caught the old man unawares. He rocked onto the balls of his feet and then backwards at an alarming angle before he managed to regain his balance. He looked me straight in the eye and whispered:

"You see, don't you? I had been forced to stand on the edge of my humanity and look into the pit. And you know, I loved what I saw there."

He searched my face for a reaction. His eyes dared me to comment, to criticise and condemn. The forest was growing darker, but his eyes remained lit with the pain and the power of memory.

"With this horror comes the sound. It comes to me at night, this scream of terrible anguish. For more than fifty years it has never left me. You think I should see someone? How can I when nobody wants to listen."

He put out his arms in a gesture of helplessness, or was he trying to recapture some retreating image? I was about to approach him and offer some words of consolation when he said suddenly very low:

"And I have a heart too. Yes, I have a heart. You saw me spit on this grave but it was not memories I was desecrating. It is those very memories and the pain that prevent me from doing the only thing that would remove that terrible image."

He threw the scarf around his face, and turning his back, he took several steps away from me. The light was fading fast, and over the tree tops, a black and rising bank of clouds reminded me where I was. I thought of myself lost at night in a strange forest, and I felt the first stirrings of fear grip at my stomach. Dusk half concealed the old man, and he seemed to merge back into the light from which he had come. And yet, I thought I could see him as I had first seen him. His chest was thrust forward, and his shoulders were pulled back. He held his head up in a commanding manner, and I heard his voice, deep but muffled through his scarf.

"It is the price you see? The price is too much for people to take."

He disappeared from view, and I decided it was time to leave and to finish my conversation with the priest. I walked quickly back along the path to Hidrizhausen with a chill grip of fear fumbling at my chest. The old man was living on some terrible past experiences. One young man I had met the previous night was spending a lot of energy forgetting them.

*

I was not sure at what moment in the evening I registered the change in weather. I had ascribed my chattering teeth to tiredness, and at some point during the film, I had felt dampness against my cheeks. When the film finally flickered to an end, and the projected light went out, it seemed to me that I was looking at the world through a grey veil. At first I thought it was just my eyes as they adjusted from glorious technicolour. The shadowy figures around us seemed to fade noiselessly away into a watery black and white, and it was then that I realised a cloud had come down on the Schlossberg.

Barbara appeared in front of me. She lifted her chin and zipped up her jacket. Her hair was glistening and wet and had fallen over her eyes. She raised her hand and pushed the hair back. I saw droplets of water sparkling like stars on her eyelashes. She reminded me I had agreed to meet her friends in the Schlosskeller. I was disoriented through tiredness but the hint of arrogance in her chin convinced me that Barbara would not take no for an answer.

She led me to a flight of sinister steps that plunged into the earth. I soon discovered that the Schlosskeller was a cellar under the ground where the film had been shown. Barbara pushed open the large wooden door, and we stepped in.

Immediately on our left was a small wooden kiosk, and inside it was a bald and thin man leaning over the hatch. He smiled at Barbara and, muttering something to her, he ushered us in. I felt his eyes watching us as we made our way into a large room with tables all around it. The room was shaped like a giant barrel sliced in half and made of bricks that seemed lined with cobwebs. The cobwebs were vibrating to the loud and aggressive noise of electronic music. I could not see the players, but the hundreds of people inside this giant barrel were like actors from a silent film. Their necks stretched and strained as they shouted at their colleagues across tables.

The players were in a second room, separated from the first by two arches. One arch was open and used as a passage to a bar. The other arch was shut off by a platform on which the band was playing. There were three guitarists, a drummer, and a saxophone player and each seemed to be doing his best to get as much noise as possible from his instrument.

Then the music stopped. The cessation of the noise released the talking and shouting from the tables, and it hit me like a roar from a football crowd.

Barbara took my forearm and led me towards a small alcove and a table at which two young men sat. When

Barbara introduced me, the men stood up and then sat down again, and immediately spoke together in German. I did not mind, I was tired and intended to have just one drink and then leave. Moreover, I had not caught their names. One of them was tall and fat with a moon-shaped face and he showed no interest in me whatsoever. The other was short and thin and he ceaselessly fidgeted on his chair. Perhaps because I had just been to the cinema, I found I had dubbed these two, Laurel and Hardy.

There was a voice, unannounced in my ear. I turned to see Laurel looking at me. His interest was clearly aroused, and he was expecting a response to some question I had not heard. Barbara put her hand on my arm.

"Thorsten asked what brings you here to Herrenberg."

"I've come to discover something of my family history," I said. "My mother came from Germany after the war."

Thorsten's smile faded from his face. He stiffened perceptibly and sank back into his chair. His eyes were so hard, I wondered if it was anger I saw there. He said:

"The war, the war."

We sat in silence for some time, and I shivered with tiredness. I heard a sigh and saw Thorsten shake his head.

"Why," he said, "do you English always mention the war?"

I was dead tired.

"Why shouldn't I mention the war?"

"Our teachers did their best," Laurel said, "to make us feel guilty about it all, did you know this?"

"Yes," I said, "but ..."

"And what happens?" Laurel said as if to an imaginary audience. "When we feel we have dealt with it, out pops another Nazi criminal, caught at last, and reminds us and the rest of the world what a horrible lot we Germans are."

"Yes, OK, but ..."

"There was one the other week," Laurel continued, "arrested for something that happened in Italy in '44 or '45."

I remained silent. It was clear that Laurel was not interested in the opinions of others.

"And it's worse than this. When a few skinheads demonstrate, do you know what happens? Of course you do. Everyone tells us that the Nazis are back, and the rest of the world had better watch out."

I struggled to keep my opinions to myself while Laurel looked intently at me with raised eyebrows.

"And then there is the question of payments to the slave workers. You have read about this? Even Barbara's father is suffering because of it."

I looked at Barbara for elaboration, but she had lowered her eyelids and was staring at the table top. Laurel was in full flow.

"Tell me," he said, "does guilt have an allotted time attached to it like a life sentence? How long must it go on? Please tell me."

He sprawled in the chair and stared at me provocatively. I avoided his gaze. I was too tired to argue. Encouraged by my silence, Laurel pressed on. He lectured us on the British Empire, and the slaughter of innocents in India and South Africa, Ireland and The Falklands. What was the difference, he asked, between what the Nazis did and what the British did?

"There's no difference," he answered, "no difference at all."

The cobwebs vibrated again as the music exploded into the bar. Barbara looked at me and motioned with her head that we should leave. We pushed our way through the crowd, and past the wooden kiosk. The thin, bald man said good night and gave us a knowing look that suggested he knew something about us that we did not. I felt uneasy.

We walked up the steps and emerged into the cold winter air. The silence of nature was restful after the noise and words of the beer keller. The bare trees that surrounded us were motionless from the cold and already white with frost. Buttoning up our coats, we made our way towards the steps, and Barbara produced her torch. In its faint light, the Schlossberg fell in front of me like the slope of a huge mountain. I looked down the black steps. They appeared like an impassable space which separated me from my hotel room and safety.

The fact was that I longed to be alone. Barbara was confronting me with a confusion of emotions, feelings, and anxiety. As I set foot on the first downward step, recollections and emotional leftovers from past sexual encounters jumped at me. I had first touched a girl when I was nineteen. The girl was several years older than me and she had seemed like a grown woman while I was far too young for what I saw was about to happen. What I wanted to do seemed intrinsically shameful. I was still too young to see that I was reacting in a way of which my mother would have approved. I ran out of that room having done nothing more than tell myself that I could do those things when I was older and more responsible. I managed to convince myself that the girl was only a rehearsal for the real thing that would come at some vague future date.

But that date never came. Occasionally, I would invite a girl to the cinema, and we held hands or I put my arm around her shoulders, but all in the knowledge that it would go no further. My upbringing would never allow it. When I was at university, I told myself that if I made love once, I would be able to do it again. I never did. Whenever a girl showed interest in me, I did not recognise the signals until it was too late. At Teacher Training College, I became something of a man's man. The drinking and the camaraderie offered a kind of camouflage under which I could be like everyone else, and I nurtured the reputation of a confirmed bachelor.

Barbara and I were half-way down the steps that led to the market square when she said:

"He's right, you know."

"Who's right?"

"Thorsten," she said. "My father owns the Daimler

concessionary here. Or perhaps I should say, the DaimlerChrysler concessionary. You may have seen it on the edge of town."

I nodded and watched her peering at me while I tried to fathom what she had in mind. Barbara said:

"I'll tell you about it one day."

A few minutes later we stood in the darkness outside my hotel door. I could barely see her face. She told me to look her up when I came back from Kleinwalsertal. She would be here and happy to see me, she claimed.

"And you should meet papa," she said, almost as an afterthought. "He loves the English."

I told her I would be delighted to meet her father. We said good night and much to my relief, Barbara walked away and left me with my thoughts. For some years, I had withdrawn into my world as a history teacher and I congratulated myself that I was well out of love, children and divorce. At the age of thirty, I was still a virgin, undeveloped in both taste and opinions but with the smouldering remains of nature's impulses and affections that had never been satisfied. Barbara had blown upon those dying embers, and they were now glowing brightly in the winter darkness.

Book Extract

Ein Soldatengrab in einem Wald. Chapter 1

In the fifties, the Tübingen City Council and the German War Graves Commission expressed their intention to take the remains of Martin Spohr and bury them with others in a communal site. However, the inhabitants of the villages in the Schönbuch area were strongly against this proposition. The following is part of the letter written to the German War Graves Commission by the mayor of Breitenholz on behalf of the people there. It was written in March 1952.

"We can obviously not make decisions on your behalf, but our personal wish would be to leave Martin Spohr in this very peaceful and well-maintained spot in the valley. So many people pass the grave, and it has come to symbolise dear memories of sons, brothers and husbands. We know that all these good people get a lot of comfort from the grave. Furthermore, we are certain that were Martin's parents alive today, they would not want him to be moved."

The German War Graves Commission replied a few weeks later.

"We understand and sympathise with what you have written, but unfortunately we can not guarantee that an individual grave in such an isolated spot will get our full attention."

The Hildrizhausen priest, Paul Fischer, wrote to the German War Graves Commission in 1954 in order to persuade them not to move Martin Spohr's remains.

"Martin Spohr's identity book and coat were found by me in April 1945. For some time, neither a body nor a grave was found, and so we were ready to report him simply as "missing". It was only by accident that the grave was found at all. Since that time, it has been respectfully looked after by people we do not know, but year after year we see the grave is cared for.

In 1949 I blessed the grave during a service there. The service was so well attended that I see it as a sure sign that the grave is well known and is often visited. The visitors are usually those who lost members of their families, but who were never able to visit their last places of rest. Martin Spohr's grave has therefore come to represent something symbolic for them.

Over the years nothing has changed. Because of this, we strongly believe that the remains of Martin Spohr should remain where they are, and where they are already looked after so well. I hope that for all these reasons, you will respect our wish that the remains stay where they were found."

Finally, in June 1956, the German War Graves Commission wrote to say that:

"The grave can stay where this soldier found his last place of rest."

Chapter 6

Hildrizhausen. 23 December. Evening

Hildrizhausen lay at a distance on the fringes of the forest. At the end of a seemingly endless avenue of trees, the town appeared as a vague and reddish-yellow glow under a mantel of stars. I was walking very quickly. The old man's story had disturbed me and given a hint of something darker and sterner than the forest itself. Even in this lonely stillness, I sensed that something was wandering up and down and brooding in the dark spaces between the trees.

On either side of me, the tops of the beech swept back and forth, an eerie shadow show majestically played out against the night sky. The show was accompanied from time to time by deep roars that sounded like jet planes taking off from a distant airport. I listened to the forest and the wind. It was gently moving as a murmur through the trees and stirring the undergrowth. The sound came without warning. It was fierce and frightening, the sound of wounded animals raging at the night. The roaring was both moving and unearthly and seemed bound to some other place or time. It was not a sound of confidence. It was a sort of howl that carried pain, resentment and sorrow. I quickened my pace to a jog.

The darkness was complete, and I was quite breathless by the time I entered Hildrizhausen. The streets were deserted, but I could hear the life of the town. It was an indistinct whispering among the eaves, and the occasional door or window banging shut against the night. The darkness was brightened in places by pools of yellowish light that shone through windows. The shadows that appeared briefly in these windows were reassuring. The shadows spoke to me and told me I was not alone. Still, I felt uncomfortable. Was it for fear of some dreadful monster that might appear from the forest that nobody dared venture out after dark? I took a deep breath and told myself to act my age. Why on earth should a thirty-year-old man worry about monsters and other unwanted things that might poke their heads out of the Schönbuch? I stared at the pavement for a second or two and tried to ignore the distant growl that still sounded from the depths of the forest.

When I saw the priest's house I made a light grunt of surprise. I had been here earlier in the day, but the building seemed new to me. I supposed it was the darkness that made me perceive objects with different eyes. Whatever the reason, I was now seeing the house for the first time. Perhaps, when I had come here earlier, my mind was on other things. I certainly had not before noticed the structure of the house. A lamp over the doorway lit up the walls and highlighted the yellow-painted and criss-crossing beams. And I did not recall that, between the beams, the wall bulged menacingly over the narrow pavement and threatened to drop its plaster onto the street below. Nor had I registered the existence of the church. But there it was, separated from the house by a low wall. The church was an ancient and crooked structure, set back from the road, but highly conspicuous with newly painted white walls that picked up the moonlight and threw it back at me in the darkness.

Peering at the cemetery, I expected to see moss-covered and leaning gravestones that would complement the age of the church. But the memorial stones were all of new and polished marble. Intrigued, I passed through a low wrought iron gate, intent on examining the headstones. It was winter, and the sharp scent of cut grass should have surprised me. Instead, the smell conjured up such a strong image of Barbara that I forgot what I had come to do. I stood amongst those dead souls while pictures of freshness and vitality passed pleasurably through my consciousness. Then, the church clock struck the half-hour.

Realising that it was getting late, I strode out of the cemetery and approached the front door of the priest's house. I lifted the knocker and let it fall on the woodwork. The crack of metal on wood set up an echoing thump which must have reached every corner and recess of the old house. I was standing with shoes in hand when the door swung open, and light flooded out to envelop me. The light was warm but so intense that it briefly dazzled me. The priest appeared as a tall and silent shape. His silence suggested that either he did not recognise me or that he was displeased to see me, but I was unable to make out the expression on his face. When I spoke to him in English, he stepped sideways, and I saw his mouth stretch into a smile. Lowering his eyes as I passed over the threshold, he closed the door behind me.

"You are late," he said.

I placed my shoes beside the floor mat and, glancing at the grandfather clock, I muttered out an apology. I was one hour late.

We made our way to the main room, and the sound of our slippers passing over the carpet was drowned out by the prominent ticking of the clocks. It was several seconds before I realised that both the priest and I were standing in the same positions we had taken up earlier - he between the windows, and me with the station clock ticking in my ear. This time though, it was night, and through the windows I noticed what I had not noticed before - neat rows of gravestones with their marble shining in the starlight. The memorial stones reminded me of what I had wanted to see just a few minutes previously.

"These graves," I said, nodding through the window,

"they are so new, and the church is so old. What happened to the older graves?"

The priest let his smile drop from his face. I watched the thin wrist emerge from the sleeve of his pullover, and the shoulder twitched irritably. I expected him to glance at his watch. He merely shook his head as though he were troubled.

"They are removed," he said, in a matter-of-fact way. "When they lie untended for some years, we take them away."

I interpreted his tone and the puzzled frown as a reprimand for my not being able to see the obvious.

"That's callous, isn't it?"

"Callous?"

"Yes," I said, and immediately decided to follow up the advantage given to me by this power of language.

"Yes, callous. Unfeeling, uncaring, perhaps disrespectful of those who remember the dead."

The priest pursed his lips and looked at me from above the rim of his glasses. The eyes held a suggestion of indecision.

"I must apologise for my poor English," he said, "but we don't get many foreign visitors here."

I gave the priest a cheerless smile, and we stared at each other, hostility gathering.

"With regard to the graves," he said, "if nobody cares for them, then it's clear that there's nobody alive who remembers the occupant of that plot of land. The dead live on only in the memory of the living, don't they? I mean, when memory is gone, then surely it is right that their piece of earth is given over to someone else. I'm sure you would agree."

The logic of this irritated me still further.

"And the grave in the forest?" I said. "Why do I get the impression that there's nobody left in the world who knew him?"

The priest clasped his hands together. I thought he was

going to offer up a prayer, but instead, he shook his head so violently that the glasses fell askew.

"If you get that impression," he said, "then you have clearly misunderstood the significance of the place."

He lifted his hand and, removing the glasses from his face, he pinched the bridge of his nose between thumb and forefinger.

"There is another reason why we leave this grave in peace," he said. "The reason is that it reminds us that we are human. It reminds us what humans can do to each other. Most of all, it reminds us to remember those things that many of us would prefer to forget."

"Then why not destroy it?"

"I told you," he said, replacing his glasses, "we need to be reminded. But we do not want to be reminded every day of our lives. After all, we had nothing to do with it."

"It?" I said. "You mean the war? The murder of the Jews?"

I heard a faint babble of voices from outside. The priest snapped his head towards the window. His hair brushed the collar of his shirt while he pushed nervously at the glasses. He stayed silent for a while and then began nodding.

"Let me tell you two things about the Germans," he said. "First, unlike you English, tomorrow, the twenty-fourth of December, we celebrate Christmas. Today, we go into the forest and take leaves and branches to decorate our dinner tables. The people are now gathering outside the church. This is the tradition."

His voice was low but trembling to an undercurrent of emotion. He was blinking rapidly into the silence of his self-restraint. Then, he said:

"The second thing you need to know is this. We do not like to dwell on the past, rather like you English do. For you, the past is part of the present. It is in your institutions - the queen for instance represents continuity. But consider what it is for us? What do we have which we should continue? What do we have on which we can look back and say, ah yes, they were the good old days? It is difficult for us. In many ways our history began in 1945. What happened before that date must be, and needs to be, filed away. Not forgotten but filed away."

"Perhaps hidden away in the forest," I said.

The priest's ears turned to pink, and in the crushing silence that followed, the stupidity of my comment overwhelmed me. I wanted to reach out, put a hand on my own shoulder and tell myself to calm down.

From outside, I heard a familiar sound that had a quality of its own. It was the sound of children. Their echoing mixture of laughter, shouts of surprise and excitement seemed to explode high in the air and hang there as bright as a Roman candle.

"So," the priest said, "I take it you have seen the grave - hidden away in the forest?"

"Yes," I said.

"It was not difficult to find? Not so hidden?"

I shook my head and tried to soften my tone.

"Not at all."

"It is a lonely and isolated spot, don't you think?"

I looked sideways at the priest, and there was a voice in my inner ear: *You are being manipulated. This man is angling for information.* I shook my head and threw the voice out. It was replaced by the troubling image of me as the good Englishman, and good Englishmen mistrusted the Germans. This was the image my mother had created for me. She would have approved of my attitude towards this man. But the troubling question remained. Did I really dislike him, or had I simply been programmed to do so?

"Did you," the priest asked, "see anyone else around?"

"I met an old man there," I said.

The priest pushed at his glasses. The eyes behind them still sparkled but it was the sparkle of hard diamonds.

"Old man?" he asked. "What old man?"

The intensity of his stare and the arrogance of his manner came together to make my unease develop still further. I tried telling myself that I was a stranger here, and that he was speaking a foreign language. I decided to give him the benefit of the doubt and I told him about my meeting with the old man. The priest searched my face as I spoke. When I finished, he turned his head to one side and said something I was not able to catch.

"What was that?" I asked.

The priest looked at the floor and then at me. There was a long silence. Then he said:

"So he did come back then. We thought he would. Somehow we knew he was here."

He spread out his arms and shrugged. Then, he looked at me and smiled in a way that suggested an attempt to involve me in a conspiracy of understanding.

"As you know," he said, "it is an illusion. Once you leave, you can never come back."

"You've lost me," I said. "Who are you talking about?"

The priest pointed to an armchair set at an angle near the window.

"Please," he said, "have a seat."

He was smiling as he said it, and I decided to accept his hospitality as genuine. I settled myself in the chair while the priest hovered at my shoulder. In the silence, my suspicions of him took on a more precise form, but they bothered me like disturbing personal questions. At last, the priest said:

"I was referring to a ghost. Someone we never met but who was, I believe, known to my father. He was to come here this afternoon - I was expecting him while you were away. In fact, I thought it was him when you knocked. No matter. He never came. It is nothing."

He had turned his back to me but his ears were burning red. He seemed restless and was fidgeting so much, he looked like a man who wanted to shed his clothes. He glanced at his watch.

"Now," he said, "it is time to tell you what I know."

He swept out of my line of vision, and I heard drawers

roughly opening and closing in an adjacent room. A few seconds later, he reappeared. Some papers and a folder were delicately balanced in the palm of his hand. He treated the papers with care and he held them close to his chest while he drew up a dining chair and sat down beside me. He was suddenly animated, a small boy who has been invited to discuss his hobby.

"What we know," he said, "is that Martin Spohr was from Ostheim. We know this from the letters. The letter you found in your attic was a letter to Martin from his mother. Probably the last letter she wrote to him."

Outside the sound of voices was getting louder. Glancing through the window, I saw that there were several shapes now gathered by the graveyard wall. A street-lamp threw an eerie light upon them so that I was unable to distinguish between the shadows and the reality.

"In 1965," the priest said, "I received a letter from your mother."

At this point he stopped, selected a paper from the pile on his lap and passed it across the gap that separated us.

"As you can see," the priest went on, "your mother wanted to know about a certain Martin Spohr, and if we knew what had happened to him."

I fingered the letter and tried to figure out why I did not want to look at it. Somehow I wanted to deny its existence. It represented a part of my mother's legacy and yet it also represented something I dared not consider, something like dishonesty.

"My father had passed away," the priest said, "so I sent your mother a translation of both the 1945 letter and the documents. These you found in the attic, I believe."

I nodded, but I was studying my mother with my mind's eye. She was sitting at the breakfast table and absorbed in the letter she held. My inner eye watched her place the letter in the trunk in the attic. She sealed the trunk and rejected her past. I heard her telling herself that there were more important things in life to get on with. I said:

"But why did she keep these things hidden away?"

I hesitated, delaying the inevitable. My heart sounded like a drum beating in time to the words of my next question.

"Did she tell you what she wanted?"

The priest licked his lips and looked me straight in the eye. Something had disturbed him. His ears, those beacons of his innermost thoughts and feelings betrayed him again. He lowered his head and whispered something I could barely catch.

"She thought that Martin Spohr might be her father."

"No, no, no."

"If the papers are correct, and there is no reason to think that they are incorrect, then, she was right."

I was shaking my head and trying to laugh.

"No, that's not possible."

I said it with conviction and with my chin thrust forward. The priest leaned sideways and placed his hand on my arm.

"I'm sorry," he said. "It is possible."

I was about to repeat my denial when the expression on his face halted my words before they really had time to form. His hand tightened its grip on my forearm. He whispered:

"The papers are correct. Your mother was right. Martin Spohr was your mother's father."

There was nothing to say. I folded and unfolded the letter I held in my hands. I was hoping that something might come out of it and tell me I was dreaming. Now I saw I had another history and another sorrow, and that I would have to come to terms with it. There was an audible creak from the joints of the priest's chair.

"So," he continued, "the grave you have just seen is the grave of your maternal grandfather."

He sat quietly, waiting for me to absorb what I had heard. It was one thing to know the truth. It was quite another to hear the words in the mouth of another. It somehow gave the words life and truth. I looked expectantly into his eyes and said:

"But why did she keep this information from me?"

He shrugged and shook his head.

"I don't know. I can't tell you that."

"But she wrote this letter," I said, "it must have been important to her."

The grip of the priest's hand remained tight. He was aware of me and sensitive to my feelings. I felt guilty that I had mistrusted him. He said:

"It was 1965. Your mother would have been twenty years old when she wrote the letter to my father, am I right? She must have reached a point in her life when she was confident enough, or interested enough, to find out about her forebears."

I took a deep breath and tried to calm myself. The priest could not know it, but 1965 was the year my parents were married. 1965 was the year my mother's life began. Before that there was darkness, a place covered with storm clouds, a secret and forbidden place in the forest where I, as the only child, was never allowed to tread. I felt like a patient awaiting an anticipated bad diagnosis from his doctor. I steeled myself for the worst.

"So," I said, "you'd better tell me the rest."

"In the letter you have, dated 1945, Martin's mother mentions someone called Mathilde. It seems that this Mathilde was Martin Spohr's wife. At least, we know she was expecting his child in April 1945. My father met Martin's uncle after the war. It was he who told my father everything he knew. It seems that Mathilde had been killed. The uncle was very keen to find evidence of Martin Spohr's death. In fact it was he who found the grave in the first place. It seems that a British soldier wanted to adopt the child and take her to England. In order to do this, it was essential to find proof that the natural parents were both dead."

From outside the window there was a sudden increase in

the number of voices. There was a shout and then a cheer. Someone sang the line of a song. Then there was silence.

"Do you have evidence of this?" I said.

The priest smiled and raised his eyebrows.

"One thing we Germans are very good at," he said, "is keeping records.

He ran his hand over the folder and then opened it.

"All the documentation is here. I have all the correspondence between my father and Martin Spohr's uncle. Of course, my father checked what he had been told. It seems that Mathilde's child was indeed taken to England and adopted by an English soldier and his wife. Sergeant Brian Humphreys was the name, and the formalities were completed early in 1948, soon after the confirmation of Martin's death. The documents are all here."

He sorted through the papers, selected one and proffered it to me. Absent-mindedly I took it. It never occurred to me that I would not understand it. It was enough to feel the weightiness of it, to see the old and faded light blue of the ink and the beautifully crafted writing. The priest seemed pleased with himself. The written evidence obviously gave him some kind of emotional satisfaction.

"At the time, there were no objections. The poor child had no family, and Germany was a country in rubble with a shameful past and an uncertain future. Our people were apparently finished, and our country flattened. Your bombers saw to that."

He nodded at me in order to reinforce his words. He then looked towards the floor in an act of apparent remembrance.

"Your mother was born a German," he said at last, "but she grew up English. Sergeant Humphreys must have told your mother everything she wanted to know about her past. At a certain point in her life, she would have wanted confirmation. And so - her letters. Is this not correct?"

I scanned my mind. I saw the photo album. There were photos of my mother in her pram, my mother taking her

76

first steps, and my mother on the beach. There were also pages of emptiness. What remained were the annotations like: "The family at Worthing," or "The family on Box Hill." But the photos had long since been torn out.

"I really can't say," I said.

"You don't know how your mother found out about her past?"

I shook my head.

"No."

"You mean, you never met this soldier? Did your mother never talk about him?"

"Not to me," I said. "And no, I never met the man. He died apparently, before I was born - a heart attack while pushing a boat off a sandbank."

"And what about the man's wife? Did you never meet her?"

"Sorry," I said, "I didn't."

A sudden gust of wind rattled the window frame. Instinctively, I turned my head. The group on the pavement had now gathered to some size. Some of them held lanterns above their heads. The downward light cast the faces in an unearthly glow.

The sandbank, the boat, the large house and the shady business dealings. These were the things about which I was forbidden to ask. It was not that I was explicitly forbidden to do so, but my mother had somehow made them dirty and taboo subjects like sex or masturbation. Perhaps by instinct, I decided to change the subject.

"What about the old man," I said, "why did you want to speak to him? Where does he fit in to all this?"

The priest raised his hand and, pushing away the hair that had fallen over his glasses, he let the hand remain on his forehead. He could have been protecting his eyes from a strong and blinding light.

"We don't exactly know," he said. "What I do know is that my father corresponded with him in the early fifties. I do not know what passed between them. My father kept no records of their dialogue. I am sorry for this, but there are no records."

He seemed genuinely ashamed.

"But why would your father want to speak to him?"

The priest looked up.

"My father was also interested in the soldier's grave. He wanted to know as much about Martin Spohr as possible. He was writing a history of the Nazi era."

He proudly held up a bundle of hand-written pages.

"He wanted to record for posterity how the period had influenced Hildrizhausen."

"But why," I repeated, "would your father want to speak to him?"

"The old man was serving in this area in 1945," the priest said. "My father thought that he had some information which might be useful to him, for his history."

"So what does this history say?"

"Nothing. My father never mentions this man in his history."

"Do you know why not?"

There was a hesitation, a second of indecision.

"No," he said.

I felt tiredness pulling at my eyelids as I struggled with the returning thought that the man was not telling me the truth.

"But surely," I said, "can't you guess?"

"Until I received your letter I was content to let things be. Your arrival threatened to change things. I wanted to speak to him before I spoke to you. He did not come. That is all."

"Why did you need to speak to him?"

The priest turned his face to mine.

"Once upon a time," he said, "that old man was a company commander. He was, in fact, your grandfather's company commander."

Outside, the gathered throng had lined up opposite the church and stood in two lines. Other people appeared at the church wall. There were large shapes and small, parents and their children.

"He knew my grandfather?"

The priest nodded.

"But there is no mention of it in my father's book. He wrote it in the fifties but for some reason he saw fit not to include the company commander's story. I am not sure why."

"How do you know so much about this?"

"The chapters I gave you," the priest said, "the ones from, 'A Soldier's Grave in a Forest,' were written by me. But much of the information in them came from my father's book. He wanted, and I want, the grave to live on as a monument to love, to peace and goodwill. This old man knew Martin Spohr. I wanted to speak to him. That is all."

Outside, a sound rose up from the shapes by the wall. It was a rendition of "Silent Night."

"Then perhaps," I said, "I had better speak to him."

Behind me, I felt the presence of the priest and then his hand on my shoulder.

"You know where he is?"

I rushed across the room towards the front door. I heard the priest step across the room and tug at my arm.

"Please," he said, "before you go, remember what your mother said. There are some things that are bigger than us. Some things are best left alone. The earth should not be turned."

I swung round to face him. The priest's face and ears were flushed.

"What did she – do you – mean by something bigger than us?" I asked. "God?"

"Perhaps. But not necessarily that."

At that point, I bent down to slip into my shoes and, putting on my coat, I opened the door. Fresh and cold air brought with it the final lines of "Silent Night." I hardly heard the priest's parting words.

"You don't know what you are doing ..."

I was not listening. I got into my car and drove down the hill into Herrenberg. I parked the car near the market square and hurried towards my hotel. Even before I walked through the door, I could hear the merriment from inside. The restaurant was full of laughter and the sound of children.

The hotel manager was extremely busy. Bustling in and out of the dining room, he handed me a note from my key hole and, in response to my enquiry, told me that the old man had left the hotel that afternoon and had yet to return. The note was from Barbara. It was an invitation to a party on the 27 December.

Forestry Commission Herrenberg

Hurricanes can cause immense damage, both directly (by wind, pressure, and rain) and indirectly (mainly by storm surges and floods). A wind of 74-93 kilometres per hour strips leaves and small branches off trees. At 111-130 kilometres per hour it can topple shallow-rooted trees or snap weaker trees outright, blow down thin walls, shift roofing material, and occasionally lift a whole roof. At about 130 kilometres per hour, lifting of roofs, uprooting, and snapping of trees is general. Wind can cause injuries and death by toppling structures and hurling loose or torn objects about with enormous force.

An action plan for the reforestation of south Germany is now in place after Hurricane Lothar destroyed the woodlands.

Klimaschutz durch Wald e.V will set up a fund for the reforestation of south Germany after Hurricane Lothar destroyed large areas of woodland on 26 December 1999.

The power of Lothar was greater than anything previously experienced. Tragically, several fatalities occurred in the Schönbuch Forest and the Black Forest. Furthermore, more than 400000 hectares of woodland were destroyed. Apart from the economic problems caused by this catastrophe, even more damage has been caused ecologically.

It will take years before the damage is cleared away, but we must start immediately with the replanting of trees.

We need your help.

Chapter 7

Kleinwalsertal - Herrenberg. 26 December

I awoke to the howls and shrieks of a storm wind. The shrieks rose to intermittent crescendos, and were followed by sounds that brought to mind huge sheets flapping and cracking in the wind. It was clear that any hopes I might have harboured, that an improvement in the weather would open the ski slopes, were dashed. It was equally clear that I had already made a decision.

I swung my legs from the bed and rushed into the bathroom. The cold water woke me up completely, and I strode back into the bedroom and dressed in a hurry. When I had finished, I went over to the window. Through a gap in the curtains, a vision of gloom hung low over the mountains. The high winds had stripped the mountains of snow before my arrival on the afternoon of the twenty-fourth. The icy beginners' slopes were still gleaming with bone-breaking menace.

The previous day, the twenty-fifth, I had seen too much of the hotel lounge, watched too much television, and had been disturbed by too many noisy and laughing children. Between bulletins of CNN news, I had peered with pessimism at the worsening weather conditions. What was more, the people around me were behaving in the wrong way, had the wrong expressions on their faces or the wrong tone in their voices. They should have been sullen and reinforcing my own frustrations by loudly complaining about the weather. Instead, they seemed to have accepted conditions as they were, and everyone happily retreated into warm and cosy family groups from which I was firmly excluded.

Being alone, even on Christmas Day, was not a new experience for me. I was an only child, and my mother had been an orphan. This meant that the cousins, uncles and aunts that other people had, were unknown to me. With my father just a vague image of what might have been, I learned to find security in myself and happiness wherever I could find it. This had always been the norm. But during those idle hours on Christmas Day, feelings of intense loneliness prompted me to question this norm, and I saw that, perhaps, there was something more. As the day wore slowly on, I recognised the birth of an urgent and aching need. I too yearned for a place where I could put my heart.

Standing at my bedroom window on the morning of the twenty-sixth, it was clear that I might face another day of inactivity, boredom and morbid introspection. The decision to leave was suddenly there as the obvious choice when there were no options. I made two calls to Herrenberg. The first was to my hotel. The call was punctuated with long silences while I listened to the crackle of static and the rustle of papers. I grew impatient at the sound of off-stage whispers that seemed to go on for an interminable length of time. When, at length, the landlord ran through the registration process, he began with a vague apology, but his manner was offhand and distant as though his concentration was elsewhere.

After breakfast I made my way down a long and narrow corridor at the end of which was a counter. Behind the counter sat the proprietor like a schoolmaster at his desk. He was a young blond, with his hair parted on one side, and a thin wispy moustache. I expressed my disappointment at an early departure. We went through the formalities and, handing me my passport, the young man looked at me with an expression of mild concern.

"We are sorry to see you leave," he said. "Have a good trip sir, and do please, drive with great care. There really is some bad weather about."

I was focused on a sense of freedom that had come over me rather than on the weather. It was a freedom made of ties cut, of things left behind, and only the future to deal with. The bad weather absolved me of the necessity to make excuses to myself. The dam of conscience was breached, and my true feelings and desires were free to pour through. I would be able see Barbara.

The previous day, her face had accompanied me during those moments of reflection and introspection. It was not a vague face I saw, but the actual one. Still, it was not enough. The face I recalled already belonged to the past. I needed to replenish the image and reconnect with it. My second call was to her. I fumbled for the phone and nervously punched out her number. I listened to the purring of the phone. There was a click, and I was connected. I heard my breathing coming fast into the mouthpiece. I tried smiling but with no returning smile I was aware only of the muscular effort.

"It's Martin," I said. "I'd like to accept your invitation."

There was a heavy silence at the other end of the line. My heart sank. Without vision I lost the quality of feeling that was associated with it. There were no facial expressions, no stolen glances or cheeky grins, and no more conversations through looking. I was shaken at my inability to replace this feeling through other channels. This loss defined my isolation. I was in a no-man's land waiting for a sigh or a sound to tell me she was happy to hear my voice. She told me she would pick me up at one o'clock the following day, and the phone died.

My hand was shaking so badly it took three attempts to return the receiver to its holder. I stared at it for some time, wondering how I should interpret her tone. Her silences had disarmed me. By the time my bags were safely in the car boot, I had managed to convince myself that no news was good news, and I was cheered by the fact that she had, at least, agreed to see me.

On the mountain, the wind was flushing out the remnants of the powder snow and blowing it high into the air in spirals of white. In the valley, it was unseasonably warm, and it was raining. Water was soon splashing and running across the road in little waves.

The road from Kleinwalsertal to the motorway ran between glistening mountain sides that loomed over the empty roads. When I came out of the valley and approached Oberstdorf I was feeling uneasy. Cars were neatly parked in rows, and flags strained in the wind and cracked like pistol shots. Nothing was out of the ordinary, and yet I was unable to shake off a distinct feeling of nervousness. Over the Nebelhorn, a low and spiralling cloud was visible. Not even thoughts of seeing Barbara could make the cloud less dense, nor did anticipation of speaking once more to the old man make the dark olive tint of the cloud less sinister.

There were very few cars on the road with me. It was as if the rest of the world was privy to some secret that had been kept from me. I sank down low in the driver's seat and tried to pretend that the daylight was not unnatural, the day itself was not threatening. No sooner had this pretence become a sort of reality than a rumble of wind shoved the car to one side, and I was forced to concentrate on my driving.

It was around eleven-thirty, and I was well out of the Alps and on my way to Stuttgart when strange things happened. The sound of flapping sheets returned. But this time it was preceded by a rush of air followed by a disarming crack and a deep vibration, which sounded like a peel of thunder over my head. The car staggered and jerked and then started on a series of sideways movements, each one worse than the other.

By midday, tense and concentrated, I was in the Stuttgart area. The air was alive with bits of tree that blew violently across the road or were sucked upwards, twirling and turning erratically in the air. I had always associated twigs and small branches with gently-stroking softness and feathery springiness. These twigs had betrayed me. They rushed downwards and smacked against the windscreen.

My knuckles were white and straining, gripping the steering wheel for support as I tried to keep a straight course. Beside the road, the trees hurled themselves from side to side. Apparently intent on throwing off the grip of some terrible illness, the trees set up a screeching howl of anger or pain. I made a vague connection between this howling and the invisible hand that had put itself on the car. And the roar, the same roar I had once heard in the depths of the forest, seemed to have escaped at last and was attacking me with an insane ferocity. I reeled beneath the storm and tried not to dwell too long on the dreadful truth. These twigs and branches were only the visible evidence of a force which was beyond my control.

I drove on into this madness in a sort of concentrated daze. My mind had turned off, but instinct made me brake sharply as the line of cars in front was suddenly lit up like a Christmas tree of red lights flickering in the chaos. Despite the presence of these other vehicles, I was isolated. The wind had singled me out and was attacking me like a personal enemy. There was another howl, and the car shook as it was caught in a powerful rush of air. The roar of the wind rose to a crescendo. A wild and shocking shriek swooped down from the sky and gripped and then released the car. I fell forward in my seat and the car lurched helplessly and staggered. It suddenly occurred to me that I might be sucked off the road. My life was in danger.

At first, I was invaded by a clear sense of coldness and a lack of emotion. I watched in fascination as hundreds of tiny whirlpools shot across the road in front of me. Coldness was soon replaced by sadness. I was sad for myself, as though my "self" were some separate identity for which nobody would care or mourn in the event of its death. And then, I was gritting my teeth and gripping the wheel in anger. Intent on hanging on to a life that I cared for even if nobody else did, I waited for the next great rush of air. It did not come. It was only later that I discovered I had driven right through the dying eye of Hurricane Lothar.

When I eventually decelerated at the Herrenberg exit, the falling engine note was overlaid with a distant humming. This faraway sound, soaring over an unnatural Sunday-afternoon quiet, rose higher and higher until I recognised the sound. Sirens were urgently screeching through the late afternoon light. I saw that many television aerials were hanging at strange or impossible angles as if held up to the sky by some invisible thread. The road and the pavements were covered in a scattering of pine needles, splinters of tree and snapped branches. These sometimes straddled the road and hindered my progress towards the town centre.

By the time I parked the car, the storm had eased. Even so, as I attempted to open the door, the wind caught it. I was almost dragged from the car and found myself fighting with an invisible enemy as I tried to shut the door. From somewhere in the distance, fragments of forlorn shouting snatched past my ear.

I grabbed my bag from the boot and struggled towards the marketplace. Smashed tiles were embedded in the neatly swept snow. The fallen chimney pots, lying in pieces on the ground, prompted me to duck and glance upwards. The wind was gradually abating to an occasional rush and howl, and a weak and watery sun broke through the clouds. The December afternoon put out its long but sickly shadows, and I followed my own as it broke on the steps of the Rathausstaffel. The lantern, now squeaking like a stuck pig, announced the presence of the hotel. The sound was as welcoming as a funeral march. There was not a living soul in sight, but somewhere near at hand there was a subdued voice with an accompanying echo that seemed to be a part of the disturbed twilight itself.

When I pushed at the hotel door, I half expected to be greeted with sounds of Christmas merriment and people sitting over the tables as I had last seen them three days previously. I was met instead by the sound of my feet on the floorboards, an empty hallway and a clock loudly ticking over the reception desk. The landlord must have heard me. At the second creak of my feet on the boards, he emerged from a back room and looked at me with eyes that were lively but sly, held an expression that was both servile and watchful. He turned his eyes downwards and mumbled words at me while he flicked through the pages of the register.

"It is good you are back, Mr Slater," he said. "We are very pleased to have you back with us. Yes, very pleased."

His dark hair was parted in the middle and fell limply over his temples while he studied the register.

"All the distance you have come today and in such terrible weather," he said. "Yes, we are glad you are with us again."

He seemed to be slightly short of breath, his forehead was lightly coated in sweat, and his movements were those of an agitated bird.

"We have had a scare. Mr Slater," he said. "Actually we are still having a slight scare."

I supposed he was talking about the storm winds so I merely nodded at him in agreement. I was about to pick up my bag when I heard the subdued voice again. I turned my head in surprise. Curiosity made me forget the case, and I looked around for the source of the sound. I took a step sideways and peered through the dining room doorway.

A man was sitting in an armchair. His back was to me. I was sure I had seen him somewhere before, but not with the legs splayed out and twisted, the head thrown back so it hung uncomfortably over the back of the armchair. If I had seen this person before he had not been asleep in front of the television.

The hotel dining room was in semi-darkness. I watched

the television images playing across the torso of the reclining figure, and I heard a man say something in German. I stood at the door while traditional German band music played and two middle-aged women in traditional costumes bounded onto the TV screen and sang. The TV images flickered up and down the sleeping man's trunk, and I observed that his clothes were similar to a policeman's clothes. The pullover was brown and matched the trousers that splayed out towards the television.

I was wondering how the man could sleep with his feet bent inwards, and his head tilted back at such an angle when I noted a change in the room. The storm had already shaken me, and now my breathing quickened, and my gaze darted from one side of the room to the other. It was the head over the back of the chair that had shifted. The man had somehow twisted it still further backwards, and his eyes were staring at me from under a curved nose and a walrus moustache. He raised his hand and twisted one end of his moustache between thumb and forefinger. Then he made a sound that could have been a sigh and he said something under his breath that I was unable to catch.

Before I had time to register that he might have been addressing me, he surprised me still further by leaping to his feet and spinning round in one energetic movement. A nervous smile was hovering around his lips.

"Global warming," he said, "yes, global warming."

We stood still and stared at each other over a distance of about three metres.

"Global warming," he repeated. "I fear it is something we will have to get used to, Martin, don't you think?"

I was extremely sensitive. On the motorway, I had nearly lost my life, and I wrapped myself around it like a protective cushion. I glared at him.

"Who are you anyway?"

He flinched as if he had been struck in the face, and the hovering smile flickered and then died.

"Correct me if I'm wrong," he said, "but you are Martin Slater, are you not?"

I nodded slowly, still trying to recall where I had seen him. It was his air of subdued authority which touched some distant memory. He had a long and thin body whose only purpose seemed to be as a support for his head. This was tilted backwards, and he was examining me through half-closed eyelids. A puffiness around the eyes was the only sign of his having been asleep just a minute earlier, but this puffiness did not disguise a sorrowful expression I had previously only associated with tired old hunting dogs. He held his hands behind his back, military fashion, and his legs were placed tightly together with the feet pointing outwards at ten minutes to two.

Without taking his eyes from mine, he leaned backwards and switched off the television. The singing ladies and the band disappeared into a pinprick of light on the television screen, and the policeman and I were immediately plunged into a deeper darkness. He waited for the television to go through its death throes, and he tapped a foot impatiently while the TV clicked and crackled its way to silence.

"My name is Maximilian Hart," he said. "Polizei Hauptwachmeister, Böblingen."

There was an awkward silence while he blinked at me and my stomach shifted.

"If I'm not mistaken," he said, "you say Police Chief Inspector in English."

He pointed a finger in the vague direction of the church and the Schlossberg.

"The Schönbuch Forest doesn't stretch quite as far as Böblingen. The trees stop, you know, on the edge of this new town. Nonetheless, the forest lies within my area of responsibility. Right now, the place is devastated. As I said, global warming is something we'll have to get used to."

I tried to fill the ensuing silence with appreciative noises, and then the policeman waved me to a chair. As I sat down, I noticed a dark shadow on the table. It was the remains of the old man's wine that had stained the tablecloth three days previously. I sent my mind back to search the day for some misdemeanour I might have committed. I waited with increasing unease as the Chief Inspector took a seat at a table on the other side of the room. I heard the trousers rub together as he crossed his legs.

"Tomorrow," the policeman said, "the foresters will begin clearing away the fallen trees from the main paths into the forest. But for the time being, we will not be able to get into the Schönbuch; at least, not on foot."

He cupped one knee between his hands, and his dark shape swayed slightly forwards and backwards. Through the window behind his head, the sky cloud was streaked and glowing red, and lingering a long time. The Chief Inspector's shoulders rose in a shrug.

"But until then Martin," he said, "we can do nothing about it."

The struggle to find something meaningful to say was accompanied by the nagging and elusive memory that continuously tugged at my consciousness. Where had I met this man before?

"Yes, it was a terrible ..."

"It is a matter of the utmost importance to us," the Chief Inspector said, twisting one end of his moustache. "It is for the old man's sake, you see. If we do not get to the bottom of the matter soon, we're going to become seriously worried. The signs are there. I have been concerned about it all day. In fact, I have been waiting for you; yes, for you, Martin. You might be able to help me."

Hart ran one hand down his pullover and brushed at his trousers in a way that suggested he was wiping away crumbs of bread. Outside, in the darkness, was the sound of brushes on the cobblestones - the cleaning had already started.

"So perhaps," the policeman said, "you could tell us what it was you talked about the other day. I saw you both, you know, together in this very room."

The dim light of memory brightened. Of course, I had seen this man some days previously. It was the day of my arrival in Herrenberg. It was the day I had met Barbara. He had been sitting at a table in this very restaurant with his wife and children. I smiled knowingly at the Chief Inspector, but I needed help. I was trying to look open, honest and decent, but in the darkening room, I was aware that he was unable to see the expression on my face. I tried to contain myself in my voice, but I sounded childish.

"I'm not sure who you're referring to," I said. "Is it the old man who sat at my table?"

I twitched uncomfortably. I was unable to deal with the quality of the long silence that fell between us. Knowing he could not see my face, I had a need to talk, to fill the silence, to verbalise everything. I tried to put a smile into my words.

"You do mean the old man I ate with, don't you?"

I imagined a flash in the policeman's eyes and a stern glare. I leaned forward and tried to see his expression, but it was his voice which came at me through the unnatural quiet.

"Do you recall what you talked about?"

"No," I snapped, unwilling to face another awkward silence. "I mean, he seemed upset about something to do with the past, the war, I think."

Another silence. I was completely unaware of what he was thinking. The darkness was like a barrier, and for the second time that day I was confronted by a sort of communicative no-man's-land. I tried smiling again but with no reinforcement, it was simply wasted effort.

"He spoke about it again," I said, "when I met him in the forest."

"You met him in the forest?"

The speed of the question surprised me, and I tried to interpret its tone. I imagined the face, animated, interested, immersed.

"Yes," I said, "two, no, three days ago."

I was left struggling to throw some light on the quality of the silence that engulfed us. I was barely able to hear the man breathing.

"Three days ago?" he said at last. "The twenty-third of December. So what exactly was the time of day?"

"Afternoon."

"When in the afternoon?"

"I'm not sure," I replied, "around three or three-thirty."

"And where did you see him? Where exactly in the forest?"

"By the grave," I said, "the soldier's grave."

I peered into the darkness and tried to see what was written on the policeman's face. I realised then that a face is not just a place where the voice comes from. I was hoping I had said the right thing. I was hoping to hear it in the man's tone of voice. I heard a rustle, and then I was blinded by the light of a table lamp.

"Mr Slater," the Chief Inspector said, "the old man we are talking of left this hotel on the afternoon of the twenty-third. He has not been seen since. Naturally we are anxious. You saw him in the forest. We have just been hit by a hurricane. The Schönbuch Forest is devastated. Falling trees are dangerous, Mr Slater."

As my eyes gradually became used to the light, I realised that I was looking at Maximilian Hart for the first time. In the darkness, I had become used to my own construction of the man. I had begun to invent a face for him. I soon saw that this creative use of memory had been neat and clever, but unsustainable. Now I was confused, and the Chief Inspector was eyeing me with what I took to be suspicion.

"So what exactly did you talk about?"

"He seemed distressed," I said.

"Distressed? Distressed people can do strange things, Martin. I need to know what might have happened to him."

I shook my head.

"He seemed to think that the grave was not what it seemed to be, that its appearance was not the reality."

The policeman turned the ends of his moustache again and raised his face to the ceiling. Then, his eyelids fluttered. The movement was so delicate I was reminded of butterflies gently winging their way from flower to flower.

"I am listening Martin," he said. "So did he tell you what that reality was?"

"No."

"And did he tell you," the Chief Inspector asked, "what he was doing there?"

"Yes – no; well, not exactly."

"Yes or no?"

"He said he mistook me for someone else."

"So he might have arranged to meet someone there?"

"He didn't say so, but it is possible."

"But, as you correctly say, Martin, he didn't say so?"

"No."

"So Martin," the policeman said, lowering his head and looking me straight in the eye, "your information is very useful to us. It may be that you were the last person to speak with the man before his disappearance. Yes, your information is of the utmost importance."

He raised his head to the ceiling once again and pushed himself back on his chair. I saw his moustache twitching, and the eyelids fluttered again as if the policeman were blinking thoughts into existence.

"Of course," he said, "the man may turn up, today, perhaps tomorrow."

Allowing the chair to fall forward, the Chief Inspector reached into an inside pocket and produced a card, which he handed to me. The written confirmation of the man's identity somehow gave him a more threatening reality.

"But do please, Martin, let us know your movements. This is also of the utmost importance until we can ascertain what exactly has happened to him."

I nodded and the understanding dawned. I had been interrogated, I had been warned, but above all, I saw that I was under suspicion.

Reuters

17.08.1999

Posters and leaflets hailing Nazi Rudolf Hess a "martyr of peace" appeared around Germany on the 12th anniversary of his death Thursday amid national concern over the far-right movement. Police broke up a torchlight parade by some 100 neo-Nazis late Wednesday in the German city of Hamburg.

This year's anniversary of Hess's death comes amid concern about the extent of far-right attitudes and racist violence in a country still painfully conscious of its Nazi past.

German parliament speaker Wolfgang Esslinger said the annual commemoration of Hess's death showed the wider problem with the far-right and neo-Nazism was not likely to go away at any time in the near future.

The government announced it would spend a further $35 million over the next three years to combat right-wing extremism with educational and social projects. One city leader warned, however, the government could not take the lead in the fight against the far-right and racist violence if the people as a whole were not more prepared to come forward and denounce the culprits of both past and present. "In the thirties and forties, people often turned away from what they knew was going on. Consequently, many crimes were committed, and many of the surviving perpetrators are still at large. These individuals should be hunted down. The people have got to learn to show their teeth, to stand up and fight the danger from the far-right and stamp it out for good," said Stuttgart mayor Hans Henke.

Chapter 8

We turned off the open road and drove across the forecourt of Joerg Eisenmann's car showrooms. Barbara nosed the Mercedes round a hedge, and we surged towards a place where many other cars were parked. Barbara dived into a space. At the end of this was a plaque with her car numberplate emblazoned on it, BB-BE-1. She turned off the engine and jumped out. Remaining seated for a while, I tried to gather my wits and prepare myself for what was about to come. The disappointing truth was that I was short on party spirit, my head was lightly throbbing, and I was finding it difficult to look others in the eye.

The continuous reliving of the storm, the post-mortems and the dark imaginings of what could have happened, had eventually shocked me. Others had not been so lucky. The evening before, I had watched television images of cars crushed by falling trees, and several people had been reported missing in the forests. The trial of the policeman's questions had left me off-balance and very insecure in unknown surroundings. Feeling the need to talk, I had tried to phone Barbara, but when I heard the answering machine click on, my heart sank still further. I left the message that I was back in town. Then I took the only option left to me and went to bed.

The following morning, I awoke late. It was ten-thirty, and the new day was already beaming strong and bright through the window. Sunlight had drawn back the darkness and stilled the turbulent air. I jumped out of bed and skipped towards the bathroom. Then, the phone rang. It was Barbara. The fiftieth anniversary celebrations of her father's company would soon be under way, she said. She would pick me up at one o'clock as arranged. I was about to protest that I surely had no right to attend such a gathering when we lost our connection.

Still clutching the phone, I glanced through the window. The shadow of the church lay obliquely across the empty marketplace. It seemed to me that the whole world had disappeared in that dark silhouette, and that I alone was alive and remembering. I blinked the thought away. There was no doubt that the company of strangers would be far better than the company of my own thoughts. I replaced the phone and went into the bathroom. My thoughts followed.

Staring into the mirror, I told my reflection that it only had itself to blame for its isolation. It was a deficient and lonely virgin, quite simply a poor reflection of Martin Spohr. He was a proper man, who lived on in the memory of thousands. I lowered my face to the basin and splashed cold water over my face, but my thoughts refused to go away. I was a useless and incompetent individual with an impossible history to emulate. Even in death, my grandfather did something positive. He offered consolation to all those people whose loved ones were listed as missing. I looked again at my reflection.

"The bereaved will expect something from you," I said, "some indication that you are the man your grandfather was. You will have to show them that you too share feelings of responsibility."

The reflection shook its head.

"Not from you," it said. "Your presence will disappoint them. After all, your grandfather is a symbol. He might last forever. You are a foreign stranger. Your flesh, blood and bones are here today but gone tomorrow."

I buried my face in a towel, but I was unable to smother

a growing sense of personal inadequacy. It developed as the morning wore on, and I was feeling very low while I sat in Barbara's Mercedes outside the company buildings.

I studied those buildings for some indication about what I had agreed to let myself in for. Eisenmann GmbH consisted of a three-storey structure. The ground floor was a long row of huge windows that reached down to the ground. This was the showroom. The upper floors resembled a medieval knight's helmet. The windows were narrow slits that prevented any glimpse of the building's interior, and the uniformly grey concrete gave the structure an oppressive air that conformed more to the once Communist east of Europe than with the Liberally-Democratic west. The showroom window was thus an eye through which one could see into the heart and soul of the company. This was partly curtained off, but through the gaps I saw dark-clad figures posturing under chandeliers that sparkled from the ceiling. Sitting alone in the car, I saw myself as the detached spectator who had been given special access to the first night of a play, but who did not belong to its world of luxury, jewels and furs. A voice rang out:

"Come Martin."

Barbara was at the company entrance. Her hair came out in fringes from under a little blue hat. The matching coat was hanging over one arm, and her dark skirt was billowing outwards as it caught the breeze. She was urgently gesturing for me to join her.

By the time I had emerged from the car, the entrance door was open, and the guardian of the company soul stood bathed in light on the threshold. It was the woman's long, splendid but dyed blond hair that caught the light and dominated the doorway. Falling in long waves that followed the curve of her back, the hair promised a beauty that could never be matched in reality. She wore simple clothes, a plain black skirt and a white blouse. She was talking to Barbara like an old friend, but when I arrived at

Barbara's side, the maid merely gave me a mirthless smile that revealed chipped and discoloured teeth. She took our coats without a murmur.

Barbara and I walked across the showroom. I heard the door shut, and its echoing thump pursued us like a shock wave as we clicked our way over the marble floor. Nearing the curtain, I heard a babble of voices and I felt Barbara nestling into my shoulder. Her voice was smiling, and her breath was warm against my cheek.

"Glad you came?" she said.

I smiled at her, but I had already turned an ear to the babbling rise and fall of voices and I was trying to assess its mood. Babbling voices have no language, but they have defining characteristics of tone. I had heard babbles of expectancy, babbles of disappointment and babbles of irritation. Bursts of laughter punctuated the babble that came from behind this curtain, and there was a theatrical quality to it that I had not often heard before.

Barbara stepped forward and, plucking at the curtain, she pulled it aside. She was suddenly distant from me as though she had disappeared into a private world of her own. She took my arm and, drawing me towards her, she placed her head so close to mine I felt she was willing me to see things as she saw them.

Through the gap in the curtain, an expansive room stretched before us. It was flooded with light from the chandeliers I had seen from the car. The light shone on a crowd of about one hundred people. Most were in formal dress and standing in small groups, talking, gesturing, and seeking out eyes with their eyes. The guests were reflected in the shining marble floor in which an identical underfoot party seemed to be taking place, and where all the people appeared to be standing on their heads.

Barbara gazed around the room.

"Wait," she said, "I'll get father."

She detached her body from mine and plunged into the crowded room. I watched her back as it weaved amongst the guests. A number of people turned to say something to her but each time, Barbara hurried on with a smile. Suddenly and disturbingly, I lost sight of her. I shifted from one foot to the other and leaned forward to catch a glimpse of her. Barbara was my link with these people, and without her, the link was broken. I was an intruder who might find his presence challenged. I turned at the sound of a voice behind me.

"English or American?"

I was looking into a face I recognised. It was older than I recalled, but the eyes were as piercing and passionate as when I had first seen them. The trigger that released the memory was neither the face nor the eyes. Nor was it the thick and white hair that curled over the nape of the neck like a lion's mane. It was the angle at with which he held his head that first struck me. This was the man I had seen on the television on the evening of my first day in Herrenberg.

"English," I said.

The old man's eyes attracted and repelled me. The sockets of both were deeply lined, and wrinkles radiated from them and resembled a road map. My gaze moved from one eye to the other until I felt shifty and guilty. The right eyebrow was considerably higher than the other. It hung like a question mark on his forehead and gave the eye beneath it a permanent suggestion of wonder. The other eye held hints of introspection, of wanting to hide away. I had the impression that this eye was not with us at all, but had turned full circle and was staring at some distant place inside his head.

He waved his finger in front of his face.

"You know," he said, "in 1945 I was in the forest here. I was running as fast as I could away from the Russians. But they were quicker than me. Then I was picked up by a couple of Englishmen in a jeep. They were splendid, let me tell you. Yes, they were simply splendid. Indeed, if it hadn't been for them, I most certainly would not be where I am today."

The voice was deep, clear and assertive, but the English was stilted to the point of absurdity. He could have learned it from books written in a bygone era or from people who live in a historical vacuum. His questioning eye searched and probed my face.

"I am really most grateful," he said.

This statement begged some sort of response. I was stumbling for something to say when a hand landed briefly - a touch like a butterfly - on my arm. Barbara arrived as a shadow in the corner of my eye. There was an immediate and easy silence between Barbara and this old man that suggested a familial bond. The man was in his seventies. I assumed he was Barbara's grandfather.

"I've been telling our friend about my rescue in '45," he said.

He turned his attention to the crowded room. The point of his curved nose lowered almost to the chin.

"You know," he said, "most of these people have their stories to tell. Many of them were not born here. They arrived in 1945 by the grace of God and a place on a train that just happened to be coming in this direction. The Russians did not take prisoners."

Barbara glanced at me and rolled her eyes towards the ceiling. Taking a deep breath, she introduced me.

"My father," she said.

I had to suppress an expression of surprise at this news, and while we shook hands, I readjusted my preconceived notions concerning fatherhood. Mr Eisenmann would have been around fifty when Barbara was born. This did not fit comfortably with my concept of the ideal or typical father. The concept was all the stronger because, as a fatherless child, an image was all I had ever known.

These thoughts were interrupted by music. Somewhere in the showroom, a band was playing "Humoresque." Its forced gaiety fitted the atmosphere perfectly. Eisenmann then excused himself and, turning his back to us, he swept through the curtains. I heard his heels clicking on the marble floor.

"We must get together," he said over his shoulder. "Barbara tells me you have come to find out about your wartime relatives. Yes, indeed, we really must discuss it. Nobody else wants to these days."

I peered through the gap in the curtains. Caught under the light of a chandelier, Mr Eisenmann himself was no more than a vague outline, but his voice was strong and clear.

"You would be forgiven for thinking the past never happened," he said. "Incredible! Is that what it all comes to? A tale told by an idiot, full of sound and fury, signifying nothing? Maybe it is."

He marched off into the crowd. Barbara was watching me intently as though she were monitoring my thoughts. Her eyes were faintly mocking.

"He learned his English as an adult," she said, "and mainly from Victorian novels and Shakespeare. Poor father still lives in the past while we younger ones have been trained to feel guilty about it so that ..."

She interrupted herself, inclined her head slightly and drew a hand slowly across the lower half of her face. I thought she was about to scratch her ear, but she turned her face the other way and ran a finger across her throat.

"We've had their past up to here," she said.

Staring at me with eyes that discouraged any comment, she then took me by the hand and led me deeper into the room and the flood of lights. The first thing I saw was the band, a quartet in dark suits at one end of the room. Three of them were seated, but one of their number, a violinist, stood above them on a rostrum. He was a striking figure who bent and twisted as he played. His beard was skin tight, and his eyes were so black they seemed permanently set in shadow. I felt him watching us as he turned and returned to his dark world inside, and when, for an instant, he stopped playing, he held the violin like a machine pistol.

The next thing I saw was the huge and tinted showroom windows. Through these windows I noticed a premature dusk lapping round the building, and the rising moon, which seemed to shimmer under a layer of frost. Along the streets, the trees were leafless, two-dimensional silhouettes against the sky and they flickered like an old black-and-white film as they were touched by the breeze.

Inside the building we were cocooned in marble and red velvet. Occasionally, I heard the squeal of mobile phones, and insistent waiters scurried and danced to the strains of the gypsy violins. Barbara and I squeezed our way through the guests, and she asked me about my trip to Kleinwalsertal. She quizzed me with great thoroughness on my journey, the storm, and my conversation with the policeman. I was under the impression that she was leading me to a particular spot, but I soon realised we were in a world of our own and going round the room in ever decreasing circles, but with no direction.

We finally came to a halt, and Barbara began conversing with two other women. As soon as Barbara spoke German, I felt she had stepped out of our little world and had gone to a place where I could not reach her. Feelings of vulnerability returned and filled me with anxiety. I tried to relax and took the opportunity to focus my mind on my surroundings.

A young man in a tuxedo was glaring nervously around him. In the middle of the gathering but part of no group, I assumed he was a waiter. Next to him, a group of middle-aged men were standing in a circle and separated from the rest of the guests by a steely protective aura. Leaning forward at the waist, they all held their glasses in front of them as if in the process of conducting a séance. Their eyes were focused at some point in the centre of this magic circle. They did not even flinch when the band struck up a waltz, and some people took to the floor to dance.

To one side of this group, I caught sight of a walrus moustache and a head, swivelling like a periscope above the gathering. The hunting-dog eyes seemed to be evaluating and assessing. Maximilian Hart was sniffing out people with something to hide. He politely returned the nods and smiles of people who passed him, but nobody stopped to talk. I averted my gaze in the hope that I would not catch his eye. We had nothing in common, except perhaps, the disappearance of an old man. From the corner of my eye, I saw him reach into a pocket and pull a mobile phone to his ear. He stood in the middle of the room with a finger in the other ear while the guests waltzed around him. I watched his face harden in concentration, and he tilted his head upwards to gaze thoughtfully at the ceiling. He muttered a few quick words into the mouthpiece and, pocketing the phone, he planted a theatrical smile on his face and mentally returned to the party.

Next, I saw Eisenmann again. He appeared to be reprimanding the waiter, who was constantly pulling his head back between his shoulders as though he was afraid of a blow in the face. The waiter's eyes occasionally sparkled with indignation. His mouth opened, and he appeared to stumble over a word. His face got redder and redder, and when Eisenmann moved away, he swayed as though he had been punched on the chin.

The room fell silent, and attention was focused on the rostrum. I followed the communal gaze, expecting to see the bearded violinist, but it was a hawk-nosed old man who was standing on the platform instead. Mr Eisenmann glared down on the proceedings and held up his hands. Barbara pulled me down on a chair and whispered in my ear.

"He's thanking everyone for coming," she said.

The voice boomed out, and Barbara translated.

"We are gathered here to celebrate the fiftieth anniversary of Eisenmann GmbH. If we are the best around today it is because of the efforts of all of us. We should thank God for the opportunities that have enabled us to move from small-time farmers to doctors and lawyers."

I noticed that he looked in the direction of Barbara when he said this. She continued translating while she looked up at her father with shining eyes.

"As you know," she whispered, "when we started, Germany lay in ruins. This brought sorrow but it also brought the opportunities that have made us what we are today."

At this point, a murmur of approval welled up around the room, and some people applauded. I wondered how accurate Barbara's translation was. The translation was filtered through a daughter's knowledge and experience of a father. When she passed this interpretation on to me, it was filtered again through my own experience. I concentrated instead on what I saw with my own eyes. The audience looked on in adoration as Old Mr Eisenmann raised a finger and wagged it between arched eyebrows.

"But," Barbara whispered, "we must fight against complacency."

There was another murmur of approval, and it occurred to me that the old man knew what the people wanted to hear and simply told them. It was an almost reciprocal arrangement. The people received confirmation of their needs and desires. The old man received his power, his position and his identity.

"Change is here," Barbara was saying, "and we must be ready to face the challenges that ..."

At this point, Eisenmann stopped and stared at some point in the crowd. I had just time to follow his gaze when a burst of shouting erupted from the centre of the room. Some men rushed to the incident while most women, with hands raised to their mouths, retreated to the walls. The man I had assumed to be a waiter had broken the séance by pushing one man out of the circle and wrestling him to the floor. Three other men were trying to pull him off but the waiter held on to the hair of his victim.

"Judas," he was shouting, "Judas."

He lifted his arm and tried to punch his adversary in the face. The striking arm was prevented from falling, and the waiter was dragged off. Other guests then joined in the accusations, and shouts came down from all sides on the sprawling victim. When he protested the accusations grew louder. This encouraged the waiter to attack again. I was about to go over and help when a voice roared over the room and silenced everyone. Eisenmann stood glaring at us from the rostrum. He was leaning into the room with his fists clenched at his sides and seemed on the point of swooping down and carrying us away. He lowered his head and stepped down from the platform, but his appeal had made an immediate impact.

The séance man was on his feet and attempting to regain some dignity by tidying his hair and protesting. The waiter was seated on a chair with his head in his hands. Two other men had their hands lightly on his shoulders, partly in a gesture of comfort, and partly I guessed, to hold him back in case he showed signs of renewed aggression. He did not move. His eyes flickered down to the floor and back up again, but they did not appear to focus on anything in particular.

A nervous but contagious laugh passed round the room. The guests began muttering, and tension trickled away. Soon the guests were talking and laughing again, and when the band struck up, it was almost as though nothing had happened. It was then that I heard a voice at my shoulder.

"It's a serious environmental problem indeed. Look at all the cars in the car park here. What will happen to them when they reach the end of their useful life? Something must be done. Recycling is one answer, I'm sure you will agree."

There was a murmur of polite and concerned agreement from the listeners. As I turned, Barbara slipped away from me and set off in a hurry to the place where the waiter was seated. I was about to follow when I caught sight of flickering eyelids beside me, and a voice stopped me in my tracks.

"Mr Slater. Good evening to you," the Chief Inspector said.

I managed to stretch my cheeks outwards to imitate a

smile. Feelings of guilt had just begun to well up again, when I caught sight of Barbara. She was kneeling at the waiter's feet and holding his hands in hers. She was looking imploringly into his face. There was a suggestion of hurt and resentment in the man's eyes but a wave of jealousy surged through my body and trivialised all other thoughts and feelings. I was about to return the policeman's greeting when I saw that he was again speaking into his mobile phone.

The waiter was still seated, and with his forearms resting on his thighs, he held his head dejectedly towards the floor. Standing over him like an executioner was Mr Eisenmann himself. On the other side of the room, the group of middle-aged men had regrouped, but they were now leaning backwards. Their magic circle had been broken by the presence of Barbara, who appeared to be rebuking them.

The policeman pocketed the phone and addressed me.

"So," he said, "global warming has claimed its casualties."

As he spoke, his eyes seemed to focus to the left of my shoulders. He smiled, and I felt Barbara's presence at my side.

"Frau Eisenmann, good evening," the policeman said.

Barbara said some words in return, but the Chief Inspector was already looking over our heads and making moves towards the exit.

"The storm," he said, "has now claimed three victims in our forest. Two bodies were discovered this morning. I have just received a call from my men. They tell me that another body has been found in Goldbachtal, by the soldier's grave."

The policeman took short but steady steps past us. He was evidently in a hurry.

"My men say that this third man is an old man, and, as you both know, an old man has been reported missing for some days."

He raised his head to the ceiling and placed both feet together.

"Mr Slater," he said, "we would like you to return to your hotel so that we can contact you if necessary. You may be needed for identification purposes."

Barbara caught at her breath, but the policeman silenced her with a wag of his finger.

"There are complications," he said. "The cause of death is giving my men problems."

He had already passed us and was speaking over his shoulder.

"Wait," Barbara cried.

Standing with her shoulders back and her head uplifted, she thrust out her chin. Her blue eyes crackled with determination.

"What is the problem exactly?" she asked.

"I told you, Madam," the policeman said, "the cause of death. I am on my way now."

"The problem," Barbara said firmly, "what, exactly, is the problem?"

The policeman was halfway towards the exit. He stopped and spun round.

"The two previous fatalities were caused by falling trees," he said. "This most recent death is somehow different."

Barbara's arm tensed and her hand turned into a fist. She took a breath to form her next words, but the policeman pre-empted her.

"It seems, madam," he said, "that this man was not killed by a falling tree. In fact my men think death was due to other and as yet unknown causes."

He turned and swept through the curtain. The blond Slav was already at the door and curtseyed as the Chief Inspector of Police stepped through the doorway and out into the car park.

BBC News: Despatches

12.12.1999

A judge in the Italian town of Verona has declared that a former Nazi SS major will have to stand trial there on war crimes charges next April. He is accused of having ordered the murder of 25 Italians. Their bodies were then strung up in public in a Square in Verona in August, 1944. Peter Winter reports from Rome.

Former SS major, Jochen Laufer, is now 88 years old and he has been located in Germany. Because of his age, the prosecution says his extradition will not be requested and he will be tried in absentia. But the murders which led to Laufer's indictment caused such sorrow during the Second World War that they cannot be justified as a military reprisal, the prosecution says. The Nazi officer ordered the killings after a bomb attack on a German army bus by Italian partisans.

The main casualties, however, were eight Italian pedestrians who were passing by. Military prosecutor, Mauro Locatelli, said he will ask for a life sentence.

Although the murders had been committed in time of war, they were a fact of common crime. 25 Italians were ordered by Major Laufer to be taken from a prison in Verona, where they were being held in custody, and shot by a firing squad in the Piazza Bra. Their bodies were then strung up outside the Roman Arena by the German military as a warning against further acts of sabotage against Nazi troops. Towards the end of the war, in 1945, when the Fascist dictator, Benito Mussolini, his mistress, and other Fascist leaders were captured by partisans, their bodies were shown to the public in the Piazzale Loretto in Turin, in memory of the Verona crime.

Chapter 9

Herrenberg. 27 December. Late afternoon

"So the missing old man," Barbara said, "is the same man I saw you with in the hotel?"

Her voice was free of emotion. She could have been checking items on a list. We were sauntering through the streets of late afternoon and heading towards my hotel. Barbara nudged against my shoulder. A few seconds later, her arm was draped through mine, and I sensed rather than saw her eyes. They were steady and questioning.

"Who is he?" she asked. "Do we know?"

From somewhere far away came the sound of a violin. Someone was playing a gypsy melody, and the tune came from everywhere as if it was part of the air itself. I looked around for the violinist, but there was not a soul in sight. I imagined that the pied piper of childhood memory had arrived in the town and led the people away to some secret and hidden place in the Schönbuch Forest. I said:

"I've no idea who he is."

My tone was defensive and it was in harmony with my mood. I had somehow stepped outside the realms of normal life and now moved in a timeless glow that protected me from the surrounding world. Everything that was happening outside that glow was ordinary, and the events which had occurred in the world of before-I-met-her were distant and irrelevant.

"So why were you at the grave?" Barbara asked.

The impatience which tugged at these words conjured up a vision of my mother when I asked her about her German roots. Her lips would change shape so that they resembled the top of a purse drawn together by a string. This effect was crowned by two disapproving eyes and a curving frown. Barbara did not know it but she was about to touch a sensitive family issue. This had been a no-go area for such a long time that I found it uncomfortable to deal with.

"I came upon the grave by accident," I said.

We turned into the square, and the sound of the violin grew louder. At the foot of the Apostles Steps, I saw the player. His black and tattered trousers and jacket seemed to grow naturally from the old suitcase on which he sat. Stopping some metres from him, Barbara and I watched the player raise his head, and a craggy face emerged from the shadow cast by his trilby hat. A distant look filled his eyes, and he smiled and played to some imaginary audience. There was a whisper, and the breath of it against my cheek.

"What did you and the man talk about?"

"The past," I said, "we just talked about the past."

The violinist finished his piece and lowered the violin. He turned his face to us but his smile was directed inwards. The people for whom he had played were far away and reflected as pools of sadness in his eyes. I cleared my throat and said:

"Who was that friend of yours at the party?"

From somewhere near at hand a dog let out a couple of short sharp barks. There was at first a silence and then a lamenting howl that faded slowly into the cold light. Barbara waited for the sound to echo away. Her back hunched, and she gazed at some point to the left of my right ear.

"Which friend?"

My mind was awash with the memory of Barbara at the feet of the man in the tuxedo.

"The one who caused the trouble," I said.

Barbara leaned heavily against my shoulder and directed me past the violinist and up the steps. We stopped at the door of my hotel. She was fiddling with the buttons of her coat. Something was preoccupying her and it hung over us like a cloud.

"That," Barbara said, "was Franz."

She smiled at me, but any pleasure her face contained was scrubbed out by the pity I saw in her eyes and the disappointed tone in her voice.

"Franz?"

For several seconds, the only sound between us was the click, clicking of her fingernails on the buttons of the coat.

"My brother," she said.

I sensed that we were straying into a no-go area of Barbara's own. She hung her head, and I noticed how attractive she looked. Her hair had fallen from behind her ear and swayed over her forehead.

"Why did he attack that man?"

The question prompted some confusion, and Barbara's eyes were soon full of rapidly passing contradictions. Love and hate, anger and calm, understanding and ignorance possessed her in quick succession. I let her live in her thoughts while I watched her. She paled, and her shoulders tensed. Then, she crossed her arms and rubbed at her shoulders. I said:

"Are you cold?"

She looked away but whether she did not want to look into my eyes or she did not want me to see into hers, I was unable to say. She remained deep in thought for several seconds, then she looked round and stared at the space above my head.

"Let's go inside," she said.

Once in the hotel, I ordered a couple of beers, and we took our seats at a table in the dining room. The afternoon was deepening into evening. High in the sky was the moon, and its rays penetrated the irregular profile of the church tower and the hotel windows. Our beers were still barely touched, and I was still hiding in myself when Barbara began to unburden herself.

"When my father started the business it was 1945, and Europe was in turmoil. Millions were uprooted and wandering around, homeless and desperate. It was the simple outcome of a conflict started by the Germans, and we have never been allowed to forgive ourselves for it. Guilt has been drummed into us. You might think that guilt itself is good for you."

She paused, and then, as though to remind herself as much as to inform me, she whispered:

"We mustn't forget the world my father comes from. It was chaos, darkness, terror and a growing realisation of what had been done, the crimes against humanity, and the guilt, the terrible guilt."

The slow shake of her head may well have been a genuine show of shock or incomprehension, but I caught myself listening to her from a moral pedestal. Perched on this high ground, I was the innocent and blameless victor who had never been obliged to deal with wickedness of this magnitude. Our different perspectives separated us, but I tried to look as though I was still attached to her.

"I suppose," she said, "you could describe father as an opportunist."

A sudden movement of her head was accompanied by a change of tone that notified me Barbara was back on a firm emotional base.

"Post-war Germany needed people like him. They have been criticised for being ruthless people, who would stop at nothing to bring certainty and security back into their lives. I don't think father's type would survive today, but at that period, the country needed him and people like him."

I dug my heels into the floor and pushed myself away from her. Leaning back in my seat, I shoved my hands into my pockets and looked at one shoe and then the other. Part of me was struggling to escape from my skin, to reach out and lose itself in this woman. Another part was screaming at her to stop involving me and pulling me to a place I was afraid of going. This inner tension prompted a feeling of tiredness to centre behind my eyes.

"I suppose you're right," I said.

Barbara laughed and wagged a finger in my face.

"I am right," she said. "You must not forget one thing about us Germans. We are always right."

Feeling reprimanded, I allowed my eyes to flicker away from hers, but I intercepted a look of sympathy on Barbara's face and I saw the faint lines around her mouth stretch into a smile. She placed her hands around the beer glass and held it tightly.

"He was only twenty when he opened a petrol station on the site where Eisenmann GmbH stands today. As the business grew, he sold second-hand cars. He developed a good relationship with the allied servicemen in this area. When they went back home, he bought their cars and resold them to incoming servicemen at a profit. In those days, there was a huge turnover of military personnel here. The company was officially formed in 1949."

The tiredness was developing into a swell of exhaustion that was threatening to overwhelm me. This was a part of my mother's inheritance that I would never shake off. Faced with the unacceptable, the shocking or the traumatic, my body would hide it all away under a wave of tiredness that slowly shut down my senses. I yearned for solitude, to think about what was happening to me and deal with it. But Barbara's expression was intent - urging me to stay with her.

"In 1950, my father met my mother. They got married two years later. My parents worked hard to build up the company. While they had a purpose in life, their marriage was successful. The struggle held them together or perhaps it made them so busy that there was no time for reflection. When Franz was born, father persuaded my mother to leave him in the hands of a succession of nannies."

She held my eyes in hers. I wondered if she could see

me fighting to be free of the emotion which quivered between us. I tried shaking my head in disbelief but it rolled limply from side to side. Barbara said:

"Perhaps this is why Franz never had a stable relationship. He can live and love only at a distance. Perhaps the torment this brings provides him with an excuse to drink. Some men never leave their mothers, do they?"

In the dining room the air went thick and heavy. I crossed my arms and rolled away from her. There was a small sound from the back of my throat. I recognised the sound as the beginning of an angry word, a rejection of Barbara's comments. I managed to swallow it. Barbara leaned forward and smiled a crooked smile.

"It was 1963 when mother and father had their big break," she said. "They won the contract to sell Daimler cars. Not long after that they won the rights to market the cars in the whole county of Baden Wuerttemberg. The company were impressed by their success. They didn't ask questions. They too were rising from the ashes."

I felt myself drifting again. I was desperate to find refuge in sleep and to lose contact with the waking world. But Barbara's voice stopped me from slipping away. Through crumbling defences, I saw her high-bridged nose, the determination of the chin and the spirit of old Eisenmann living inside her.

"So," she continued, "they let him develop their business. He sold their cars and serviced the trucks, and he and the company grew together. It suited both parties. Nobody ever thought that times would change. Father ran the company with a fist of iron. There was never any attempt to delegate authority, never any attempt to develop consultative management practices. He was the boss and he made sure that everyone knew it. If employees questioned or disagreed, father interpreted it as disloyalty and he sacked them without mercy."

Barbara was speaking in a monotone. She could have

been reading from the printed word. It gave her voice a curiously cold touch.

"When I was born, and mother insisted on staying at home to take care of me, she sealed her own fate. Father insisted that she go back to work but mother saw what had happened to Franz and she refused. The marriage never survived this rift. Mother left fifteen years ago, when I was ten."

Barbara took her hands from the beer glass and placed them over her eyes. I wondered if she was reliving, if only for an instant, the very moment when her mother had said goodbye. She lowered her hands and rubbed at her arms.

"So mother escaped too," she said. "She remarried and now lives happily in Switzerland. Father's success has come at a heavy price."

During the silence that followed, I wondered if Barbara could see the adjustments that were going on inside me. My perceptions of myself were shifting, but they were not going to give up without a fight. They grabbed at the chance to put the conversation on an impersonal level.

"Depends how you define success," I said.

Barbara hesitated. I had the impression that she was listening to some inner voice or that what I said was being filtered through some kind of interpretive process. At any rate, it seemed that it was a voice other than mine that prompted a grim smile to appear on her face.

"There is only one success for him," she said. "Father is what father has. Success is what he sees every day when he goes to work. Success is the company he created, the car he drives, and the money he has in the bank. Above all, success is the power that comes from all that."

I watched her shoulders tense and I heard a short intake of breath. Barbara blinked and she opened her mouth to say more, but then she appeared to choke as she came up against some internal resistance. She blinked again, and I saw her eyes were filled with sadness. I had the impression that I was witnessing some internal struggle, and it held me in a trance. Eventually, she simply let out a long sigh of acceptance.

"Yes," she whispered. "Father has never accepted disloyalty, and those who say anything against him are not to be trusted. In other words, if you are not for him, you are against him. But as with most tyrants, people have started rebelling against him."

She held her breath for a moment, and a faint pulse in her temple revealed the presence of a deeper feeling. I fidgeted inside myself, tried to climb out of my skin, to reach her, to tell her that I admired and respected her for finding the courage to explain her life to a stranger. At the same time, I recognised the need for my mother's blessing. I wanted to tell her to come out of hiding, that I was tired of playing hide-and-seek, and that I had something important to tell her - I had found a wonderful woman. Barbara's voice sounded loudly in the silence of these private thoughts.

"Father got so used to having things his own way he lost the ability to judge people. When DaimlerChrysler was formed some time ago, there was a lot of pressure to modernise the company and the dealership network. Among other things, this meant a modernisation of management style. Father's paternalistic view of the world was no longer in fashion."

She cocked her head and appeared to study my eyes. When she spoke again, bitterness had crept into her voice.

"So," she said, "the company pushed for a flatter management style - more transparent, more accountable, a style that would suit the new-look DaimlerChrysler. It wasn't long before the company gave their support to a group of younger Eisenmann managers who were pressurising my father to step down. These are the very people who have been given their chance by father himself. They are his management team and now they want a system that will effectively give them control of Eisenmann. It was one of these people who took the brunt of my brother's aggression today."

She stopped and held down a shuddering breath. Her voice dropped a tone but it was alive with feeling.

"Everyone knows what is happening. Everyone at the party today knows what is going on. But nobody talks about it. They have filed it away, turned their backs on it as though they do not want to recognise the existence of a problem. Why can't they face it ...?"

I watched her eyes darting wildly from side to side as she searched for some explanation. When she looked directly at me, there was an expression of infinite sadness on her face and it reached right to my heart. My identity melted away, and with a serene detachment, I saw it had been turning round a void. Where there might have been a son or a teacher there was just a gaping hole. And in this emptiness a new fact of life was emerging, and I accepted it without a murmur. The fact was Barbara and it changed everything. Just being there with her, at that place and that moment was a delight. Her act of trust deserved repayment in kind.

"About the old man," I began, "I told you something ..."

Full of the importance of the moment, I was unreasonably disappointed to see that Barbara was not listening to me. She was still chasing her own thoughts.

"While he still makes a profit," she was saying, "father thinks he is safe. But he is constantly under pressure to resign. He is seventy-four years old, and he has no successor. He thinks Franz is a worthless drunk, and I've got my own life to lead."

Her voice was now trembling, and the power of her forced me to listen. She continued in a breathless rush.

"I love him, but I have to become a person in my own right. This Christmas is the first one I have spent with father for three years."

I was about to make a polite comment when she pouted her lips, lifted her chin and studied me through the veil of hair that had fallen over her forehead.

"I can not let myself fall into the same position as my

mother," she said. "I will not become just a rich man's daughter."

I was distracted by a growling roar and the appearance of two spots of light that pierced the darkness and swung erratically round the square as if searching for something lost. Dogs suddenly appeared from doorways and flung themselves barking at this apparition. Then I heard the squealing of brakes. The sound of a purring engine and the word Polizei, emblazoned on a jeep door, invaded the room together. I saw Barbara glance through the window but she was still living in her own thoughts.

It was at this time of disconnection that I realised the jeep had come for me. Once I knew it was there, it remained like a stain that would not go away. The driver had parked right under the street-lamp outside the hotel. The jeep's idling engine encouraged me to believe that its presence might be only temporary. This hope was short lived. The headlights dimmed and died, and the engine cut out with a sickening finality. A door opened and slammed shut, and two uniformed men appeared in the corner of my eye. One of them put a foot on the jeep's fender and lit a cigarette.

"Father's private life has been disastrous," Barbara was saying. "Now his business interests are threatened. If the business is taken away from him, he will have nothing. It will destroy him and ..."

She jerked upright as her phone squealed. She fumbled for the handset like a person fumbling to shut off an alarm clock in a darkened room. She lifted the phone to her ear, and I watched in fascination as a variety of emotions passed like clouds across her face. Eventually, her cheeks turned pale, and her eyes opened wide in astonishment. Then she rested her forehead on an open palm and slowly replaced the handset on the table. She shook her head.

"What is going on?" she asked.

My own unease rose with her tone. It rose still further with the creaking of the front door, the sound of muffled voices and the scraping of feet on the hotel doormat. Barbara blinked and spoke rapidly.

"That was the Chief Inspector," she said.

"And?"

"And he wants you to come into the forest immediately."

I turned my head towards the sound of footsteps making their way across the hall to the dining room.

"It's a bit late," I said.

"He says two things are worrying him ..."

The policemen came straight through the doorway and stepped smartly up to our table. One of them pulled himself upright and his head back.

"Martin Slater?"

I folded my arms over my chest to protect myself from the voice which boomed around the room. My heart was beating wildly. The policeman looked me up and down.

"You must come with us, sir. You must come and identify a body in the forest."

The man spoke the heavily-accented English of the Hollywood Nazi. My head told me that the associations of accent with authoritarian behaviour were false. My stomach sent out shivers that reached to the very tip of my being. I disguised my fear with an expression of annoyance.

"Me? Why me?"

"Yes sir, you. Our Chief says you are the last person to see the dead man alive. We need you as a ... to ..."

"... to identify the body," Barbara interrupted.

She turned her head and blurted out a question of her own.

"What about the grave?" she asked.

The policeman's upper lip lifted to reveal yellow-stained teeth.

"What about it, miss?"

Barbara opened her mouth to offer a reply and then shut it with a snap. She hesitated and then she said coldly:

"The Chief Inspector said there was something strange about it."

"Strange?"

"Yes, strange, different. You know, not as it should be."

The policeman shook his head and shrugged.

"Well," he said, "we only know Mr Slater must come with us."

Barbara jumped to her feet, her eyes glinting, and her chin thrust forward.

"Then I shall come too," she said, "in case an interpreter is needed."

The policeman glanced at his colleague. He seemed to be studying his fingernails and said under his breath:

"Very well, but we should go immediately."

Barbara glanced at me and grabbed at my hand. We followed the two policemen out of the hotel and hurried towards the jeep. As it pulled away and roared out of the square, I heard Barbara whispering in my ear:

"I've never told anyone about my family before."

We were soon swaying side by side in the back of the jeep. I should have been able to predict my reaction to the extraordinary events that were going on. My shifting perceptions of self, the dead man in the forest, the discovery of my grandfather, and now Barbara was gripping my arm with ever tightening fingers. It was all too much for me, and I dozed off.

I vaguely noticed that we were driving through a forest and I dreamed that the dark shadows of the trees in the moonlight were the shadows of time itself. In my half-asleep and half-awake state, I knew that the forest held the key to my existence.

BBC News

November 1998

Shares in the newly merged DaimlerChrysler Company have started trading on the Frankfurt stock exchange. The shares rose 1.70 marks to 142.20 in early trade. The company was formed in the $42bn transatlantic merger, announced in May, of Germany's biggest industrial company Daimler and US carmaker Chrysler Corporation. Jürgen Schrempp and Robert Eaton, the joint bosses of the new organisation, celebrated Monday with a reception at Germany's main stock market in Frankfurt, before flying off to Wall Street, where both will ring the opening bell at the start of trading at the New York Stock Exchange.

Many of the workers at Chrysler and Daimler factories were invited to participate in the celebrations.

The DaimlerChrysler merger is projected to generate savings of $1.4bn next year, rising to $3bn in three to five years. The new combined management has promised that there will be no plant-closures or lay-offs.

Mr Schrempp described the merger as, "a marriage made in heaven". However, he has stressed that there will be a modernisation of the dealership network in Germany, and that all dealers must be ready to face the challenges that lay ahead. "The world is global," Mr Schrempp said, "and our dealers must be ready to change and adapt to the global world."

Chapter 10

The forest. 27 December. Evening

I was not expecting it to disappear. The warning signs had been in my dreams for some time, but I had given them only cursory attention. Even while we were driving up the winding road to Hildrizhausen, I did not understand what was happening. A part of me was dying. One moment that part was there and the next moment it was gone. I did not even see it leave.

We had left Herrenberg town centre behind us, and none of the people in the jeep said a word. Barbara's shoulder was pressed tightly against mine and, in front of us, the two capped heads swayed lazily to the movement of the vehicle. We all seemed to be following our own thoughts accompanied by the throaty snarl of a noisy motor. The jeep's window glass was splashed by mud and rain so that the outside world filtered through to me as a grey, distorted and desolate place. We continued to ride for a few minutes in silence and without exchanging glances. The jeep rattled and plunged its way through the fringes of Herrenberg, and we entered the Schönbuch Forest to the light of the moon, that appeared and disappeared behind the clouds. We drove on in a ghostly landscape full of high trees and moonlight shadows. The motor roared and deafened us as the jeep struggled up the winding road that led to Hildrizhausen.

It was then that I saw the dark shapes peeping through the trees. The shapes were the outlines of small houses crouching defensively in the undergrowth. I leaned forward. The houses were gingerbread houses. They were the houses in the forest where Hansel and Gretel lived and breathed in the warmth and comfort of my childhood memories. And was it a trick of the light or were there snowdrops decorating the lawns, and small animals or fairies dancing to the light of the moon? The plants and the trees that framed these enchanted houses looked as though they were leaning out and hoping to reach me and invite me to join them. I pressed my head still further forward to hear them, but I only banged my forehead with some violence on the windowpane. I must have blinked for when I opened my eyes, this vision of innocence had gone.

The road flattened out, and the roar of the jeep receded but my ears rang with the sound of it, or was it that same mournful echo of times past that I had heard some days previously while making my way out of the wood? If this were the case, my childhood had gone, and I had not even found the time to say goodbye.

I pulled my jacket around me and closed myself in my thoughts. Bumping along in the back of the jeep, I scarcely noticed that at a point near the top of the hill there was a barrier across the road. We had already decelerated and were moving at walking speed when a man in uniform appeared in the headlights. We pulled up when he raised his hand. I saw his shape through the glass. He was short, thick and powerful and said something in German to the driver of our jeep. His companion turned, and making a crossing movement with his arm, he spoke to Barbara. She translated for me.

"He said the road's been closed to traffic. And there is why."

She detached herself from my shoulder and, leaning over my chest, she pointed through the window. Following the direction of her arm, I saw immediately that she was referring to the aftermath of the hurricane and its terrible devastation. So many trees had fallen that the lower parts of the forest were a bristling and impenetrable wall of different shades of darkness. Above this wall, the outline of the tree trunks leaned at various and impossible angles. Once so lofty and aloof, the pines seemed to be apologetic and surprised at their misfortune. Stunned by an incredible blow, they lay floundering and incapable, ashamed that their private and highest parts were now exposed to the rest of the world. I could almost hear the life of these proud trees fading away like a dying breath.

"The roots are so shallow here," Barbara said, "and the snow had already weakened the surface soil. When the wind came, there was nothing to hold on to."

It was not long before we turned off the road, and the jeep bounced along a dirt track that apparently led into the heart of the forest. We were again moving at walking speed and gently shaken by the uneven ground. I absently watched the trees and the dark disorder of the forest on either side. The driver muttered something over his shoulder.

"He says it took their men a lot of hard work to clear this track," Barbara said.

But her words were vague and distant. The slow bumping, the warmth and proximity of Barbara, but above all, the need to turn away from what was happening, combined to overcome me with tiredness and I dozed again. In wakeful periods, I saw toppled and broken trunks, upturned roots and tree tops bristling at my shoulder. They were briefly caught in a blaze of passing light and occasionally brushed noisily against the side of our jeep before disappearing into the darkness. In sleep, I dreamed that from the ruin of the forest, people put out their quaking limbs and were pleading with us for help. They were skeletal shapes in ragged clothes and with shaven heads. Then I saw that many of them were already dead, and somehow I knew I was going to have to identify them. Awake or asleep, the smell of pine was everywhere, and our wheels cracked over piles of bark, which lay like scabs where they had been left by the barking-machine. To my right, where the foliage had thinned, the lights of some town or village winked at me as we passed.

I am not certain how long I allowed myself to be carried along in this hallucinatory state. We drove very carefully down the narrowing track and occasionally we had to make slow and bumpy detours around enormous roots that rose like serpents through the broken soil. It was after one such detour, followed by a sharp descent, that I saw the lights. This peculiar image, the queerness of such blazing white light in the middle of the forest woke me from the fantasies to which I had abandoned myself. The source of the light was three enormous spotlights that blazed angrily. So bright was their light that everything behind and above was covered under a mantel of black. I glanced at Barbara and then, invaded by a calm so unnatural that I felt it with hilarity, I imagined we had walked on to a film set - a programme for local TV on the ravages of the hurricane.

We stopped by the side of the dirt track. I fumbled for the door handle and, pushing the door open, I emerged into the freezing air with my eyes screwed up against the light, and something wet and cold intermittently touching my cheeks. I blinked, and rubbing my eyes, I saw shapes in white overalls padding around what looked like a large Punch and Judy tent. In the middle of it all, and directing proceedings with exaggerated movements of the head, was the familiar figure of Maximilian Hart, Chief Inspector of Police. He was darting around with enormous and energetic strides. Occasionally he stopped and, thrusting his heels together, he lifted his head to the stars.

The wetness on my cheeks was caused by snow flakes, small stinging flakes, which whirled in the light wind and melted when they touched the ground. The smell of snow, pine, and a mild odour of antiseptic and paraffin was effectively sealed off under a canopy of darkness. We could have been anywhere in the forest. And yet, the faint but unmistakable sound of trickling water stirred my memory so that I knew I had been there before.

I saw the policeman from the corner of my eye. He was standing with his head up, his shoulders back, and his hands clasped firmly behind him. Slowly lowering his head, he fixed us with a long, hard stare before beckoning us over to him with a wide and oblique movement of the head.

As we walked towards him, I noticed the irregular stream of vapour coming from Barbara's nose, and I heard her breathing, quick and nervous.

"OK?" I said.

She nodded but in the unnatural light I saw her face was tense, and the eyes fearful. In contrast, my mind was clear, and my thoughts were serene and easy. The Chief Inspector was kicking at the bark that lay at his feet. When we were within hearing distance, he said:

"It is interesting, is it not, that certain types of tree must be cleared away before others. I am told that some trees rot more quickly. These must go first ... for environmental reasons, you understand. And do you know, have you any idea, how much dead wood there is here?"

I felt the heat of the floodlight against my cheek. The driver was looking at his motor, and the seconds passed slowly while we waited for the Chief Inspector to answer his own question. He seemed pleased with himself for being in possession of knowledge we did not have.

"There is enough," he said, "to satisfy the energy needs of Herrenberg for the next ten years. Just think of that."

He pulled himself upright and set his feet so that they pointed outwards at ten minutes to two. He pulled and twisted at the ends of his moustache while he reflected on this information. Then, swivelling on his heel, he held his arm out for us to follow. He walked ahead, but he frequently turned to satisfy himself that we were still there. He stopped outside the Punch and Judy tent and poked his head inside the flap. He withdrew, and a man in white emerged from the canvas doorway. The Chief Inspector gave Barbara a worried look. Then he said to me:

"Have you seen a dead body before, Mr Slater?"

"Only on the television," I said.

"There is nothing so lifeless as a dead body," the Chief Inspector said. "But you can be consoled by the fact that the moment of death is the one moment in our lives that we can not experience. In a sense, death does not exist for us as it did not exist for him. Remember this. Please be prepared, and come with me."

With the cold finding its way to my bones, I followed the Chief Inspector through the flap. The body was lit up by a paraffin lamp and lay stretched out on the ground. The legs were lost in the thin and spidery branches of a fallen tree. The left arm was flung up towards his head, and the hand was closed like a claw. The dead face seemed to look at me with motionless and distorted eyes, and the once immaculately combed hair was in disarray. The mouth was open, and a sliver of spittle had dried on the chin. It might easily have been the same spittle that he had ejected onto the grave. The Chief Inspector was right. The body had as much life as a discarded teddy bear.

"Is this the man you met in the forest?" he asked. "Is this the man who you sat in the restaurant with?"

I nodded. It seemed obscene that I should be the one to identify the man. I had known him for barely two days. If there was nobody who knew him better than me, then the life and experiences of this body at my feet had never been. Maybe the priest had been right. The dead live on but only in the memory of those who remain.

"Are you sure?" the policeman asked. "Please look carefully."

I nodded again, and the Chief Inspector clapped his hands together.

"I knew it," he said, "but we needed identification."

He led the way out of the tent. Barbara was waiting. The policemen said:

"The doctor tells us that death was between five and seven o'clock on the evening of the 23 December. And you last saw him when?"

The policeman had lifted his head and was apparently studying the stars. I felt Barbara frowning at me from one side.

"I am not sure," I said, "some time earlier ..."

The policeman's head dropped forward as if the neck muscles had given up. He glared at me.

"It would hardly be later, Mr Slater, would it?"

He lifted his head once more to the heavens.

"At first we thought that he was hit by a tree during the storm. That would have made the time of death between twelve o'clock and three o'clock yesterday afternoon."

He broke off for a while and, still smiling at the unseen sky, he let out a mild chuckle. To us he said:

"No, no, that is just not possible. Forensics tell us he had been dead a long time before that."

I exchanged a conspiratorial glance with Barbara. It was only a glance, but it bound us together and confirmed our little world, our togetherness and our separateness from this odd man with the walrus moustache. I cleared my throat and glanced again at Barbara. This time, I saw she was smiling.

"How was he killed," I asked.

"Who said he was killed," the policeman said with the rapidity of a machine gun. "The exact cause of death could have been anything, heart attack, hypothermia, who knows? And we won't know, Mr Slater, until forensics have found the time to have a good look at him."

I looked away from his face and gazed at the wall of blackness around us. The Chief Inspector was turning his head slowly. Then he closed his eyes and spoke softly under his breath.

"What is more," he said, "one or two things are worrying me."

He let his head fall forward, steepled his hands and held them to his chest.

"Please, Mr Slater. What you tell us may be of the utmost importance. So think carefully, I beg you. When exactly did you see him, Mr Slater? Do you remember the time?"

I focused my eyes at some point over his left shoulder and examined my memory. At the priest's house I had been surrounded by clocks. But once I had entered the forest, I moved and breathed in a sort of endless world of childhood where an hour was a universe, and history stagnated. I had no idea what time it had been.

"No," I said, looking straight into his eyes, "it was late afternoon, still light but it was getting dark when we parted."

"And the sun, Mr Slater," the policeman said, "was it setting or not?"

When I looked again over his shoulder and into the past, that afternoon in the forest refused to end. I recalled the sun between the trees and in my memory, it seemed all too comfortable amongst the clouds.

"I really don't remember," I said.

The policeman made an almost silent grunt.

"And was he well when you left each other?"

I looked again over the man's shoulder and into the depths of darkness. The moon suddenly appeared through the clouds and its light filtered through the pines above us. I made out distant trees and the shapes of clouds, dark in the darkness. I heard again the tinkling sound of water flowing nearby, and the almost indistinguishable sound of the wind as it played on the water's surface. It was not that I recognised the place, but I suddenly knew exactly where I was. I looked around for the grave and said with an absent mind:

"He seemed physically all right. But as I told you yesterday, something was troubling him."

"The grave you said."

"That's right."

The policeman raised his hand and twisted the ends of his moustache.

"So, what did he say about the grave, exactly?"

I looked again into the blackness, and suddenly bats appeared in the darkness and flew in undecided circles around us. They were as black as the night itself and just as far away. There was a world out there, but it was barely visible.

"I don't remember exactly. I told you yesterday that he seemed to think the grave was not what it seemed to be."

"And that was all?"

"Yes," I said, "he did not say what he meant."

The policeman turned his head to one side and then raised his eyes to search the heavens for the solution to some difficult problem. He was so absorbed in his meditation that for some seconds he seemed unaware of our presence. I realised then that I was getting cold. The air was humid and drifting over my face like an invisible but freezing mist. From the corner of my eye, I saw that Barbara had all but buried her head in her jacket, and my teeth were chattering. A sliver of spittle formed in the corner of my mouth. Suddenly remembering, I said:

"He did something that shocked me."

The Chief Inspector's response was so rapid that I flinched in the face of it.

"Shocked you?" he said. "You say shocked you? Why did you not mention this before?"

I shook my head and blew through impatiently pursed lips. A cloud of vapour appeared between me and my inquisitor.

"Oh, I don't know," I said with a shrug. "I forgot."

"Then perhaps it was not such a shock as you say. What did he do that shocked you so much that you forgot it?"

The speed and power of the question and its accusatorial tone temporarily stunned me. After some hesitation, I hung my head and said:

"He spat on the grave."

"Why did he do that?"

Once again, I peered over the man's shoulder. It was not that I was trying to recall. I remembered exactly what the old man had said. It was his feelings that were impossible to verbalise. In the end, I gave up trying.

"He mentioned something about memories," I said. "He said he was not spitting on memories."

"Did he elaborate further?"

I gazed at the ground, wondering how I would be able to translate the man's emotional power into words.

"He told me a story, a memory from the war I think. If I recall correctly, he mentioned that over fifty years had passed."

"And?"

"He mentioned a church, a dead body and how he felt about it."

"And how did he feel about it?"

"Resentful," I said, aware of the inadequacy of the word.

The Chief Inspector frowned and looked towards Barbara. When she muttered something in German, the policeman looked back to me.

"Did he tell you why he felt like that?"

"Yes," I said. "He told me he had been forced to confront his own emotions. I think he enjoyed what he saw."

"And did he appear frightened in any way?"

"As I told you, he was distressed, angry and bitter about something."

"But not frightened, like a man who knows he is being followed."

I recalled him swaying around the cloud shadow and his first words about an old soldier's trick.

"He said something about the enemy being around. He said they were always around, and that was why he walked in the shadow."

"But he didn't actually say to you that he was being followed?"

"Not in so many words. But as I told you yesterday, I got the impression he had mistaken me for another person."

"Which suggests he had arranged to meet someone there, does it not?"

"Maybe," I said, "but he did not tell me."

The policeman kicked again at the bark on the forest floor.

"We can see no signs of robbery," he said. "Can you think of why anyone would want to kill him?"

There was a gasp of fright from my shoulder. Looking round I saw that Barbara had raised her head from her coat and was covering her mouth with her hands. Her face had picked up the moonlight, and the whites of her eyes seemed unnaturally bright in the surrounding night. The policeman contemplated the stars again.

"Of course," he said, "we don't know for sure that he was killed, but the forensics boys say he was struck on the back of the head. Whether it was the blow itself that killed him or the shock that followed we are not sure. However, we must be prepared. I am treating this as a murder inquiry."

"And I was the last person to see him alive."

"It is highly likely," the Chief Inspector corrected, "that you were the last person to see him before his death, Mr Slater. As I told you, what you have to tell us is of the utmost importance."

There was a stifled sob at my elbow. Barbara's voice emerged from the darkness.

"Is there no possibility that it was an accident? I mean, are you sure he was murdered?"

"Not until the body has been examined. And you know we have no motive. There was no robbery. In fact Frau Eisenmann, we don't even know who the man was and what he was doing here at this time of year. Most of us are with our families at Christmas time, are we not Mr Slater?"

I decided to ignore the provocation, but I guessed it would not be long before I was put under intense interrogation.

"With regard to his identity," I said, "you can ask the priest."

"The priest?"

"Yes."

"There are many priests, Mr Slater. To which priest are you referring?"

I turned and pointed through the forest in the vague direction of Hildrizhausen.

"The priest in the next village."

"You mean Hugo Fischer?"

"Yes, that's him. I think the priest invited him here. Something to do with the war."

A look of distaste passed rapidly across the policeman's face. He peered through the trees that surrounded us. I got the feeling that he was trying to control his emotions.

"I think," I said, "that he knew the man."

"Who knew what man?"

"I think the dead man knew the man in the grave there."

I looked around with the intention of indicating the grave of Martin Spohr. I pointed in one direction, but I was vaguely aware that the grave was invisible to me.

"Did the deceased tell you this?"

"No, he didn't."

"Then how do you know?"

"The priest told me."

"And why would the priest tell you, Mr Slater? Why would the priest tell you that the deceased knew Martin Spohr?"

"I am a historian," I said. "I am interested in all things past. It seems that this Martin Spohr is something of a celebrity."

"And celebrity is immortality, isn't it?"

I barely nodded. I did not know how to respond. The policeman said:

"We are all trying to escape mortality, don't you think?"

"I suppose so," I said, "but this man did not."

I made another lazy movement of the arm to indicate the Punch and Judy tent. The policeman mused for several seconds, his eyelids fluttering like a butterfly.

"All our myths are connected to mortality," he said. "And myths, in turn, are connected to a sort of collective subconscious - something much more important than us."

I stared at him in silence. I heard Barbara ask:

"What do you mean?"

The policeman considered this question for so long, I wondered if he had ignored it. Then he said:

"I will show you something. And for the time being, this something must remain a secret between us. Do you agree?"

Barbara and I glanced at each other. Barbara nodded. I shrugged.

"I agree."

"Then, please come this way," the policeman said.

He walked past the tent, out of the glare of the lights, and into complete blackness. For several seconds the Chief Inspector was swallowed up by the night. I heard his feet rustling through the grass, and Barbara tightly held on to my hand as we followed. Then silence. As my eyes grew accustomed to the darkness, I pulled up sharply when a dark shape materialised in front of me.

"We thought at first that this tree fell and killed the man back there. As I told you, we now suspect that this is not the case."

It took some time to see what it was to which the man was referring. An enormous tree had fallen, and we were standing at the upturned root. It appeared like a gigantic saucer whose rim was over my head. And from the saucer I was gradually able to discern the roots that still connected it to the forest floor. At the base of the saucer was a deep and black hole. I heard the policeman's voice from below. I assumed he had gone down on his haunches. I heard him scratching about in the earth, and then his shape loomed beside me. He lifted an object in front of him and at arm's length. In the darkness, a cross appeared.

"When the tree fell," the policeman said, "its roots came up from under the grave."

He lowered the cross, and I heard it fall to the ground.

"The grave is completely destroyed."

I heard him fumbling around in his belt. Then there was a click, and he shone the beam of a torch on the ground. The first thing I saw was the cross lying upside down on the pieces of concrete that had once surrounded the grave. The next thing I saw was a huge hole where the grave had been. The earth was fresh and glistening in the torchlight. The policeman lowered himself onto one knee.

"I have taken liberties," he said, "and I have dug further down ... there, you see, at least another metre at the head of the grave, there ... look."

Barbara moved closer and nestled into my shoulder. I felt her breath upon my cheek, and she grabbed at my arm. We looked. There was just the upturned earth and the smell of freshly turned soil. It was now lightly covered in snow.

"What do you see, Mr Slater?"

"Nothing," I said.

"Frau Eisenmann?"

Barbara shook her head.

"Exactly," the policeman whispered, "nothing. No bones, no items of clothing. Nothing at all."

He rose to his feet, and the three of us stood with bowed heads and staring in silence at the spot where the grave had been. Behind us I heard the policeman's colleagues padding around, and the occasional hiss as a flake of snow burned against the heat of the spotlights. Eventually Hart said:

"And what does the presence of nothing suggest to you?"

I opened and closed my mouth until the chief inspector put the unacceptable into my mouth.

"It suggests to me," he said, "that perhaps this grave is not what it seemed. Perhaps the dead man was right."

"But surely," Barbara broke in, "it is possible that the bones have disintegrated, isn't it?"

There was a light grunt of dissent from my side.

"In fifty years? I don't think so."

"Then perhaps the bones were removed and put somewhere else."

"No," the policeman said with finality. "The villagers here fought for years to prevent that very thing from happening."

We stood in silence for some time. I heard the policeman breathing and saw the vapour streaming from his nose. When he spoke, his voice was charged with emotion.

"To many Germans, this grave represents something of huge importance. It enables them to do something that has been denied to us. We have not been able to commemorate our dead and glorify them as you British do, Mr Slater."

He looked up and seemed to consult his memory before continuing in a more authoritarian tone.

"We must keep this a secret," he said. "We can not trample on the memories of so many people. We have never seen this. Life must go on, and people must be allowed to grieve for their loved ones. We may have lost the war, Mr Slater, but that does not mean that our dead should not be remembered by those who wish to remember."

"I don't understand," said Barbara, "what must be kept a secret?"

There was a silence, and then I heard the policeman whisper:

"It is entirely possible," he said, "unless either of you can think of a good explanation, it is entirely possible that the presence of nothing means ..."

He broke off in a way that suggested he was searching for a word or phrase in English with which he was unfamiliar. Then he said:

"What I want to say is if there are no bones, no items of clothing like buttons or metal buckles, there is every probability that there was never a body here in the first place."

BBC News

1 December 1999

Germany has not budged from a "final offer" of DM8bn ($4.2bn) to compensate people forced to work as slaves for the Nazis.

Chancellor Gerhard Schroeder repeated the offer on the day set by German and American Government negotiators as the deadline for agreeing a settlement. In an interview on television in Germany, he said: "The contribution cannot be increased."

This came only hours after the victims' US lawyers and the World Jewish Congress rejected the offer as insufficient. The latest offer follows months of negotiations between German Government and businesses, and US lawyers representing about 1.5m to 2.3m survivors.

About 60 German companies, including DaimlerChrysler and Siemens, agreed in November to double their offer to DM5bn ($2.6bn), with the German Government providing the remaining DM3bn ($1.6bn). The firms set up the fund in February under threat of US class-action lawsuits, and are seeking total legal immunity in exchange for making the payments.

It is possible that more German companies could add to the fund. The American Jewish Committee last week published a list of companies which it believes were involved in using slave labour.

BBC correspondents say that difficult negotiations still

lie ahead about how the money should be distributed among the victims.

The issue is extraordinarily sensitive. The DaimlerChrysler merger was nearly blocked because of the German company's associations with the Nazi regime and its use of slave labour. Jewish organisations in the US objected to the merger on these grounds. They still describe the new company as immoral, unjustifiable and a slap in the face for all those who suffered as slave labourers.

Chapter 11

Herrenberg. 27 December. Night

The arm startled me at first. Its appearance over the driver's seat seemed like the moves of a nervous boy with his girl in the back row of a cinema. The driver of the jeep seemed unconcerned about the arm, but glanced nervously at the person to whom it was connected. One side of this person's face caught the orange light from the instrument panel. The other side of the face was as dark as the dark side of the moon. A walrus moustache swung into vision and bristled towards the back seats. Above the moustache a questioning eye picked up the light from the dashboard and bore down on me from over the shoulder and along the arm.

"Mr Slater," the inspector said, "it's time you told us exactly what it is you are doing here in Herrenberg."

My eyes flickered sideways. Barbara was no more than a shape in the corner of the back seat. She was half turned towards me, and her head was angled in such a way that suggested she was asking questions of her own. Maximilian Hart's orange eye was locked to mine and shone like a cat's eye in the night.

"You see, don't you?" he continued. "Things that we have just witnessed do not happen here in our town. It is true that some people go into the wood, and they are never seen again. Usually, it turns out that they are abused husbands who do not wish to be found. But murder, or to be more precise, suspicion of murder, this is really out of the ordinary. It does not happen in our … let us say … in our neck of the woods."

He seemed proud of his command of English idiom and chuckled at his joke. We were bumping along the forest track with considerable speed. It was obviously too fast for Maximilian Hart. He snapped his head towards the windscreen and made a short command to the driver. The jeep slowed. The questioning eye turned back to me.

"Look at it all from my perspective," the Chief Inspector said. "It is Christmas, a time for celebration, a time to be with loved ones, family and children and so on, and so on."

There was another alarming bump. Turning and re-turning his face from the windscreen, to the driver and then to me, the policeman's voice rose and fell like a poorly tuned radio. I missed a good number of his words altogether and had to guess at others.

"Then, out of the clear blue sky, two strangers arrive in our community. One is an Englishman who has, shall we say, his own business to attend to. What this business is, nobody knows. Second, an old man arrives. Who he might be is also unknown. But the old man is found dead in mysterious circumstances, and the other stranger, this Englishman, was the last person to see him alive. As far as we know, the Englishman was alone, and nobody can verify his story. Is this a fair construction of the situation?"

My eyes were dry and stinging, and my eyelids twitched out their protestation that they were tired and longed to close. The forest brushed and scratched at the window while I looked for an answer to the policeman's question. The inspector slapped the driver's seat with the palm of his hand.

"Yes, that's it," he said, in a tone that suggested he had suddenly stumbled on some eternal truth. "You both arrive in Herrenberg at the same time. You meet in the hotel and you arrange to go to the forest together; yes, just the two of you. And only one comes out alive. What does that suggest?"

Hart paused and watched my face closely. I shook my head from side to side but managed no sound other than that of my back teeth grinding together. The policeman said:

"It suggests that you might have argued and that you hit him. Of course, you did not mean to kill him, did you? But the man is old, and his heart is weak. How does that sound Mr Slater?"

I was about to object when the shape in my peripheral vision shook itself. Barbara leaned forward and spoke with increasing volume into the policeman's ear. Occasionally, she thumped the back of the seat to emphasise a point. When she had finished, she fell back against the door with her arms folded, her chin jutting aggressively and the whites of her eyes flashing. Impressed by the intensity of her defence, I turned towards her and tried to find her eyes in the darkness. But she refused to return my gaze. It was almost as though she had made this spirited defence for her benefit, to chase away gathering doubts of her own. Hart said:

"And what does the priest have to do with all this?"

With one sudden and smooth movement, he coiled his body round and faced me squarely with both arms draped over the back of the seat. He looked like a cat preparing to pounce on an unfortunate victim. His right eye twinkled orange and it stared straight at me.

"That is a very interesting question, Mr Slater, isn't it?"

I was stammering out a reply when the car lurched alarmingly, and we emerged on the metalled road. While we accelerated towards Herrenberg, the policeman untwisted his body and let out a string of oaths at his driver.

We drove on in silence, and the jeep plunged in and out of the moon shadow. The full moon cast a bluish light over the tree tops and flooded the interior of the vehicle. There was a low mumble and a deep breath from the front of the jeep. The mumbling gradually developed into clearly recognisable but disembodied words. I had the feeling that the words were directed at nobody in particular, but the policeman was speaking English. His words were intended for me.

"I am simply searching for answers," the policeman said. "This is what I do. It is my role. This particular event in the forest is struggling with history. It is causing some contradictions, don't you think?"

I was about to ask for clarification when the policeman continued with a direct question.

"So, Mr Slater, my problem is this. Who, basically, are you? And what are you doing here?"

The jeep had now picked up speed and was hurtling through the forest and down the hill towards Herrenberg. I started a deep breath, and in the lengthy yawn that followed, I saw the roofs of the town. And rising from them was the church tower, its onion dome glistening in the cold blue light of the moon. I rubbed my eyes between thumb and forefinger.

"I came to go skiing over the Christmas holidays."

"Alone?"

The tone of the question contained an element of criticism that touched a recently exposed nerve.

"Yes, alone," I snapped. "Is there something wrong with skiing alone?"

In the ensuing silence, I examined the policeman's profile, the eye which questioned me, and the forward thrust of the neck, which worried me. I watched the jaw move slightly forward and waited helplessly for the next question.

"Are there not better skiing resorts in Austria or Switzerland?" he asked. "And where in Germany did you go - alone - exactly?"

"Kleinwalsertal. Riezlern, to be exact."

"But why Germany?"

"Because it seemed a good idea to kill two birds with one stone."

"Ah, but let us stick to this one bird for the moment," the policeman said. "So why are you not skiing now?"

"Because the conditions were bad and ..."

I stopped. The policeman had begun speaking to the driver. We turned off the main road and drove slowly along the shopping precinct towards the square. I heard the church bell tolling the hours. I started counting.

"And so," the policeman said, "you came to Herrenberg before you went skiing, that is correct, isn't it? You came here first in order to meet the, how shall I call him, the deceased?"

We decelerated into the square and rocked to a halt. The driver applied the handbrake and switched off the engine.

"No," I said, counting the fifth hour. "I did not come to meet the deceased. I came to speak to the priest. I had booked the hotel in Riezlern from the twenty-fourth. I arrived here on the twenty-second of December. I came two days early to meet the priest."

The policeman became suddenly agitated. He spun round and draping his arms over the front seat, he leaned towards me.

"No, no," he cried, "surely that is not the beginning. Start from the beginning, man. Why did you want to speak to the priest? You must have decided that before you came. Did you know him?"

I became suddenly aware of my hands. They were clasped so tightly in my lap that they were hurting.

"No," I said as I reached the twelfth hour, "I did not know him."

"Then why did you want to speak to him."

"Because I thought he would be able to tell me something about my past."

"Like what exactly?"

I focused my eyes on the seat in front of me and tried to control my shaking voice.

"Last November my mother died. That is when it started."

At this point I heard Barbara stirring beside me. The pressure of her hand over mine was reassuring. Her warmth told me I was not alone, that there was someone who was willing to share my feelings.

"I found some letters in the attic of our house," I said. "Until then, I thought my mother had never had any contact with Germany."

"And why should your mother have had any contact with Germany at all Mr Slater?"

"Because she was born here in 1945. My mother was born a German. She was adopted by an English soldier and taken to England. She never talked much about it. My mother wanted to be English, and that was what she became."

The Chief Inspector made a non-committal grunt. He leaned back against the jeep's door and, steepling his hands, he fixed his eyes at some point above the driver's head.

"And these letters," Hart said, "why did you find them so interesting?"

"Because for the first time I saw that she had not cut herself off from Germany. I saw that there was something here that interested her."

I would never have consciously chosen this moment, but I knew that I was about to tell my story. The thought of revealing private corners of my life touched off a burst of embarrassment and stoked up already aggravated feelings of vulnerability. Telling the world was going to be like removing my trousers in public or unwinding the bandage from a badly cut and stitched finger that had barely had time to heal. It was not a question of fear. I just did not want to look.

"And do you know what that something was?" the policeman asked.

"Yes."

"What was it?"

"My mother wrote to the priest at Hildrizhausen because

she wanted information about a man called Martin Spohr. The letters I found in the attic were the priest's replies. Apparently, she wrote to thank the priest, but there was no more correspondence after that."

"Your mother was interested in Martin Spohr? Why was that?"

"That was why I came here," I said, "to find out. Before leaving England, I contacted the priest and arranged to see him."

"And you have seen him?"

"Yes."

"When exactly?"

"The day I met the old man in the forest. It must have been the twenty-third."

"Four days ago."

"I suppose so."

"And what was the result of your meeting? Did you find out what you wanted to know?"

"Yes," I said.

"So, what did you discover?"

I opened my mouth and closed it again lest the emotion that filled me should burst out like air from a balloon. I gritted my teeth and steadied myself. Breathing deeply through my nose, I blurted out:

"Martin Spohr was my mother's father."

Once the words were spoken, I leaned my head against the seat in front of me. I remained there motionless for some time and waited for the cries of surprise that I was sure would follow. There was simply a silence. And in that silence, an image of my mother appeared briefly in front of me. The lips were tight and disapproving. Then, the image seemed to slide away and it disappeared into the grey light. From the greyness came another voice.

"And that was why you visited the grave?"

"Yes."

There was another silence. Then the policeman said:

"Martin. Why did you not tell me this before?"

I raised my head and leaned back heavily in my seat. Staring through the windscreen, I saw the ragged edge of a cloud passing across the moon. For a brief moment, a shadow spread itself over the town.

"I didn't tell you," I said, "because I wasn't ready to tell you."

"Not because you had something to hide?"

"No."

The policeman placed the tips of his fingers under his chin and gave me a worried look.

"And so you met the old man there. At the grave I mean."

"Absolutely by chance."

"Can you think of any reason why he should have been there?"

"I told you," I said. "He mistook me for someone else. Perhaps he had arranged a meeting with someone. Who knows?"

It was then that the swift shock of a memory hit me. I glanced at the policeman and then out of the window. I brought my hand to my mouth.

"Is something the matter, Mr Slater?"

I shook my head. The memory had lodged firmly in my consciousness. I breathed in deeply as the implications of the memory took root. Then I whispered:

"He did have an appointment with the priest."

My statement had the tone of a question, and when I glanced at the policeman, I was aware of a questioning expression on my face. Hart appeared to consider the information I had given him and then he said:

"Sorry? The old man had an appointment with Hugo Fischer? In the forest?"

"No," I said. "I don't think so. Not in the forest. In his house."

"Why would the priest want to speak to the old man, do you know?"

The shock of the first memory had marginalised the

others. My mind was blank. The policeman drummed his fingertips together.

"Come on Mr Slater, think. What is the connection between the deceased and the priest?"

The Chief Inspector's impatient tone loosened my memory.

"There was a connection between the old man and the priest's father. They corresponded apparently, but you had better speak to the priest yourself."

"Oh I will, Mr Slater, I most certainly will. But I return to my question. Now think. What is the connection between the priest and the deceased?"

There was another long silence as I tried to remember. The policeman stared through the window. Barbara still had her hand over mine. The driver's head seemed to have fallen forward. I wondered if he had nodded off.

"The priest invited the man to Herrenberg," I said.

"So, can you tell me why he invited the deceased to Herrenberg?"

"No," I said with something approaching finality. "But I can tell you that according to the priest, the old man was my grandfather's company commander during the time they spent here in 1945."

Maximilian Hart placed his steepled hands under his chin and began a stroking movement that started at the Adam's apple and finished at the chin.

"How do you feel now, Mr Slater?"

"What about?"

"About yourself. You have seen that your grandfather has become something of a celebrity, immortal almost."

"I'm not sure I feel anything at the moment."

I braced myself for another question, but the policeman was in a world of his own.

"You know," he said, "communities are built around myth. Myth is an integral part of culture, of identity even. If you destroy myth, you destroy a people. We can not do such a thing. Nobody must know that the grave was empty. In fact, even if we told them, I am sure that the people here would choose not to believe it. This is the German way, Mr Slater."

There was something about the tone of the voice that suggested Maximilian Hart would not accept any argument that contradicted his eternal, God-given truth. If that was the German way, then so be it. I moved my hand towards the door and pulled at the door handle.

"One last thing before you go, Mr Slater."

I was outside the jeep, and a cold wind was already ripping through my trousers.

"Yes?"

"When are you planning to go home? Back to the UK I mean?"

"My return ticket is for the second of January," I said.

"And you intend to stay here until then?"

I looked at Barbara. She had already got out of the car and was standing over me.

"Yes," I said.

"Just so we know where we can contact you," the policeman said.

The car pulled away and made a circle around us. Barbara was watching me. She was searching my eyes, my cheeks, and my forehead for some clue or answer to a question that troubled her. Eventually, she shook her head, and in a tone of voice that sounded like an ultimatum, she said:

"We have to speak. Not tonight, tomorrow... We have to speak ..."

The police jeep reversed towards us, the window rolled down and Maximilian Hart's head appeared through it.

"I'd like to say," he said, "welcome back home to Germany, Mr Slater."

The car accelerated away and disappeared into the cold and unfeeling darkness of the night.

Herrenberger Zeitung

20 December: English version.

Joerg Eisenmann, the distributor of Mercedes Benz cars, is synonymous with Herrenberg's progress since the war. Like most German businessmen, Herr Eisenmann has seen prosperous times and he has struggled for survival. His toughest battle has come in recent years as the overwhelming tide of global supercompetiviness has seen many companies modernise and restructure.

Herr Eisenmann has been selling cars in Herrenberg since 1950, and the company has made a valuable contribution to the prosperity of the town. Our sources indicate that Herr Eisenmann (73) is himself is under pressure to step down as the head of the company. Parent company, DaimlerChrysler has made no comment, but it is well known that the newly merged giant is keen to modernise all its dealerships in Germany. Eisenmann is about to celebrate his fiftieth anniversary. There is speculation that this celebration could be his swan song.

Chapter 12

Herrenberg. 28 December. Late morning

The taxi driver dropped me outside a café in a part of Herrenberg that grated in contrast to the medieval town centre. Identical modern houses, their walls darkened by the sooty fumes of passing traffic, lined the road. Grubby plastic blinds were firmly shut against the outside world. Even the slats of the blinds beside me were cast downwards like sorrowful eyes. Hidden behind these eyes was the place at which Barbara had suggested we meet, La Dolce Vita Café.

Deep voices, thumping music and dark shapes filtered through frosted glass and invited me to push through the outer door. The room was so full of swirling smoke that I felt I had entered another world. When the music stopped, there was an immediate and exaggerated moment of silence. It was soon broken by monosyllabic sounds that I took to be curses in a Slavic language.

The counter was a turmoil of overflowing ashtrays and spilled beer. Everything seemed to be covered in ash. Skirting a pool of liquid at my feet, I found a space between two drinkers and waited to be served. It was barely eleven o'clock, but one customer was slumped on a stool in a corner. His head was thrown back, and his mouth hung open in a silent scream. Another man stood unsteadily beside him. He had flung one arm across the shoulders of the sleeping man in a gesture of comfort. Such dissolute behaviour prompted the immediate reactions of embarrassment, disgust, and feelings of moral superiority. When my mother's face appeared frowning in the foul air above me, I grabbed hold of myself and stopped this slide into conditioned reflex. Nobody else in the bar appeared to be upset about the two drunks, so why should I?

I ordered coffee from a young woman and took it to a table in one corner. A blind at my shoulder had stubbornly refused to fully open and it knocked and rattled against the wall as it caught the draft from an ill-fitting window. I turned my head and, lifting one of the sorrowful slats with a finger, I looked through the window and down the street. There was no sign of Barbara. I wondered if the taxi driver had made a mistake or perhaps there was another Dolce Vita Café in Herrenberg. I could not understand why Barbara had chosen to meet me on the edge of town and in a place that was full of misfits.

The entrance door opened, and fresh air flooded into the bar. As the smoke dispersed, the room partly revealed itself. It was about twenty metres square. The floor and walls were of wood, and red and black designs had been painted on the ceiling. There were two doors - the one I had entered by - and the other, open and revealing cobwebbed walls, a painted finger, and the letters, WC.

The two drunks from the counter had disappeared, but the stirrings of cold air from the street outside brought with it their muted shouts and curses. Under the red and black ceiling there were video jukeboxes. Placed well beyond the reach of clutching hands, the screens urged people to spend their money on a favourite tune. They were playing a song called, "Durch Deine Leben." The music was so loud that even the smoke appeared to vibrate before being sucked out of the open door. I was drifting into the song, when it stopped whilst in full flow, and English words flashed up on the screen: "Did you like that? If you want to hear it please put in the money and press F456."

The song was ringing in my ears when I saw Barbara. I

had not seen her arrive but she was standing in front of me. She was wearing blue jeans under a long black coat that reached down to her ankles. The coat was unbuttoned and revealed a coloured shirt that was full of fullness and flowers. I blinked. Barely twelve hours had passed since we had last seen each other, and yet she somehow did not fit the mental image I had created for myself.

"This is one place in town," she said, "where father can not reach us."

I hardly heard her. I was coming to terms with the realisation that it was not Barbara who had changed, it was my reaction to her that was different. I was seeing her as a woman, and I wanted to touch her. I rose to my feet, stepped round the table and kissed her on the cheek. Holding her waist just a little longer than was necessary, I was already standing nervously on the edge of foreign territory. I gave Barbara a warm smile, and we stood staring at each other. Initially she looked pleased to see me, but her expression of pleasure quickly changed to one of concern.

"Martin," she said, "I have to clarify things. Before we go on, I have to ..."

With a boom, someone's favourite song played. My stomach tightened. I knew what was coming next: the rebuke, the rejection, and the expressed intention of staying friends. I had heard them all so many times before.

But for a while, neither Barbara nor I attempted to raise our voices above the din. I scanned her face for a sign. There was indecision or reluctance in the way she held her head, and I thought she appeared hesitant as though she were unable to decide whether to go or to stay. She dug deep into her pocket, pulled out a mobile phone, and placed it on the table. Then, I watched her lift the long tails of the coat and sweep them under her as she sat down.

I sat down opposite her, and at first, her eyes refused to meet mine directly. I suspected that I had made a mistake, that I should not have touched her. It was the wrong time I had chosen, or I had misread the signals. Perhaps the pressure of my fingers had been too strong, or my grip had been too long. I searched her eyes for a suggestion of the mood that might be mirrored in them. I looked for coldness, distance, a suspicious touch to the eyelids that would tell me she was fearful or defensive.

The sudden cessation of the music released the conversations that were going on around us. Half-words, ragged sentences and grunts reached out to us from the bar area. Amongst these sounds were Barbara's words, but my ears were still ringing, and I was distracted by my own voices. A sort of fatalism came over me as I tuned in to her.

"... the grave," she was saying.

I blinked and refocused. She was leaning forward, and her hand was on my forearm.

"I'm confused," she said. "I can't get a grip on it all. This dead man, the grave, the fact that it's empty, and you ..."

My concerns were replaced by a pleasant tingling sensation. It started in the stomach and spread to my face, which glowed alarmingly. But the pressure of Barbara's hand on my arm prompted the surge of another worry. What if my feelings were reciprocated? Barbara would surely expect something more from a thirty-year-old man than fumbling inefficiency.

The look of concern returned to Barbara's face with lines on the forehead and creases around the eyes.

"You are here," she said, "and an old man is found dead by a grave. The grave is unearthed during a violent storm, and there's nothing in it. I want to know what's happening. Something is going out of control."

She looked obliquely towards the table top and, removing her hand from my arm, she ran a finger in circles on the plastic cloth, drawing a picture with her fingertip. She turned her head from side to side as though she were assessing her work.

"What does it mean," she said, "for you, for me, for all of us?"

She was watching her finger as she spoke. The finger moved round and round in ever tightening circles.

"It all seems so unreal," she said. "I feel I'm being forced to see things differently, almost against my will."

Her arm was trembling, and her temple was pulsating. I tentatively held out my hand and tried to put a reassuring tone to my voice.

"I'm sure they will discover that the man's death was an accident," I said. "The police have probably made a mistake with the time of death. Wait a while. You will see that he was hit by a falling tree."

She made no movement so I took her hand from the table top and squeezed it. When I made to take my hand away, Barbara hung on to it. She moved herself closer to the table. At this point the music got louder. It exploded through the bar, and the table top vibrated under our clasped hands. My grip on time gave way. Embarrassment forced me to turn my eyes away from Barbara and to look down at the stains and burns that marked the wooden floor. When the music stopped, Barbara laid her other hand on top of mine.

"The grave was always a part of my consciousness," she said, "part of the natural order of things. But I never visited it. I've never wanted to visit it. It means nothing to me."

Barbara had already lifted her hand from mine and she used it to emphasise her final words. Although it was only the table top which took her slaps, it was my heart which felt the full force of the blows.

"But now," she added, "it's different. The grave seems so important to you, and I too see things differently. I understand why you came here, Martin; but what are you really looking for?"

I shifted uncomfortably while I considered this question. Looking past Barbara's shoulder, I took in snatches of conversation, fragments of words and phrases that reached me from the bar. The drinkers seemed to be an assortment of nationalities: Russian, Turkish, and Italian. They had arrived at this down-at-heel bar from places far away and they had got no further than the next drop of oblivion. Most of them were simply staring into emptiness. I wondered if this was what it looked like, the time of the day when these immigrants turned their thoughts to that ideal place called home. And was there anyone at home to return their thoughts? For those who had stayed behind in the motherland, perhaps these drinkers were simply half-forgotten ghosts or vague myths which were as difficult to bring to mind as a barely remembered song. And if there was nobody at home to remember them, perhaps the people in the bar were already dead.

"There are ghosts from my past in the forest," I said. "Wouldn't you like these ghosts to explain themselves? Wouldn't you feel curious?"

Barbara was staring again at her imaginary picture, her head inclined to one side. She slowly turned her eyes towards me. Then she shook her head to deny the existence of some unwanted image.

"Maybe I would feel that," she said quietly. "But what do you feel Martin?"

I looked into my heart, but I was looking through a glass window that would not open. I was shocked at this disconnection from my feelings. Without words they would remain only shadows.

"I want to know what's hidden here," I said. "After all, Martin Spohr represents part of my past."

"Poor Martin," Barbara said. "Now you've come all that way from England, and the grave's empty."

I was distracted by a voice that thundered around the bar. The voice dropped like a fading siren. An arm was raised, and a finger was pointed. Then silence. The shout had been a useless, brief burst of anger at the world, this town and a journey that had brought these people no further than the Dolce Vita Café. The video jukebox put up a comforting message: "Now we present you a nice music video."

"The absence of bones proves nothing," I said. "Someone might have removed them or maybe the grave never contained anything. Martin Spohr could have been hit by a shell - a direct hit would have obliterated all physical evidence that he had ever existed. The grave would have been dug and left as a simple memorial, containing nothing except a name."

Barbara was drawing again. I watched the top of her head, and wondered what was going through her mind. I heard her say:

"What is it that the past can give you or any of us? The past is dead, vanished and gone. The present is the place to be."

"The past can give you a lot," I said, "especially if you don't have one."

Barbara lifted her head and peered at me with an expression of interested compassion. Time passed, a minute, perhaps two. I raised my eyes to the television screens that hung beneath the ceiling. We were being entertained with sporting accidents of the motorised type. I watched for a while until I found myself hoping for more and more dramatic accidents and shots of the victims. I looked away in disgust. Nobody at the bar seemed interested in the programme. They were huddled over their beers and stared vacantly at their unhappiness while the television images flickered on their faces.

"Perhaps it's family I've come to find," I said at last. "Something I can belong to."

"And if you find it," Barbara said, "what then?"

"I shall go back to England."

"And then I too will become part of the past, is that it?"

She was drawing circles again, and her vitality seemed to have left her. She had recoiled and withdrawn from me and vanished in herself.

"In order to know where I'm going," I said weakly, "I have to know where I've been."

With a flourish, Barbara finished her imaginary picture.

She lifted her finger and brought it down hard, like a full stop.

"Why are you English so obsessed with the past? When I lived in England, the war always came up sooner or later. And what's it got to do with you and me?"

"You can't just bury the past in the forest and pretend it isn't there."

Barbara closed her eyes and held the eyelids together while she let out a long sigh.

"Then let's hope," she said, "that neither the past nor the future are as empty as the grave itself."

"That's not fair …," I began.

"Martin, we are living today. We can create the past to suit ourselves."

I decided to remain silent as a flowering of tenderness for Barbara inextricably bound itself to frustration at the turn the conversation was taking. She leaned forward and cupped her chin with one hand and rested her elbow on the other.

"And with regard to the present," she said, "we've been summoned."

"Summoned?"

Barbara lifted her eyes to mine and, twisting her mouth sideways, she gave me a conspiratorial look.

"We've been summoned to lunch, today. He said he wanted to meet you. Remember?"

"Who said he wanted to meet me?"

"My father," Barbara said.

"I thought he was just being polite."

"That might be the case in England," Barbara said. "When a German makes an invitation, it is an invitation."

She raised her eyebrows to reassure me of her playful intentions, but I felt I had been roundly ticked off. I lowered my eyes.

"I see."

"Before we go," she was saying, "before you meet him again, there's something you should know."

I breathed deeply. So here at last was the punch line. She was going to tell me that we were just friends. I hunched my shoulders as if in protection from driving rain.

"Father isn't himself," she said. "He's under pressure to resign. Daimler grants him a licence to sell cars. But it's only for one year renewable."

I scratched at my head.

"One year? Are you saying that technically speaking, he could be out of a job at the end of each year?"

"Technically yes. There is never, and there was never, a guarantee that the licence would be renewed."

"And when ...?"

"The renewal is coming up at the end of the month," Barbara said.

I made a quick calculation.

"This month? In a couple of days?"

The telephone rang. It seemed too loud, too intrusive. I looked on helplessly as Barbara picked up the mobile and lifted it to her ear.

"Eisenmann."

Barbara gave some numbers in German. The way it rattled off her tongue, I assumed it was her telephone number. Her eyes darted around the bar. I sensed that she was interpreting, analysing. She dropped the phone onto the table without saying goodbye. She took a deep breath.

"That was Chief Inspector Maximilian Hart," she said.

I raised my eyebrows.

"He wanted to know father's phone number."

She ran her finger over the table top and, with an energetic movement, she destroyed her imaginary picture.

"Why didn't he look it up in the phone book?" she murmured.

"Maybe he had other things to ask you," I said.

"Indeed," she said, sounding like her father. "He wants us to come to the priest's house this afternoon. He says he has some information we need to know."

"What," I said, "do we need to know?"

"He didn't say."

She rose quickly to her feet and buttoned up her coat.

"Ready?"

We walked out of the Good Life Café. Nothing was stirring outside but the air was refreshing after the stuffiness of the café. I would have liked to stroll about for a while in order to clear my head, and to clear away the debris of the past, but Barbara was striding on ahead of me.

I looked up and saw that although it was early afternoon, the sky seemed to hold a promise of darkness. My imagination told me that it was not the approaching night, but the shadow of another great force, and it was gathering to engulf us all.

Herrenberger Zeitung

27 December: English version

Rumours of a management takeover battle at the Eisenmann dealership intensified this week. Sources indicate that in the light of the merger with the US car maker Chrysler, question marks have been raised over Joerg Eisenmann's wartime past. In a recent local television interview, Eisenmann laughed off any suggestions of a criminal past. He admitted that he had served in the army, but that he was just a frightened 19-year-old who simply tried to stay alive. He said that he was never at any time involved with the Nazi party.

The rumours suggest that the struggle for leadership of the company is becoming increasingly bitter. Jewish groups in the US have already objected on moral grounds to the DaimlerChrysler merger while both the company and the German Government are extremely sensitive to the issue of compensation for Nazi slave workers. However, it is likely that the outcome of the dispute will centre on company finances rather than on rumour. Eisenmann's yearly results will become know later this month.

Chapter 13

Herrenberg. 28 December. Afternoon

We drove under a stone arch and turned into a long driveway, the car wheels crackling loudly on the gravel. The moment Barbara switched off the engine, a vague sense of detached enchantment fell upon me. I imagined airy spirits playing in the pines that flanked the driveway of Joerg Eisenmann's house. The trees stood as straight and tall as sentries, and from between them danced the fallen leaves, whirling around in circles as if they were dogs chasing their own tails. Stillness enveloped the house itself. It was crouching and low and appeared to be protecting itself from an invisible enemy. The windows were watchful eyes, looking out towards the fringes of the Schönbuch Forest.

We got out of the car and Barbara said:

"In four days time to be exact."

"Sorry … what?"

"The renewal of father's contract," Barbara said.

"Is there any reason why they shouldn't renew it?"

She shrugged but there was a flicker of concern in her face as she said:

"If father does not meet the financial targets set by the company, they have the right to appoint their own sales and management team."

"That seems rather unfair," I said.

Barbara pushed out her bottom lip as a signal of partial agreement.

"Yes and no," she said. "Both parties have done well out of this agreement for fifty years."

She set off for the front door with me following in her wake. The door was made of a heavy and thick wood and was flanked by two suits of armour. There were peculiar metal objects on the lawns which bordered the parking area. These objects had apparently been left by some rough magic, or else at random as though they had dropped from the sky. They could have been construed as modern art, but to me, the pointed and angular objects suggested a gloomy, grotesque and barbarous period in the distant past. My detached enchantment melted slowly away into the thin air. My palms were clammy, my right leg shaking.

"Will he meet the requirements?" I asked.

"There are complications."

"Like?"

Barbara gripped my arm.

"Let's forget it for the moment," she said. "I'm looking forward to the lunch. I feel good about it."

I smiled at her and tried to catch her optimism. But that magical stillness that had lain on the world was already turning, and a bristling atmosphere now hung over the house, the trees and the parking area. A dog barked angrily, and others answered him from corners near and far.

Evidently we were expected because the front door swung ponderously open, and the woman who had welcomed us at Eisenmann's party stood sentinel on the threshold. This time, I did not admire her blond hair. I merely noticed the chipped and discoloured teeth.

Not a word passed amongst us as the maid stood aside, and Barbara and I stepped into the house. In the hallway, my nostrils twitched at the musty smell of oldness which seemed to seep from the woodwork, the furniture and the walls. The door thumped shut behind us. From a little round table, a familiar face peered at me from amid a variety of newspapers. I pulled out what I saw to be a morning edition of a local paper. The front of this paper consisted almost entirely of the face of the old man, whose body had been discovered the previous day. I scanned the article while Barbara and Nadia, the maid, exchanged quiet words. My heart leaped when I read the word "morder". I wanted to ask whether or not the cause of death had been determined, but from behind, I sensed the hostility of the maid. I heard her say:

"It's time you went in."

I glanced over my shoulder and smiled at Barbara, who was hovering in the middle of the hall. She took my arm, and we walked along a panelled corridor. At the end of this corridor, some steps led upwards through a low archway, and we entered a room which was sparkling with bright light and dappled with weak shadow. The light flooded through a window that took up one wall in its entirety. The struggling sun was already hanging low in the sky. The shadows of the forest trees stretched out like tentacles over the undulating land and, with a final and breathless lunge, invaded the room in which we stood.

Eisenmann was sitting deep in an armchair and contemplating the view through the window. He was resting his chin in the palm of his hand. Barbara walked over to him and gently kissed his cheek. I ambled round to one side of him - clearly in view, but careful lest I should interrupt his view of the forest. Without shifting his chin from the apparent comfort of his hand, and without uttering any form of greeting, he spoke into his palm:

"I have just spoken to Hart. He tells me that things are going on in the forest here."

The tone was flat and defensive as though he had taken offence at some critical comment that had never been made. He said:

"What Hart says may be true, but from this distance, the forest looks the same. And I know the forest well. I am acquainted with almost every mound and hollow, and almost every patch of shadow. I often look at the forest - to remind me."

There was a long silence. I was unwilling to intrude on his reflections, but I felt some sort of question was demanded of me.

"To remind you of what?" I said quietly.

He replied into the palm of his hand.

"What it was once like."

He removed the supporting presence of his hand and stuck out his jaw.

"What terrifies me," he said, "is how ordinary it has all become. And yet, what was once so ordinary also had the power to become terrifying."

He emitted a sort of grunt. Whether what we heard was a failed attempt at a laugh, I was unable to tell. But it was not a sound that invited us to comment. He remained deep in thought for a while and then he put out his arm and pointed through the window. Herrenberg's church tower dominated the land between the house and the forest, but Eisenmann seemed to be indicating the passage of the Herrenberg to Stuttgart road. It was clearly visible as car roofs which zipped along behind hedges and which disappeared every now and then behind buildings under construction. Eisenmann's deeply lined eye sockets creased up still further.

"This land you see now has become a non-place. Look there ...," he said. "What you see is just a road that people use to get from one place to another. They see and notice nothing apart from the car lights in front. The rest is no more than a blur of green, a faint realisation of something more, of something else beyond the comfortable and protective confines of the car."

There was silence for a while save the sound of his breathing. Then he cocked his head to one side.

"Yes," he said, "just a blur. They see it in the same way that they see their own faces when they look out at the world. They have a vague sense of their hairline, the shape of the face, and so on and so on. In fact, they see nothing. And this is normal. This is how it should be, normal times and normal people doing normal things."

I had opened my mouth to say something but I felt Barbara tugging at my arm. She smiled at me. Her eyes bade me be silent.

"Once," Eisenmann continued, "and I remember it well, if you set foot on that road you were a dead man."

He leaned forward, his body blending into the tired shadows.

"And there, do you see that green and grassy blur? It was suddenly alive - and there ... it was ripped up in fountains right front of your eyes. The empty backdrop of sky was alive with the roar of their planes. The ground around you leapt and spat where the bullets raked it. That is what made it so shocking. It was so unexpected. They came from nowhere and to nowhere they returned. And when they had gone, they left behind a low sound, a sort of moaning. It was the sound of the earth itself sobbing."

Eisenmann looked down and scanned the floor at his feet. He made an almost imperceptible movement of his head and raised his right eyebrow so that a question mark appeared on his forehead.

"How can a farmer defend himself against bombs? Can you tell me that? And the bombs smashed and broke, and obliterated people. I wondered why then. I wonder why now. Those who drive here every day have either forgotten these deaths or perhaps they never knew about them. What separates these drivers from that terrible period is more than time itself. They worry about their houses and their cars, but this land is tainted with the blood and the pain of their fathers. Most of the living spend their time trying not to remember. You understand don't you? They try hard not to remember."

His voice faded away to indistinct breathing. I was left trying to digest what I had heard. It was not what Eisenmann said that was important, it was the way he said it. I could not help but be moved. He was no stranger in his own memories. They were part of his present. Eisenmann stirred, and in a stronger voice, he said:

"I used to go into the forest - but no longer. I have no

need. If I sit still long enough and listen, I can hear the forest quivering with life - a stream that trickles, birds that cry out a warning, small beasts rustling in the undergrowth. And the trees - I see their branches bending, their tops swaying, and the branches creaking where the birds dance lightly on them. And all the time, the damp earth crackles and settles at your feet. When I walked there, I always heard sounds like footfalls on the leaves and you know, even now when I am sitting here and thinking about it, I turn and I expect to see someone behind me."

Eisenmann sat completely still, his hands now resting in his lap. For some seconds the silence in the room was broken only by the distant sound of a light wind gusting in the trees.

"But there is never anyone there," he continued. "There was never anyone in the forest either - only the trees that surrounded me. The whole forest is living and breathing in my mind. It waits and watches us as we go through it and pass on to the other side. And when we have gone, the forest remains - the same but invisible, and as silent as the grave. The forest is untouchable. But it is there. It is always there."

I looked at Barbara's affectionately smiling face as she leaned over her father's body. She resembled a loving parent adoringly bent over its charge. Eisenmann took a deep breath to indicate, perhaps, that he had finished with his memories for the day.

"We all live in the shadow of what we did and experienced in the past," he said, "but I rarely go into the forest these days."

He looked up at me and leaned his head to one side.

"You must excuse the imperfections of my English," he said. "Shakespeare and Conrad do not help us much in these times. They do not help us understand this forest and its heart of immense darkness do they?"

He rose to his feet, and Barbara put out her arm to aid him. He ignored the arm and stood bolt upright while he turned his head to gaze a little longer through the window. Without a word more, he led the way into an adjacent room. Taking a seat at the head of a large wooden table, he was framed in a window which was flanked by shutters. When he sat still, he reminded me of a Christ figure in the central panel of a triptych over a church altar.

Barbara and I took our seats opposite each other. The large mahogany table reflected the cutlery, the plates and our own faces when we leaned forward on our elbows. Nadia brought in steaming bowls, and Eisenmann motioned with his arms for us to help ourselves. I felt uncomfortably aware that he was staring at me, and his chin and jaw jutted aggressively.

"Max has told me that things have been happening here since your arrival Mr Slater," he said, "and Babs has talked about it too."

The shortening of her name and the formal use of mine surprised me. It indicated emotional distance, a refusal to accept me as Barbara's friend.

"Hart's men have found a body," Eisenmann said, "in the forest I believe. And you too have found something that interests you, am I right Mr Slater?"

I glanced at Barbara. What I saw surprised and somehow disappointed me. She was sitting low in her seat with her hands folded neatly in her lap and her eyes lowered towards the table top. This was the same person with whom I had entered the house but there was now someone I could not recognise living inside her skin.

"Yes," I said. "There's a grave in the forest ..."

"I know it," Eisenmann snapped.

He was sitting so still, I would not have been surprised to see his feet tucked up under him like a Buddha. There was a clatter as Barbara bent forward and removed the cover from one of the bowls. As she did so, clouds of steam billowed upwards and momentarily obscured her face. Eisenmann said:

"There are many more graves in the forest. Perhaps

hundreds, who knows? But they'll never be found now."

I heard Barbara stirring the contents of the bowl with a ladle. She leaned over to put some in my plate, and I recognised that she had fallen into the obedient role demanded of her by her father. I picked up my spoon and turned my eyes away from Eisenmann's intrusive stare. But when I leaned forward to bring the spoon to my lips, the reflection of his lined and wrinkled face leaped at me from the table top. He continued to stare at me while I brought the spoon up to my mouth. My thoughts were derailed. I was left floundering and wondering what I was doing in that house with two strangers.

"Well," I said, "it seems that the man in that particular grave, Martin Spohr, was my grandfather."

I lifted my head and stared back at old Eisenmann. I was, perhaps, expecting an encouraging slap on the back or some exclamation. There was nothing. Not a movement, not a grimace, save perhaps the flicker of some unrecognisable emotion from deep inside and reflected in his eye. Or was it simply the trees in the driveway I saw mirrored in his eyes? Whatever it was, I was much more concerned with myself and my own emotions. I lowered my head to the bowl and brought the spoon again to my lips. In the polished table top, I saw Barbara's bowed head and Eisenmann's stare. He had hardly moved.

"So, your grandfather is famous around here," he said flatly. "How does it feel?"

I stopped chewing in order to show him that I was consulting my emotions. I was surprised to find disappointment lurking there, disappointment that my newly found knowledge was about to become part of the natural order of unquestioned things. I swallowed the food and shrugged.

"Difficult to say," I said.

"Would you not like to go to one of the villages here?" he said. "Would you not like to go to Breitenholz and say to the people that you are Martin Spohr's grandson, and have your photograph taken by the side of the grave? Would that not be appropriate?"

I looked hard at his reflection before replying.

"Right now," I said, "there is no grave and there is nothing to ..."

I looked towards Barbara for confirmation, but Old Eisenmann interrupted.

"Yes, yes," he said, "Max has told me everything."

"So you know there is no body."

"I told you," he said sharply, "Max has told me. But body or no body, the place itself is a holy spot. The policeman is right. The truth must remain what people think it is."

There was the slightest lowering of the eyes as he said this.

"No, really," he added in order to pre-empt some kind of objection, "it is far too late to change anything now."

The maid appeared at his elbow, and at the slightest nod of his head, she helped him to some of the soup.

"It is all very well," I said, "for you to talk about your truth ..."

"How," Eisenmann interrupted, "did Mr Slater discover all this?"

"The point is that ...," I began, but before I could get any further, Eisenmann had turned sideways and addressed Barbara.

"Perhaps," he said, "the past is best left alone."

Barbara had lowered her head so far forward that I wondered if she had fallen asleep.

"He found some letters," she muttered, the downward intonation at the end of her utterance suggesting she had only just started.

"Indeed. That must have been a surprise for him."

There was a flash in front of my eyes. Disappointment at Barbara's inability to confront her father's behaviour, and shame on her behalf drove me to challenge him.

"The point is," I said, "that one moment you berate people for not wishing to remember, and now you are saying that the past is best left alone. What exactly do you think Mr Eisenmann?"

I glared at him, expecting my assertiveness to pay off. Eisenmann merely put out his hand and laid it on Barbara's forearm.

"Some letters you say?"

Barbara nodded. Her face was white and taut, and her words, spoken on a breath were almost inaudible.

"Yes, it was a surprise."

"And does he know where these letters came from?"

"The priest," she said.

"The priest? The letters came from the priest?"

From the corner of my eye I saw Barbara nod. Embarrassment prevented me from looking at her directly. I looked instead at her reflection, but I was unable to make out her expression - only the downward angle of the head and the dropped eyelids.

"He came to ask his own questions," I heard her say.

"An inquisitive young man," Eisenmann said, "who refused to follow the example of his elders. He should have left it alone, you know. Why? Because the forgetting has become automatic."

He was old, mysterious and elusive, and it was this that inspired respect like a conditioned response. Perhaps he was just mean and stupid. I glanced up at him with a wince of surprise. The surprise was at my own action. I dropped the spoon with a clatter and rubbed my eyes as if waking from sleep.

"Why don't you speak to me?" I said straight to his face.

Silence swelled between the three of us. Eisenmann moved. He pushed his plate to one side and looked obliquely towards the top of the table. A splash of dying light lay across his back. I watched his cheeks swell to the pressure of his tongue as it moved inside his mouth. I sat frozen, shaken by my outburst. Anger hung over the table like a cloud but it was received in silence. A drop of liquid, quivering on Eisenmann's chin, betrayed a tremor in his face. This old man whose manner to me, and perhaps to most who knew him, was that of a man as hard as nails, seemed shaken. His eyes were red and weary, and he lifted his hand and rubbed at his cheek with the back of a fist.

"Tell your friend," he said to Barbara, "nobody has to work at it any more, the forgetting I mean. But nobody will thank him for telling them they have made a mistake. You know, the Chief Inspector is correct. The truth must remain what the people think it is."

In the silence that followed, I heard the wind outside moaning like wind through a pipe. On the hillside, the shadows of the forest seemed to have moved further towards us. Eisenman said something else while his hand massaged his cheek. His voice was so low that I had to strain to catch what it was he said. His gaze seemed to hold the distance for such a long time that I turned to see if someone had entered the room. There were only the walls that surrounded us, and the reflection of the trees in his eyes. I thought I heard him say:

"The shadows of the forest are closing in around us."

Then, using the table top to steady himself, Eisenmann rose to his feet. He stood swaying for a second, apparently shocked or startled, while he looked down and frowned at his own reflection. Turning quickly away, he strode proudly towards the archway through which we had come. He stopped and staggered on the threshold, and I wondered if he had struck his head on the low ceiling. Then, he turned to face us, and his eyes were wide open and filled with an expression of horror. It seemed to me that in a flash of clarity he was confronted with some dreadful reality. He muttered something, but his words were drowned out by the tolling of the church bells coming to us from over the fields. He clenched his fists, and his arms shook.

"No," he said, "it's impossible, just impossible."

Unblinking eyes stared at us for a second, and then he plunged into the archway. On the other side of that arch I sensed an empty darkness opening out into the hallway, the heavy door and the courtyard with its strange art forms. A continuous roaring then grabbed at the air and seemed to come down on me. I rose to my feet and, surrounded by this noise, I made my way towards the window. I was expecting to see a car roaring past the pine trees that flanked the driveway. There was nothing but the leaves, still whirling around in circles and chasing their tails.

I looked out across the fields and to the rooftops of Herrenberg. The ringing of the bells was still running over them, and the lowering sun, in the midst of an iron grey sky, allowed its rays to come through the slits in the clouds and descend obliquely over the houses and the forest. I heard a sound from behind. Barbara had found some escape in routine. She was tidying and stacking the unused plates and gathering the unused cutlery. I could think of nothing meaningful to say. The sky closed in. The clouds pressed one against the other, and the slanting rays of the sun thinned and paled, were quenched and, finally, disappeared.

Letter from Ulrich Schneider

June 1955

Not all thoughts are allowed. Too much feeling is with them. I am not in good health. Have ten years really passed or were those years a dream? We are talking about the Schönbuch Forest. It was April 1945. What happened there is not known to many people. There were very few battles. The French and Americans did not dare go into the wood. The chaos is something that I shall never forget. The war was lost. It was a useless, pointless situation. We had to fight on to the bitter end.

My section of air defence was motorised. We had half-tracks, and self-propelled guns. We had already crossed the Rhine. We were retreating towards Stuttgart and we found ourselves near Herrenberg. We helped as best we could in battles with American planes. There were no military targets for them. They came and attacked the farms and farmers. We did what we could to help. Every time the planes came, they left the dead behind them. They were pointless deaths in a pointless situation. I could not and I can not understand what the Americans hoped to achieve.

I do not remember when Martin Spohr joined us. He was young but not inexperienced. We tried to help him. Spohr belongs to a period of complete chaos. Most details are difficult to recall. But not the deaths – never, never those deaths.

177

We were weak. We had no rations. It was not a question of defending Stuttgart. We wandered into the Schönbuch Forest near Sulz in order to reach the German lines. Then we were ordered to support the battle for Herrenberg. We advanced, and in Küppingen, we were forced to halt. Without heavy weapons it was impossible to go on. The only way forward was to go through the forest. We did not have enough fuel to do anything else. On 18 April we entered the wood.

We arrived in Nüfringen and surprised a group of twenty or so French soldiers who were drinking wine in a house there. They seemed to think that the war was already over. We did not know what to do with them. We could not take prisoners with us. Then, the women from the village emerged from the wood where they had been hiding. They were in a sorry state. They told us they had been in the wood for days, and without proper food and nothing to drink. They begged us not to leave them in the hands of the French. The soldiers had already raped and killed a number of them.

We did what we could. We tied the prisoners together and locked them in the church until we could decide what to do. One thing was certain. If these men had committed crimes, I was going to make sure they would stand trial. I left Spohr in temporary charge of the prisoners while the rest of us tried to make the short distance to Herrenberg under cover of darkness.

We reached the main road and machine gun fire forced us to keep low. When we arrived at the main street in Herrenberg a more concentrated shell fire began, and then the planes came over. I gave orders to take shelter. Some did not hear me. Several were killed. Our half-track was positioned near a guesthouse by the church. We took refuge in the cellar. We gave the wounded men opium, but many of them died. Then I heard that the prisoners had been killed. I assumed they had been hit during the bombardment. These men had been my responsibility. I wanted them to answer for their crimes. I don't recall when Spohr came back to the unit. We were relieved that he was still alive. I could not believe what was going on around us. How could it happen in the last moments of the war?

Chapter 14

Hildrizhausen. 28 December. Evening

We roared through the outskirts of Herrenberg and sped up the road to Hildrizhausen. The sun was playing a game of hide-and-seek between the trees, and we plunged in and out of blinding light and deepening shadows. Barbara drove so fast I wondered if the devil himself was chasing us. On reflection, I realised that this image was not so fanciful. There was no horned man with a three-pronged fork behind us. Barbara was rushing away from her own personal demon. In the presence of her father, the child she had been escaping from her whole life long had returned and taken possession of her body.

The urgency of her expression discouraged my reassuring comments, and the roar of the engine prevented speculative conversation about why we had been summoned to the priest's house. Neither of us spoke until, at the top of the hill, Barbara changed up a gear and struck the steering wheel with the palm of her hand.

"Poor father. It's so unfair. Why doesn't someone stop them?"

The car lurched alarmingly towards the left side of the road and then slowed to walking speed.

"Stop them from what?" I said.

Barbara sat stony-faced, her arms rigid, her eyes mere slits.

"From digging into his past. No wonder he's so unhappy."

I turned away and breathed deeply as a pang of nervousness shot through me. I did not want to lose her to things dead and buried.

"Daimler used slave workers during the war," she said. "This nearly blocked the merger with Chrysler in the first place. At the first hint of some connection with the Nazis, the company wouldn't hesitate to drop him."

Barbara forced the gear lever into third and pressed down hard on the accelerator. The star at the end of the bonnet seemed to lift as we surged off and away from the thoughts and the demons that tormented her.

The trees passed in a flash, and the sky between their trunks changed from blue to blood red. Up ahead, wood smoke drifted lazily over the roofs of Hildrizhausen. Glancing sideways, I saw Barbara's eyes. They were damp and pink.

"And nobody would blame them," she said. "Even the German Government is under pressure to rid itself of its dark past. There are still Nazis around. Everyone is afraid of what happened in former times and they are fearful of the present. And what can we do to help?"

She turned her face towards me, but I kept my eyes fixed on the road ahead. I thought I detected a sullen touch to her expression which pictured exactly what was going on inside her head. It reinforced my growing feelings of impotence and inadequacy. I wanted to scream out my frustration.

"Just show him you are there for him," I said.

Up ahead, a freshly painted church threw its whiteness at me in the gathering dusk and announced our arrival in Hildrizhausen. I waited for Barbara to acknowledge my comment, but she was away and rambling in her own thoughts.

"They know," she said, "that Daimler are very sensitive to its past."

"Who are they?" I asked.

"Those people you saw at his party, remember? Father's

managers. They know that the contract is up for renewal. They have already been ingratiating themselves with Daimler bosses and now they are digging up all the dirt they can find and ... oh why is everything falling apart?"

We pulled up on a grass verge outside the graveyard. The sun had finally set, the shadows of the forest had retreated, and the Schönbuch was now an impenetrable and darkening wall.

"In four days time," she said, "the dealership contract is to be renewed. They intend to see that it isn't."

The church clock struck the half-hour. I looked through the car window and at the graves lying in neat rows on the other side of the low wall.

"So what you are saying," I said, "is that in theory, in four days time, he could be driven out of the company he created."

Barbara bit her bottom lip and nodded.

"It's really not my problem," she said.

Her words were rendered meaningless by the frustrated and bitter tone on which they rode. There seemed little else to do but stare into the graveyard. What I really ached to do was put my arm round her and protect her, but she was as brittle and as sensitive as a dried flower, and I dared not touch her for fear that she would disintegrate and fly away from me. I swung away from her and got out of the car.

A few seconds later I was knocking at the door of the priest's house. The anticipation of what was soon to come somehow gave Barbara and me a joint focus and helped to ease the tension that had fallen between us. The front door shifted, opened a few inches, and then hung still. A shaft of light cut through the opening and splashed across our shoes. Barbara and I exchanged quick anxious glances, and I pushed at the door. It swung slowly back until it gently struck the inside wall. Standing with one foot in the hallway, I noticed the ticking of the clocks. I heard them because they seemed to be ticking faster than normal, and frantically like a heart recovering from a panic attack.

The next thing I noticed was the dark shape of a retreating figure making its way towards the sitting area. I closed the door, and Barbara and I followed the shape down the hallway and into the lounge. There were no voices. Apart from the ticking of the clocks there was only the creaking of our feet on the floorboards.

The main lights had yet to be switched on, and with the house in semi-darkness I was first drawn to the familiar musty smell of oldness that had either followed me from Eisenmann's house, or it had permeated my clothes like cigarette smoke. But wherever the smell had come from, the living room was full of it.

A figure materialised in the struggling light. The figure was a shape that occupied the armchair, but as my eyes became accustomed to the dim light, I recognised the priest. He was sitting bolt upright, and his feet were pulled together, his ankles crossed under him. His hands lay palm downwards on his thighs. He wore similar clothes to the ones in which I had seen him before, but it seemed that someone else was now living inside them. He looked as though he had been physically picked up in the air and shaken roughly. And while being shaken, someone else had taken possession of his body. His hair hung untidily over his neck and shoulders, his lips were pulled back over his teeth, and his glasses were askew on his face.

Chief Inspector Maximilian Hart was settling himself comfortably in the armchair nearest the door. With his legs stretched out in front of him, he steepled his hands, placed his chin on the tips of his fingers, and lifted his face to the ceiling. The priest did not offer a greeting. He merely glanced at Barbara and me, his face begging us for assistance. When the policeman spoke, he was clearly picking up the threads of a conversation that had been interrupted by our arrival. Excluded from the proceedings, Barbara and I looked on while the priest stared wildly around the room.

"So yes," the policeman was saying, "I am suggesting

that were he alive today, he would be wanted for war crimes, and crimes against humanity. Maybe you read the paper some few weeks ago. A former major in the SS is to stand trial in Verona on charges of war crimes. 1944 I think it was."

The clocks ticked loudly. Barbara and I moved towards the sofa. Lit up as it was in the blaze of a reading lamp, it seemed to invite us to use it. The policeman stroked his throat with his fingers.

"Yes, crimes against humanity," he said, "whatever they are. Is global warming a crime against humanity? Are corporations which put profit before everything guilty of crimes against humanity? These are interesting questions, are they not?"

The leather sofa creaked and puffed as Barbara and I took our seats on it. The policeman appeared to be reflecting on his own question, and nobody else attempted to respond. Outside, a sharp wind whined through the forest. Glancing through the window, I saw a dark figure shambling along the pavement. A bell sounded from the old church. It was five o'clock.

"The question is this," Hart said. "Can we allow the information we have to leak out? And if we did, would anyone believe us? To whom do we have a duty? As a man of God, I am sure you would agree that it is not only the law that determines what is right and what is just."

The Inspector lowered his chin to his breast bone. With his hands still steepled together and under the chin, he appeared to say a short prayer before raising his hunting-dog eyes and allowing them to flicker around the room as if in search of a new victim. He fixed the priest with a long stare.

"But perhaps," he said, "you had better tell our friends what we are discussing."

The priest stiffened, and his eyes darted nervously around the room. His mouth opened and closed as he searched for words, and an attempt to straighten his glasses set them further askew on his face.

"Where shall I begin?"

The policeman took a deep breath and blew out slowly and noisily through his teeth. He sounded like a snake.

"It might be useful," he said, "to start at the beginning."

The priest let his head fall forward. He was mouthing silently to himself, and even in that shaded room, I saw his ears were burning red.

"It was me," he said, "who asked the old man to come here. We had kept our secret for so long. I did not know what to tell the young man."

He rubbed his forehead with the palm of one hand.

"I mean you Mr Slater. What could I tell you? Was I to continue the lie? Did I really have to continue with something I could not comfortably live with? Should I tell you the truth about your grandfather? That is why I asked Mr Schneider to come here. I didn't know whether he would agree to continue with the lie."

There was another loud intake of breath from the policeman.

"No, no. You haven't told them who Mr Schneider was. Tell them man. Tell them."

The priest buried his head in his hands. A sliver of saliva fell from his lips and swayed over the carpet.

"As you know," he said, "Ulrich Schneider was your grandfather's company commander. He was the only one alive who knew what happened … the only one who experienced it all."

I frowned and turned towards Barbara. She was looking at the priest with expressionless eyes. Her lips were moving but her mind had wandered away to ask itself questions in private. While I formulated questions of my own, the policeman raised his eyes skywards and interrupted again.

"No, no," he said. "Start from the beginning. Our friend here has no idea what you are talking about. Start from the beginning, you understand? The beginning."

I expected the man of God to protest or protect himself. Instead, he looked up at the policeman with the hurt and questioning expression of the schoolboy who knows he is guilty and awaits punishment. The Chief Inspector blew noisily through his teeth again. He was barely able to conceal his impatience.

"The book," he said. "Why don't you begin with the book?"

"The book?" the priest muttered. "In the beginning was the word. This is always the case, isn't it?"

He looked at the policeman and then at me. I was feeling self-conscious, aware that my presence in the house was critical. I was also aware that although I was the star performer, I had no part to play and no lines to speak.

"You already know," the priest said, "that my father wrote his history of Hildrizhausen during the Fascist years. The book was entitled, 'Hildrizhausen and the Nazi Times.' He decided never to publish it because of ..."

At this point he bent sideways to pick up some papers. The policeman lazily stretched out an arm and raised his palm. He could have been controlling the traffic, but the movement stopped the priest as if he had been struck by magic and turned to stone. He remained immobile and twisted, and holding the papers over the table. The policeman said:

"No. Not yet. Keep to the logical order of events. It helps."

The priest returned the papers to the table and turned towards me.

"My father had first-hand experience of those terrible years," he said. "He wanted to put it all down for the sake of posterity. He was particularly interested in the soldier's grave in Goldbachtal. He knew its story and he had watched as the grave developed into a sort of shrine. Perhaps because nobody knew about Martin Spohr, the grave assumed such a mysterious and mystical quality. Who was the man buried there? What had happened to him? My father decided to investigate."

It was now dark outside. Nobody had bothered to turn

on the main light but my lateral vision caught Barbara's face in the light of the reading lamp behind us. Her eyebrows were gathered up. I thought she looked moody or displeased, but she said nothing. The policeman was a silent shadow, motionless and stretched out in the chair. The priest was a bent silhouette with a hanging head, his hair falling like a curtain over his temples and cheeks. He was speaking so quietly that I had to strain to catch every word.

"My father received many dead soldiers. They were brought from the forest and into his church, but he was never able to forget the two who had died in the arms of the other. Partly he recalled them because he saw that the need for human contact in death was so at odds with the violent way in which they had died. Partly he was not allowed to forget them because of the initial confusion over their identities. As you know, Spohr's soldbuch and greatcoat were found next to the two men. But it soon became clear that neither of the dead men was, in fact, Martin Spohr."

The priest's voice faded away to silence. As it did so, I felt Barbara's hand on top of mine. I felt the light pulse in the flesh around her wrist. There was a sharp intake of breath from the priest.

"When Spohr's uncle came," he said, "my father tried to help him in any way he could. As you know, the grave was discovered by accident in the winter of forty-seven to forty-eight. Over the years, the spot took on its almost magical qualities, and my father was asked again and again the same questions."

The priest paused as though for breath. I stifled the sounds of my own breathing so that I would not miss a word.

"Who was this man, and what had happened to him?"

The priest's shape swung towards the table, and the papers rustled and cracked under fumbling fingers. There was no sound from the policeman. In the light of the reading lamp, a hand appeared. Between its fingers, a piece of paper hovered over the ground at my feet. Catching the light, the handwriting was revealed as small, spidery and uneven. The paper slipped into my fingers, and the priest's hand withdrew into the faint light.

"My father made enquiries," he said, "and in 1954 he wrote to Martin Spohr's company commander. My father did not know whether or not the man was still alive, so he was pleased when he received a reply. They corresponded further and in June 1955, Ulrich Schneider sent this letter to my father. Until his death, my father kept the letter a secret. He didn't show it to anyone - not even to me. It was only when my father died in 1964 that the letter came into my possession. What you have there is my English translation. I knew that if your mother asked for more information about Martin Spohr, I would have to make a decision. Would I give her the information in that letter or would I deny it? For a year, I dreaded the arrival of the postmen. Fortunately, she only wrote to thank me for what I had already sent her. She never wrote again. I never had to make the decision."

I let the page lie on my lap. Barbara leaned against me. I supposed she knew by instinct that a letter intended for my mother might rekindle feelings of loss. But there was no time left for crying. My heart jumped when I saw my grandfather's name at the bottom of the page. To see those letters, scribbled on the paper by someone who had known him, somehow made him more real to me.

I was struggling to find the words to express my excitement when I heard a stifled sob coming at us through the darkness. I thought I must have misheard, but it came again as a sort of high-pitched and broken moan like a child whining. Then came the voice, watery and choking. It was the priest who was crying.

"It was never Spohr," he said through gaps in the sobbing, "never Spohr who governed my actions."

Silence, and then, in an angry tone, he added:

"No, nor was it only my villagers. I had to think about

all those Germans who had lost loved ones. And there was your mother too. How could I tell them all something as terrible as this? Was it really my decision to make?"

There was a clicking sound from the back of his throat, followed by a strangled sob and the fast and uneven breaths of a man trying to control himself.

"This is not what you told me when we met," I said. "If I recall correctly, you told me you did not know what passed between your father and Schneider. You told me you didn't know why your father excluded this letter from his book."

Unable as I was to see the man's face, my provocative remarks bounced off the darkness.

"There is something bigger than us," the priest spluttered, "something bigger than us had developed. By the time I found out what had happened, it was too late. The decision was not mine to make. The grave had become a shrine. The truth had decided on itself."

I was not really listening at this point. I had begun to re-read the page on my lap. The authority of the written word was somehow at odds with the spoken words of the priest. Schneider's account of the useless situation and the pointless death of innocent civilians was shocking and permanent. Most of all, the letter was full of pain. The pain was in the silences. His anguish lived between the phrases. His feelings were between the full stops and the following letters. He had tried hard to put down the facts, nothing but the facts. What he had done was to reveal the intensity of his emotions.

The priest leaned towards me and handed me another page.

"What would you have done?"

Stretched out in the chair, the policeman's shape stirred. I heard his clothes rustling and the static crackling. The Chief Inspector lowered his head and, separating his palms, he held them apart for a second before clapping them loudly together.

"Nothing is always an alternative," he said. "So why did you not leave things as they were? Why did you not simply do nothing?"

I heard the two men, but their words reached me as vague sounds with no real meaning. I was absorbed in Schneider's story. His style was simple and direct, but the man's essential goodness, his integrity and his sincerity shone through his words so that I felt I would have liked to know him better.

I let the page rest in my lap while I watched the two men sparring. The priest had leaned forward. He seemed to have been expecting the policeman's question. His reply was pre-packaged and forceful.

"I did nothing," he said, "because while Spohr was merely a spirit, he presented no problem. But with the arrival of Mr Slater, Spohr's flesh and blood came back to life. I didn't know what Schneider would do. I didn't know what questions Mr Slater would ask. I had no idea what I would tell him. I needed to discuss it with the only other person who knew what had happened. Should we leave things as they were? Or should we, could we, tell the truth?"

The policeman waved a deprecatory hand.

"Then go back to the story," he said. "The young man does not yet know what the truth was."

The priest turned his body towards me again. I was unable to see the expression in his eyes, but there was something about the way he held his body that told me he was afraid and hesitant. Then, out of the darkness came the third and fourth sheets of paper. The silence of expectation lay heavy on the room as I took the papers and began to read. As I did so, I heard the policeman continue with his interrogation of the priest.

"Is it not true to say," he said, "that you wanted to know whether or not the old man would keep silent? If the truth was to come out then you wanted be the one to come out with it, didn't you? In this way, you could claim the glory for uncovering something that you had been covering up for so long. Is this not a good reason?"

"No," the priest said, "that was not my motivation."

"So you say," the policeman countered. "But my guess is that your motivation is not as simple as you think. In my experience, it ..."

At that point I stopped listening. Something was happening inside me. My heart was beating hard against my ribs. A film of sweat covered my forehead. My hand was shaking. I grabbed hold of Barbara's hand to feel my own, to convince myself that I was contacted to some physical entity. The sofa beneath me cracked and puffed. I thought it might be my sense of identity cracking. My breathing was fast but the sound of it seemed to come from the other side of the room.

"Are you all right Mr Slater?"

There was a pause.

"Mr Slater?"

I shook my head. I dared not look up. The objects in the room suddenly seemed to swell, and I became Tom Thumb living in a world of giants. I was drifting away from myself and falling into sleep when there was Barbara's voice.

"Take a deep breath," she was saying. "Take a deep breath."

I did so, and some sense of normality returned.

"Another," she said.

I obeyed and as I relaxed, the sheets of paper slid from my lap and landed neatly on the floor at my feet.

Letter from Ulrich Schneider

June 1955

The half-track was positioned next to a house. When I came back to Herrenberg in 1950, the house had been converted into a guesthouse and it was opposite the cemetery. In 1945, during the bombardment, we used the cellar for shelter. We had to go on. There was no fuel. I should have destroyed the half-track. I did not do it because we would have had to destroy the building too, and the people in it.

In the forest there were many soldiers going east and no enemy. There were many wounded, and smashed and broken vehicles of all sorts. We were on foot. Someone told me that the French prisoners had been machine-gunned. I refused to believe this. They were my responsibility, and we were at the war's end. I called for Spohr, but he had disappeared.

There was no time to think. We had to survive. We split up into smaller groups, and I went east with fifteen men. We found a hunter's lodge and we ate a lot. When we emerged from the hut, we saw American soldiers on the other side of the field. I could not send my men across an open field. It would have meant certain death for them. So we had to go back westwards. We saw no more soldiers. There must be many unmarked graves in the Schönbuch Forest.

When we arrived back in Nüfringen, we found the French prisoners. They were still tied together inside the church. They were huddled in a corner. They had been riddled with bullets. There were no other men, and all the younger women seemed to have disappeared. Some old men and women were digging around in the rubble. They told me that the German had shot the prisoners soon after the planes had gone. The memory of the carnage will never leave me. The bodies of the murdered soldiers had been abused in the most shocking way. Spohr had committed this atrocious butchery and he had been under my command. I was responsible for what had happened.

I roared like a bull. My anger was a terrible thing. Had we come so far and with so much honour that it should end in murder? My anguish echoed in the forest, and my men were afraid that the enemy would hear us. I promised myself that, one day, I would find Spohr and make him pay for his actions.

At the time, there were more urgent problems. How could I keep my men alive? A farmer allowed us to sleep in his stable. In the morning we split up into groups of three. We cried on parting. We had been through so much together. We swore we would meet again. We never did. To this day, I do not know how many of the groups survived. I heard that Altner had been killed along with Spohr.

Our group made it through the forest to Baden Baden. We brought one of our men back home. We stayed at his house until the end. On 10 May, I heard that all my family had been killed.

At the end I want to say this. In 1950, I came back to Herrenberg. I found two of my soldiers in the cemetery. There will be many more graves in the forest. I went to the house which is now a hotel. I told the owner about the war. I told him how I had saved his building and the lives of the people in it. He was not interested. The war was over he said. That may be true for those who did not fight. But the past will not leave old soldiers in peace. Spohr may be dead, but this damned murderer's grave has become a place of pilgrimage. I can do nothing. So many people get so much comfort from this shrine. What right do I have to tell the truth and take this comfort away? I dream but I can do nothing.

This inner conflict comes often to me at night when I am about to fall asleep. The memory of that day returns in all its terrible reality. It will not let me go - this sound of my own anguish roaring in the depths of the forest.

Chapter 15

Hildrizhausen. 28 December. Evening

I was swaying on the brink, clawing at air. Then, I lost balance. I grabbed at Barbara's hand, hoping that it would prevent me from toppling. My thirty years of life flashed across my consciousness. Everything else in the room happened in a slow and detached way. The policeman took an eternity to get up from his chair and when he switched on the main light, he was on the other side of a huge chasm. The priest was swivelling a pencil between one finger and another. The brushing of wood against skin was loudly grating.

Barbara leaned forward and picked up the pages I had been reading. Her movements took several seconds, but they were the worst seconds of my life and they involved a lifetime. In those seconds, I managed to evaluate my life and the person to whom that life belonged. I could only use metaphors to describe my reactions, but my identity was on the gallows. The support had been kicked away, and I was struggling.

If my grandfather were alive today, he would be a war criminal, hunted down for crimes against humanity. It fell to me to atone for what my grandfather had done. My mind rolled on to consider whether the propensity to mass murder could pass from one generation to another. My heart beat wildly as I scanned my life for signs of it. At the same time, I felt the first shadow of guilt pass over the world in front of me. I was no longer the casual observer making judgements from afar. I was now the observed and the judged. I was one of them, the condemned, the war criminal and the guilty.

In my peripheral vision I saw the outline of the Chief Inspector. His face was directed at me, and he seemed to have read my thoughts.

"There is no evidence," he said, with a grim smile, "that suggests criminality is genetic. And of course, you are not responsible for Spohr's actions."

I managed to find my voice. Somehow it surprised me. I was expecting it to have changed.

"No," I said, "maybe not. But I have to live with the guilt."

The Chief Inspector chuckled.

"Then stay in Germany," Mr Slater. "We Germans are used to living with guilt."

Time shifted. Images from the recent past flashed up in my consciousness. I was back in the hotel. The old man was sitting in front of me, and his voice was ringing in my head: *Tell me, how would you feel if you looked at someone over whom you once had the power of life and death?*

A stubby glass thumped down on the table beside me. It contained a clear liquid. There was another voice in my ear. It was Barbara's.

"Drink it."

I tossed the liquid into my mouth. I felt better as the schnapps slowed down my thoughts. It was only a temporary respite. I grasped her hand ever more tightly to reassure myself of my reality. But the old man's voice was again sounding in my skull: *For what did we suffer if future generations choose to forget?*

I shook my head in an attempt to throw the voice out. But still it persisted and rattled through my bones like an ague*: What was the point of it all?*

"There is no need to make useless speculations," another voice was saying. "I have a modern day murder to investigate."

The policeman was looking at me, an expression of concern straining his features. Did he guess that all the dependable facts and all the certainties upon which I had built my existence were in question?

Releasing Barbara's hand, I refused another glass of schnapps and cleared my throat to signal that I had something to say. I raised my head and took in great gulps of air. Barbara put her hand over mine. Her palm was warm and calming. The Chief Inspector resumed his position in the armchair. Stretched out and relaxed, he was once again staring at the ceiling, his chin resting on his fingers.

"Are you better?" he asked with concern. "Can we now go forward? It really is the only place to go, believe me. We Germans discovered this some time ago."

"I'm OK," I said.

This was not exactly true. I heard the calmness of my voice, but I could hardly get the words out. My cheeks were so rigid they could have been frozen, and my mouth was tingling.

"So," the policeman said, "we need to look at the facts. In 1945, two bodies are brought in from the forest. Although Spohr's soldbuch and greatcoat are beside them, it appears that he is not one of the dead men. Is this a reasonable summary of the facts so far?"

The priest made a gesture of helplessness.

"We already know this. We ..."

"The facts," the policeman snapped, "we are looking at the facts, you understand?"

The priest's shoulder twitched violently, and the policeman said:

"As I understand it, the only evidence we have that wrongdoing of some sort took place is the letter the young man has just read. What do you think? Am I correct?"

He had removed the supporting presence of his fingertips so that his head fell forward onto his chest. He looked at the priest with raised eyebrows.

"I asked you a question," he said. "Am I correct?"

The priest removed his glasses and rubbed at his eyes with thumb and forefinger.

"Yes, yes," he said, "you are right."

"And the facts are," the policeman said, "that a grave was found in 1947, and that the grave had the name Martin Spohr inscribed on it, is this not so?"

"1948," the priest said.

"And the fact is that this grave has become a shrine to those who were killed in the war, correct? It reminds us of the monster lurking within us all, and it tells us that this monster must be tamed."

The policeman rubbed his nose with the tips of his fingers and then placed them again under his chin.

"And the facts are that the body was never exhumed. Despite the protests from the authorities, it was allowed to stay where it was. A most unusual decision for Germans to make, but nevertheless, that decision was made I believe."

"That's right," the priest said. "My father helped to convince the authorities that the grave would serve a useful purpose where it was."

Now the truth was out, the priest's identity was slowly re-establishing itself. His shoulder was twitching irritably, and his ears were a healthy pink.

"Quite," the policeman said. "And your father had his own interest in the grave, didn't he? He wrote his history of Hildrizhausen during the Nazi era, is this not correct?"

The priest leaned back in his chair. He replaced his glasses and pushed them onto the bridge of his nose.

"Yes, that is correct," he said.

"And yet," the policeman said, "your father did not publish it. Tell our young friends why he did not publish it. Go on, tell them."

The twitching in the priest's shoulder became almost spasmodic and his ears were now burning red.

"In order to write the history, my father contacted Ulrich Schneider. I recall well the day he received and read Schneider's account. I had never seen my father so upset.

What could he do? The grave had taken on a meaning of its own. To tell the truth, that the shrine had been erected to a war criminal would have been unacceptable. My father decided never to publish his findings."

If the priest had been expecting some sort of comment, he would have been disappointed. The policeman remained absolutely still and stared at the ceiling.

"I told you," he said, "to tell our friends here, and not to direct your story to me. But no matter. Perhaps you could tell us this. Did you or did you not know of this letter's contents?"

The priest hesitated.

"I guessed at its contents," he said, "but I never saw the letter itself until after my father's death."

The Chief Inspector's face remained expressionless. For several seconds, he continued to stare at the ceiling while he took several deep breaths.

"So," he said, "there we have it. But let us go on. We must continue to deal in facts. In 1999, something happens that disturbs our little conspiracy. That something was the arrival in Herrenberg of Martin Slater. He is intent on making enquiries about his mother's father. Some letters that turned up after his mother's death prompted these enquiries, and it turns out that his maternal grandfather was Martin Spohr. Is this right?"

"Yes," I said.

"And at the same time," the policeman mused, "our priest here sees fit to invite Ulrich Schneider to Herrenberg."

Spreading his elbows outwards and clasping his hands behind his head, he stared along his nose and focused his eyes on the priest.

"You said you wanted to speak to him about Spohr, if I recall correctly. You wanted to know whether or not Schneider would keep quiet about Spohr and his connection with the deaths of those French soldiers. As you put it, you wanted to know whether you would have to continue with the lie or whether you would be forced to tell Mr Slater the truth. In short, you and Schneider needed a united front, am I correct?"

When the priest nodded, Chief Inspector Hart opened his mouth and exhaled noisily through his back teeth. For a while he sat still while his eyelids fluttered.

"All that duplicity," the policeman whispered, "and yet, there is no evidence that Spohr did kill the prisoners, is there? The facts are that he was guarding them, and they were killed, probably during a bombing raid. It is unfortunate that Spohr chose this particular time to disappear. Allow me to speculate for one moment. Schneider mentions that the women were afraid. Maybe they killed the French soldiers. This is entirely possible, is it not?"

The priest looked up and shrugged.

"Perhaps," he said. "But in the letter, Schneider writes that some old people told him the killings were committed by the German soldier."

The Chief Inspector shook his head.

"There were many German soldiers at that time," he said with a cheerless smile. "And those old people are a long time dead. What Schneider has written hardly counts as incontrovertible evidence."

"But we have Mr Slater's word," the priest said, "that Schneider was upset about something. He ..."

"Right," I interrupted, suddenly finding my voice. "Schneider was upset about the grave. He said something about desecrating memories. He said it was the memories that prevented him from doing what he believed to be right. I suppose now that he meant the memories of the bereaved and the ..."

"That," the policeman said, "is merely supposition and your own memory, Mr Slater. And supposition and memory do not count as fact. The fact is that on 27 December, one day after the storm that had already taken the lives of two other people, Ulrich Schneider is found dead by the side of Spohr's grave. Time of death has been given as early evening on the twenty-third. In other words, he had been dead for nearly four days by the time he was found."

There was a deathly hush. The policeman raised his head towards the ceiling.

"Fact," he said. "A falling tree during the storm collapsed the grave. The grave revealed nothing. No bones, nothing. This is fact. How we interpret the facts is another matter. Thousands of people have already interpreted the facts to suit their particular circumstances. The grave has become a shrine. This too is fact. Does anyone disagree?"

"What about the letter," I said. "Is it not a fact that my grandfather was a war criminal?"

"Not necessarily," the policeman said. "The only evidence we have is the letter itself. Its contents are entirely circumstantial. Damning? Certainly, but solid facts? No."

"And is it a fact that Schneider was murdered?"

The policeman pursed his lips and wagged his head.

"The facts are these. Forensics have determined that Schneider was struck on the back of the head. He was struck from behind by a blow that would almost certainly have rendered him unconscious. There are traces of material in the back of his neck that are consistent with him having been struck by a piece of wood. Whether he was struck by a falling tree or clubbed, we do not know. Anyway, it was not the blow which killed him. The actual cause of death was heart failure."

"But why," Barbara broke in, "would anyone wish to strike an old man?"

The policeman shrugged.

"We could," he said, "speculate for hours. There is no obvious motive, you see? But let us stick to the facts."

I was getting impatient with facts. Released from the paralysing effect of shock, my mind was overactive. It needed to speculate, to interpret.

"Just a second," I said, "one person might have had a motive for killing the old man."

All eyes turned towards me.

"Martin Spohr," I said, "my grandfather might have had the motive and ..."

The policeman interrupted.

"Martin Spohr is dead," he said flatly. "He died in 1945."

"Yes," I insisted, "but you showed us the grave. You said that if there were no bones in it then it was probable that there had never been anyone in it in the first place. Perhaps he was not killed."

"The lack of bones proves nothing," the Chief Inspector said. "Perhaps the man was killed elsewhere and the grave erected as a simple memorial."

"Then why," I said, "did the priest here at the time insist that the grave remain untouched?"

"Because of what it had become," the priest said.

Chief Inspector Hart blew impatiently through his front teeth.

"Look," he said, "Martin Spohr was killed in 1945. And it will remain that way. I shall see to it. And the fact of the empty grave, Mr Slater, must remain our secret. We have a duty to the dead and to the living who remember them."

"But it is surely not a fact," I said, "that my grandfather was killed in the first place."

The policeman hesitated.

"It has become fact," he said. "We can and we will do nothing to change it."

From the corner of my eye I watched the priest remove his glasses.

"Let us return to the facts," he said. "Do we know whether or not Schneider had contact with anyone while he was here?"

"Two people," the policeman said, "and one of them is sitting here in front of you."

"And the other?"

There was a slight hesitation. The policeman kept his eyes focused on the ceiling.

"The other?" he repeated. "Let me just say that we are following up enquiries."

I was about to protest when the policeman raised his arm and cut me short.

"But we must tread very carefully," he said, "for we are treading on dreams."

Then he removed his steepled fingers from his chin and, lowering his head, he turned his eyes to mine.

"Mr Slater, I advise you to return to England and never come here again."

The intensity of his stare and the gravity of his words shocked me.

"I believe your mother said there was something bigger than us," he said. "She was right. If this something is God, then his purpose is unknown to us. But I believe in some kind of ultimate harmony. This is something so precious that it forgives all war and killings. It is something that will justify everything that has happened with men. You see, Mr Slater, for me this grave represents the hope for a world which is more peaceful and more humane. It represents the hope that we can understand more about ourselves so that we can create a world with less misery. Yes, we need to examine the monsters inside us, but we need to cage them, and the grave is part of our attempt to do just that."

I opened my mouth to object, but before I had a chance to make even the slightest sound, the Chief Inspector was away with his own thoughts.

"Go home," he said, "go home and forget us all. This is a friendly warning Mr Slater but please take this advice or you will certainly live to regret it."

The policeman lowered his head. He looked at Barbara and me from below his eyelids.

"Listen to me please," he said. "When two people fall in love they have no idea about the person they are falling in love with. Listen to me and remember this. The truth about the grave must remain what people think it is. There can be no other way."

"But why," I asked, "why should I leave? I have done nothing wrong."

The Chief Inspector looked up at the ceiling again and balanced his chin on his fingertips.

"Think of this," he began. "I deal in facts, simple facts. I told you, memory does not count as fact. When people remember, they usually add things, things that come from their own experience. This is normal. For example, two people will remember and interpret the same room in a different way. The colours change. The size is different. When it comes to people, the same is true."

He lifted one hand to his moustache and rolled its ends so that they were pointed and bristling.

"Yes, I deal in facts," he said, "but since you like to speculate, Mr Slater, let me do some speculation for you. You meet Schneider in the forest and you argue. You do not mean to hurt him but you strike him. He falls to the ground and you ..."

"That is preposterous," I began. "That is ..."

The policeman interrupted.

"Preposterous or not," he said, "you will listen to what I have to say. You certainly had the opportunity to kill him. And you also had the motive, didn't you? We know that Schneider had information about your grandfather. He tells you. You refuse to accept it and you hit him."

I stared in disbelief.

"You do not believe me Mr Slater? You have just experienced it. I saw your reaction with my own eyes. You find out that your grandfather was a war criminal. This is unacceptable to you and your perception of yourself. Oh yes, we Germans understand this, Mr Slater. Believe me, we understand this only too well. But you? You are angry. You wish to silence the person, the only person who knows about your dark secret. This is quite understandable really. Yes, quite understandable, and enough to make you a suspect. Take my advice and leave. It is for your own good. And be thankful that I have other avenues to explore. If I were you I would go, now."

*

"You know," Barbara said, "there are two things which are important here."

We were sitting in my hotel dining room. I was still holding on to her hand and enjoying a proper sense of where I was. I mumbled out some encouragement for her to continue.

"Yes, two things," she said. "First, what that policeman said to you, could also apply to him."

"What do you mean?"

"I mean that he too had a motive for killing Schneider. Our policeman obviously feels that the grave has an importance that goes beyond Martin Spohr and what he may have done. Maximilian Hart is unconventional. He is a man of strong convictions. He would only see right and justice prevail and right and justice for him obviously go beyond the law. If Schneider threatened to reveal what he knew, the policeman might have thought it necessary to remove him."

I was unable to stifle a laugh.

"That is theoretically true," I said.

"No less likely than you killing him."

"I suppose not," I said. "And what was the second thing."

There was a silence. Then Barbara said:

"I will not leave you tonight."

And suddenly I was not scared. I merely looked at her, and keeping her hand in mine, I rose to my feet and searched in my pocket for the room key.

Herrenberger Zeitung

29 December: English version

All change at Eisenmann. Preliminary results for 1999 suggest that profits have fallen slightly short of expectations. This could mean the final blow for founder Joerg Eisenmann (73). DaimlerChrysler have made no secret of the fact that they want to modernise their dealership network. Furthermore, it is well known that Eisenmann is under intense pressure to step down as head of the company and to give way to younger men. The new millennium will almost certainly see new management installed at the well-regarded Herrenberg dealership.

Over the past fifty years, Joerg Eisenmann has shown himself to be a pillar of the community. Much of his personal wealth has gone towards a betterment of the town and its people. It is feared that with the changes at the dealership, such acts may well be a thing of the past.

Chapter 16

Herrenberg. 29 December. Morning

I awoke early and found myself staring at the ceiling with my eyes so wide open that it seemed odd that they had ever been closed in sleep. I felt the presence of Barbara. Her body warmth and the sound of her breathing reached out to wrap me in contentment and the feeling that of all the places on earth, I was in the right place. Even the fading memory of a dream could not detract from the knowledge that I was exactly where I should be. In sleep, I had recognised the people lying at my feet. I had dreamed of these skeletal shapes in ragged clothes less than two days previously while on my way into the forest. I had thought that they were reaching out for help. Now, I saw that they were reaching out across time and through blood to pull me back into the past, where I would wallow in guilt.

Voices of busyness from the market square prompted me to swing my legs to the floor and creep towards the window. Parting the curtains, I pushed the window open. Light and motion enveloped me, and the rays of the sun seemed to penetrate even the most hidden places. Against my face, the air was cold and it held a babble of voices from those who mingled in the square, the hum of faraway traffic, and music from a not-too-distant radio.

I knew I was precariously balanced on the edge. I could fall forwards and convince myself that my grandfather was an accident to me. What he had done was too far away to merit anything but cursory attention. The dream-induced guilt then hit me and settled like a stone in my stomach. Maybe my grandfather was out of sight but his sins would never be entirely out of mind. They would always be there waiting for me, somewhere near - perhaps just around the next corner. His crimes would haunt me, and the guilt-stone would weigh heavy again in my stomach.

Barbara was shifting in sleep. I closed the window and tiptoed into the bathroom. Carefully pulling the door shut behind me, I leaned heavily against it and focused on the present. The previous day I had been a virgin. Today, I was not. I felt the lightness of a man who has at last been relieved of a burden. I smiled into the mirror and punched the air with my fist. If there were vague feelings of disappointment stirring somewhere in my consciousness, I managed to stifle them. I had been yearning to pass that sexual milestone for years. Now, in a moment, in a sigh, I had done it. Unseen, the line had passed me by.

Why of all the possible women on the planet did it have to be Barbara? I told myself that it was more than her physical attributes. It was true that I was so taken by her looks that Barbara's character was dominated by them. It was easier for me to say that what I liked was in the blue of her eyes, the high-bridged nose and the arrogance of the chin. It was not so easy to identify the aspects of her character that attracted me. There was also the special bond I had felt at our first meting in the hotel. We belonged together. I knew, because my stomach told me, that we had known each other for a long time.

I turned on the hot tap and watched the basin fill. Dragging the razor through the water, I raised my hand and wiped the mirror clear of condensation. With a sharp intake of breath, I recoiled. The razor must have fallen from my hands. I vaguely heard the plop as it struck the water. I made no attempt to rescue the razor. I stared open-mouthed at the mirror, and my mother's face stared back at me.

I blinked and vigorously rubbed again at the mirror. The

face stubbornly remained, its expression critical and disapproving. I shook my head in a vain attempt to obliterate this vision. The face and the life it represented bore little relation to mine. I pinched myself to ensure I was not asleep and still dreaming, but the face of the woman who had given me life, the woman who had raised me and influenced my way of thinking refused to disappear. But something had changed.

It was my world which had shifted dramatically. I still respected the woman in the mirror, but I had no real desire and no need to argue with her. I looked down at the sink. Taking a deep breath, I raised my head and looked again into the mirror. I wiped my hand over the reflecting glass, and my mother's image was gone.

When I emerged from the bathroom, Barbara was dressed and sitting on the edge of the bed. The curtains were drawn back, and sunlight filled the room. I was not sure what was expected of me, so I sat down on the bed and put my arm around her. We sat that way without speaking. Then, Barbara's mobile telephone rang.

She broke away from me and barked her name into the mouthpiece. I felt a shiver of doubt run through me. I knew human beings to be contradictory and not all of one piece. Yet it was difficult to reconcile the person beside me with the person who, just a few hours previously, had pulled me towards her and circled my head with her hands. The voice that had softly called out my name was now hard and cold. I looked into her eyes and into every line and shadow on her face, but she was locked on to another world with another voice unseen.

I walked to the window and looked outside. I listened to the faraway and indistinct roar of the traffic and I allowed the sound to drift by. A cloud passed over the sun, and the room was plunged into shadow. It seemed that there was nothing but emptiness behind me, until out of the air I heard a voice without a face.

"That was Nadia," the voice said. "She says that father has gone."

I turned and resumed my position beside her. Simultaneously, Barbara jumped up and walked towards the window. I was left feeling slightly foolish, abandoned and alone on the edge of the bed.

"What do you mean?" I said. "Gone where?"

"Gone," she said, her voice as shaky as her hands, "and Nadia said he has taken his gun with him and left a letter for me."

I shook my head to reject this news. Barbara folded her arms.

"Apparently, he has not taken his dogs. Just the gun."

Through the open window I heard the striking of the quarter-hour from the bell tower. The word "gun" had a sickening finality to it. Gun spelled menace and death, and was associated with places I had never been before. I jumped to my feet and was about to utter some inane comment when Barbara glanced at me. She may have caught the expression of concern written in my face. Perhaps it reinforced her own sense of urgency. She was suddenly stimulated into a whirl of activity.

She grabbed at her bag and pushed through the door. It swung back with a crash against the wall. Barbara was down the stairs in a flash, and I rushed down after her. I emerged into the cold air of the marketplace with my head held high for fear of losing her. She was some metres out in front of me, pushing her way through small knots of people who were lingering to talk over their lives. Barbara's voice rang out harshly in the cold morning air.

"We must get to him," she said, "we must try and stop him."

I was so utterly absorbed in the importance of what we were doing that I had no time to consider what exactly we had to stop Eisenmann from doing. But the word "gun" had changed everything to such an extent that I was out of my depth. The people in the square appeared to me in a haze. Occasionally, the astonished face of a passer-by looked up at me with a clarity that branded itself on my memory.

Barbara hardly waited for me to get into the car before she pulled away from the parking place.

She drove like a person possessed. She leaned forward in the driving seat and fiddled nervously with the mobile phone. Within minutes we pulled up in the driveway. Nadia was waiting at the doorway of Eisenmann's house. She was covering her mouth with a handkerchief. Above the handkerchief her eyes were scared. We emerged from the car, and she pulled the handkerchief away from her face.

"Mr Eisenmann, he is gone," she said.

She ushered us into the house and waved the handkerchief in front of her while speaking loudly in German. It occurred to me that she was partly enjoying the satisfaction of power that came from knowledge that only she possessed. This knowledge abolished the limitations of her position, and made her mistress for a minute. When she had finished with her monologue, she led us over to a table in the lounge. She almost lost her balance as she bent to pick up an envelope that was lying on a table by an open fire. She handed the envelope to Barbara and then she wept into the handkerchief.

Barbara tried to push Nadia out of the room. The maid looked at us both with the sweet eyes of a young child, but she refused to go.

"Mr Eisenmann - he is gone," she said to me.

Barbara ripped open the envelope and dropped into an armchair in a way that suggested her legs had lost their strength. Nadia was now silent, but I could hear the deep tones of a television from another corner of the house. Unable to keep still, I walked up and down the room and gazed through the window that looked towards the forest. I turned and took a tentative step towards Barbara. She looked up and snapped away from me as if she had seen a ghost. She put her hand over her heart.

"It's from father," she whispered.

Shaking her head in a movement of denial, she lowered her eyelids and stared at the floor. She was suddenly breathless and agitated but I stayed where I was. There was a wall around her that I dared not even try to scale.

"What does he say?" I said.

A slight nod indicated that she had heard me. At first, she seemed reluctant to reply. Then she closed her eyes and breathed deeply as though she were willing herself to go on.

"It's in German," she said. "I shall try and translate it."

And then, against the sound of the crackling fire, she read. She spoke in a flat tone, hesitating now and then in order to find a word or a turn of phrase.

"My dearest Barbara," she said. "This you must know. And once you know it, visit the forest sometimes and think not the worst of me for it. Burn this letter immediately, and when you have burned it you must say goodbye to Mr Slater. Now you must know the truth."

During this introduction, Nadia continued to sob. Between one sob and another, she wiped her eyes with the handkerchief. I supposed she must have been susceptible to atmosphere and tone of voice. I knew her knowledge of English was limited.

"The person in me who fought the war is gone," Barbara read. "The person I was before the war is also long gone. In 1944, that man was eighteen. He was desperate to establish an identity for himself in a world that saw military prowess as the height of masculinity. He joined an elite regiment and was taught how to accept absolutely the authority of those in command. He was given a false sense of self-worth. Above all, he was taught how to value aggression and how to dehumanise those who were the enemy. He was given permission to use any level of violence and without moral restraint. In 1944 he was on the Eastern Front. Within two weeks, there was nothing much left of the old him. Only his name remained. And even that he buried. He buried it without hesitation just before the war ended."

Barbara stopped reading and, dropping the letter to one

side, she looked at me. I saw the firm chin with its uplifted hint of arrogance but there was something else I had never seen before. There was a suggestion of wildness, of running away in her eyes.

"In 1944," she continued, "it took but one month for him to become someone else. He had become a person who no longer needed an imagination to see horrors. He no longer needed sleep to have nightmares. He knew the smell of a man's intestines hanging out. He knew the smell of shit mixed with blood. He had seen the scorched skulls that grinned at him from tank turrets as though they had been laughing and not screaming when they had burned to death.

By the time he joined Schneider in 1945 he had already been to the very edge of hell itself. He had stared down into the eyes of Satan. What had happened to him had developed so slowly that he had not even noticed it. It began with the first death and with the first casualty. But there were so many deaths and so may wounded that he became hardened to the point of inhumanity. His mind was unable to accept such suffering and survive it all. Barbara, he was only nineteen."

A sob from Nadia accompanied Barbara's pause. Nadia presented a picture of perfect sorrow. It was so perfect that it was not altogether convincing. She was sad but at the same time she was performing. But it was the performance of one who believed completely in the role she was playing. I was sure that once we had gone, she would dry her eyes and go back to the television programme our arrival had interrupted for her.

"At Nüfringen," Barbara read, "Schneider told him to watch over the French prisoners until a decision was taken with regard to the future of these criminals. It was then that the explosion happened. And it was triggered by the bombing. They were in the church when the American planes came over. A bomb landed in the square outside the church. A group of women were still trying to take in their washing when the bomb struck. All of them except one were killed instantly. The one who survived had both her feet blown off. Her legs were torn to pieces. The whole groin area was completely blown away. He had seen such sights before, but not women collecting their washing. It was the most shocking sight he had seen in the war. He did not know that it had made him snap."

Barbara was staring in front of her. Her head was planted on her neck like a flower. Her expression told me nothing. She betrayed no feeling except perhaps an affected boredom. Then, she lowered her head, read in silence for a few seconds and then continued with the translation.

"When he went back inside the church, he saw the Frenchmen laughing and joking. The women were German women. It was funny that they had been blown to pieces. And the one who was slowly dying? They would find her groin and let the animals screw it. There would be no struggle. No more little Germans from her they laughed. And then he started losing his sense of what is normal. He wanted them to stop. At first, he asked them, but they ignored him. They fell about laughing as the woman screamed her way to an agonising death. He went back outside and shot the woman. Then, he re-entered the church and screamed at the Frenchmen to stop. They did not even listen. He shot the soldier nearest to him. Then it all came out, the training, the programming. Once he had started it was easier to kill the next man and then the next. When one magazine was empty he put in another. He turned those men into sieves. He had no feeling, no emotion, he just killed. And that was not enough for him. Those men were scum, the lowest of the low, animals whose bodies should be rightly desecrated. He emptied his bowels on them. He pissed and spat on them and dismembered their hideous bodies."

From the television I heard the sound of muted laughter. Barbara had tilted back her head and shut her eyes. As the sound of applause drifted through from the television room, I heard Barbara take a sharp intake of breath.

"It was later," she continued, "that he became appalled at what he had done. At first, he went back to his unit, but he was frightened, scared out of his wits. He ran off into the forest. He must have wandered around for a day or two before he stumbled on the bodies of Altner and Kleine. He decided to leave his greatcoat and soldbuch with them. He had some vague idea of faking his own death. But in his emotional state, it did not occur to him that the description of himself and his photo matched neither of the dead men. He was terrified you see - terrified of what he had become. It was only later, when he calmed down, that he decided he would have to do more. So he buried himself. He dug a grave at some spot in Goldbachtal and he engraved his own name on the cross and put his helmet on top of it. He said no prayers. He knew even then that Spohr had died long ago."

I am not sure at what point that morning I realised the implications of what I was hearing. At first I watched Barbara as she massaged her forehead between her fingers. I was trying to suppress the pleasure with which I observed her pain and discomfort. I was, perhaps, savouring the fact that it was she who was suffering while I could look on as the sympathetic observer. Then, it hit me. It hit me at the same time as another burst of applause came from the television. I felt panicky. The sequence of events became obscure. I did not accept it at first. Like a vague but interesting idea, the truth came like the moon which appears and disappears through rents in the clouds.

"Even then," Barbara read, "the more he thought about it, the riskier it all was. He would need a new identity. He wandered around for days in the forest until he got his chance. He nearly missed him. The dying man was lying in a rut, one of those deep ruts you can sometimes find that seem to have no right to be there other than the fact that they had already been there for so long. The man was on his back and he seemed to have sprung up spontaneously from his own patch of earth. The light of the sun flickered on his young face. It had been painted green and this camouflage was like an imitation of the shade itself. He was lying still as though dead already. Then his eyes rolled. This man, emerging from the earth that had claimed Spohr, would be my saviour."

I closed my eyes and let myself be carried along by the smell of wood smoke from the fire. It conjured up memories of past times, of Christmas Days once enjoyed and now lost forever. I recognised this remembrance as nothing but the desire to immerse myself in the protection of the familiar and the comfortable. I breathed in deeply. I needed something familiar and comfortable to hold on to.

"His name," Barbara read, "was Eisenmann. The boy was nineteen. He had big brown eyes and a bigger hole in the stomach where the French had got him. Before he died, he talked about himself. His parents had been killed. He had no family except his section but he did not know where they were. I saw my chance. Spohr was dead. Eisenmann would live. He would live on in me. I was indeed picked up by two Englishmen in a jeep some days before the end. I was taken to a camp near Herrenberg, and there I have stayed."

At this point I wanted to cry out and tell her to stop. But how could she? How could she stop the flow of words, the flow of detail, the flow of facts that led to the truth that Martin Spohr and Joerg Eisenmann were the same person.

"The grave," Barbara was reading, "the grave in Goldbachtal never had anything in it, except fear and the shadow of a man who once had been. It was found by accident, after the war. How could I have known that it would become so famous? How could I have known that it would come to mean so much to so many people? But it was this power that saved me. The priest knew what Martin Spohr had done. His son knew too. Because of the power, they decided to do nothing about it."

I leaned back against the wall. I suddenly felt so tired I could barely hold up my head. My eyes refused to meet

Barbara's. I dreaded finding confirmation there of my own fears. But Barbara continued reading in a monotone. I guessed that translating prevented her from thinking too much about the meaning and implications of her own words. Later, and not too much later, her emotions would be struck by the tidal wave.

"Barbara, you may ask how Spohr could have done such a thing. How could he have disappeared like that when he had a family and a pregnant wife back home? It was easy then. There was so much death it would not be difficult for them to accept another. Spohr was dead anyway. The person he had been was obliterated and disfigured beyond recognition. He did not feel the need to be a father. He had seen death close up. He had sometimes felt excitement at killing and destruction. There is a heightened sexuality attached to all this that troubles him and haunts him to this day. I have concluded Barbara that war for him, at some terrible level, was the closest thing to what childbirth and motherhood are for women. It was initiation into the power of life and death Barbara - the power of life and death. Being a father meant nothing after that.

I buried Martin Spohr a long time ago. Eisenmann was my creation and he lives in my company. But now, at long last, the shadows of the forest are closing in around me. Mr Slater came. Mr Slater is Spohr's ghost. The priest knew that by coming to Herrenberg, Slater would upset things. His mother had already guessed the truth. Some things are bigger than all of us. His mother - how could I have known she would survive? She was my daughter."

The stifled sob surprised me. I looked across at Nadia, only to find that she was looking at me with an expression of sympathy on her face. Then I realised that it was me who had made the noise. Tears rolled down my face, and I fumbled in my pocket for a handkerchief. I hoped I was dreaming but I heard Barbara continuing to the bitter end.

"But the priest had already contacted Schneider. I suppose the priest wanted to know whether or not

Schneider would keep quiet. Just before Christmas I received the call. It was Schneider. He had seen Spohr he said, on the television. Fifty-five years had passed but still he recognised Spohr. And do you know how he recognised him? He said it was the way I held my head, cocked to one side. Schneider said he would go to the police if I did not agree to meet him. I suggested the forest. It was his idea to meet at the grave.

It was the twenty-third of December. I arrived first and hid myself in a place where I could see across the valley. I saw Schneider, and there was someone with him for a while, but he hurried away. I think it was Mr Slater, but it could have been anybody. So, at dusk, and after more than fifty years, I came out of hiding. At first, Schneider simply stared at me with an expression on his face that was pained and shocked. He could not believe what he was confronted with. I can not say what he saw. Perhaps it was that part of himself which he had left behind in the forest over fifty years before. Then he burst out crying. He continued to stare at me while tremors ran through his body. His sobs were uncontrollable but there were no tears.

Eventually, he started shouting so loudly that I thought he would wake the dead. He was uncompromising. He said he would expose me. I did not argue with him. One word from him, and my whole life, the life of Eisenmann, would be destroyed. It was unthinkable. I had not come so far in life to have my creation threatened by something that happened so long ago. I picked up a branch from the ground and I hit him. He fell, and I left him. In a sense we were both dead already."

There were several seconds of stunned silence. In that silence, I felt myself cut off from my surroundings by a wall of fog or perhaps a smoke screen of my own making. Trapped inside, I gasped for breath while images assaulted me from all sides. Faster and faster these images flew, and my world became a jumble of thoughts and feelings, wriggling from my grasp and lying beyond comprehension.

From the other side of the wall, I heard Barbara's voice.

"Maximilian Hart knows. We have spoken together. He says that the grave must remain what people think it is. The man is right. He who created life can also take it away. I created myself in my company and now, even that may be taken from me. It is too late now. Eisenmann's time has come."

Her last words returned "gun" to my consciousness. I was suddenly filled with anxiety. The smoke screen thinned, and I replaced it with a protective blanket of anger and frustration.

"Is that it?" I cried.

"No. He says, Woher die Dinge ihre Entstehung haben, dahin mussen sie auch zugrunde gehen, nach der Notwendigkeit."

"And?" I said. "What does that mean?"

That was the moment when time stopped for us on that battlefield of life, love and feeling. Barbara glanced at me, and in her eyes I saw what she herself, perhaps, could not see. It was the beginning of our end. Barbara said:

"It means, according to necessity, where things come into being, so must they also go to earth."

Taking refuge in action, I shouted at Nadia.

"He has gone to the grave."

My peripheral vision caught Barbara. She had turned towards the open fire and tossed the letter into it. I watched in fascination as the bundle of pages browned at the edges and flared up in a brief flame. The flames died down, and the charred and smouldering pages were snapped up by the smoke of time past and sucked into the chimney and oblivion.

Barbara was looking at me with her chin uplifted, but I saw her wondering expression, and with it, the first glimmer of self-doubt I had seen in her. I gathered myself as the wind of necessity swept aside any doubts or questions.

"Contact the policeman," I shouted. "Tell him to meet us there."

I watched as Barbara put out a hand to pick up the telephone. She seemed so nervous it needed three attempts to pick up the handset. She stabbed at the knobs and lifted the handset to her ear. There was silence. I heard her speaking in German. Then she pocketed the phone and, without looking at me, she made for the door. I followed - thankful for the necessity of action and trying desperately hard to focus on finding her father. It was then that the policeman's words came ringing back in my ears: *When two people fall in love they have no idea of whom they are falling in love with.*

Had he guessed that Eisenmann and Spohr were the same person? Did he therefore know that Barbara's father and my grandfather were also one and the same?

EU Directive 1997, No. 607, p.812

The crime of incest consists of sexual intercourse between near relatives. Intercourse between close relatives is forbidden in most societies, but there are differences among the systems in the relationships within which intercourse is forbidden. Most systems forbid intercourse between immediate relatives - father and daughter, brother and sister, mother and son. The majority of states in the European Union now describe incest in the following way:

A person commits incest if he marries or engages in sexual intercourse with a person he knows to be, either legitimately or illegitimately:

- his brother or descendant by blood or adoption; or
- his brother or sister of the whole or half-blood or by adoption; or
- his stepchild or stepparent, while the marriage creating the relationship exists; or
- his aunt, uncle, nephew or niece of the whole or half-blood.

Chapter 17

The forest. 29 December. Evening

We roared up the Hildrizhausen road. I tried to focus on the task at hand and push away the ugly thoughts that were pressing around my head. Each time the thoughts appeared, I overlaid and crushed them with the sound of my voice.

"He must be an hour ahead of us."

But I was like a child attempting to flatten a balloon. No sooner had I flattened one thought when another bubbled up and took its place.

"Why the gun, why ...?"

Barbara was not listening to my attempts to obliterate the silence. She was jealously guarding her own protective mechanism by continuously babbling to herself.

"Poor father ... poor father ... fifty-five years ..."

"We'll never catch him," I said.

"Why didn't he tell us?"

Without changing her expression, except now and then to frown in concentration, Barbara addressed the unacceptable. As though this was waiting to pounce at the first hint of silence, she emitted a non-stop stream of language.

"How he must have suffered ... why did he never share it? ... Fifty five years ... Poor father ..."

"He's probably just gone for a walk in the forest," I said.

"What a terrible secret ... to live with that ..."

There was a shocking squeal of tyres as Barbara hauled the car out of the path of an oncoming lorry. The sight of the driver, gesticulating wildly, momentarily cleared my head of anything other than the need for self-preservation. Barbara put her foot down, and the car surged through the forest. Objects sprang into sharp focus, and as suddenly, blurred and vanished. I saw a cluster of people, walkers perhaps, under a tree. Away in the middle distance a single point of silver brilliance pierced the daylight. Barbara must have seen it before I did. The car suddenly lurched forward, and I was propelled towards the windscreen as the wheels locked. There was a crunching of gravel and the sound of stones bouncing off the car chassis. The back wheels came round as we skidded to a halt in a clearing by the side of the road. The point of brilliance was the chrome fender of a car, parked in the shadow of the trees.

Barbara leaned over the steering wheel, her breath coming in short and shaky gasps.

"That," she said, "is his car."

We jumped out into a cloud of dust that swam at our feet and billowed upwards. Barbara plunged into the swirling dust and prowled around the car. I stood looking down at my shoes as the dust settled on them. The need to articulate the thoughts that tormented me was so strong that my fists clenched and my forearms trembled. At the point of no return, some inner voice spoke harshly and prevented me from opening my mouth. Barbara was still carefully circling the car as though she were unwilling to touch it. A bewildered expression crossed her face.

"Someone must wait here for the policeman," she said, "but you go. Please go. I would only hold you back. Please, you are quicker alone."

Still avoiding her eyes, I nodded vaguely. Through the dust, Barbara materialised in front of me. I felt her hand upon my arm. Her fingers tightened as though she were willing me to look at her. I heard her whispering on a breath.

"Be gentle with yourself. We didn't know. We aren't to blame."

I managed to raise my head and stare at the harsh reality.

"Where does that leave us?"

Barbara looked imploringly into my eyes, and I watched her mouth open and close as she tried to construct her own understanding and transform it into words. These began as almost childlike sounds and monosyllabic utterances which gradually strung together with other sounds and formed meaningful language. I strained to catch the words that sighed through the dust. She said:

"I ... am your mother's half-sister."

She smiled and held on to my trembling arm. Her voice persisted, and somehow, its tone contained the joy of a child who has discovered words for the first time.

"That means I am your aunt, of half-blood."

Barbara repeated this horror under her breath in what appeared to be an attempt to hold the information fast in her mind. I wanted to back away from her, to tell her to stop her foolishness, that the joke had gone too far. From the shadows of my self, someone alien approached. I turned my head and heard the person say:

"Then we must finish here and separate for ever. You know it must be. There is no other way."

Barbara tossed her head. Her hair, a pale cloud in the wind, fell over her forehead. Forcing myself to keep my eyes and ears open to common sense, I said:

"We dare not, we must not, see each other again."

Barbara frowned painfully. I stretched out my free hand in the hope, perhaps, that she would rescue me from myself. The sound of her voice surprised me by its ferocity.

"It's so unfair," she said.

Her lips were set hard. The grip of her hand was released from my arm, and she took a step backwards. Her words rattled around my ears. Her clenched fists and bloodless face shook me from a dream. I had known the truth but now I was possessed by it, and the harsh reality I had been trying to escape from flowed from head to heart. I stared at her expressionless face and I knew my heart was right. Straightening my shoulders and facing Barbara squarely, I held down a shuddering breath and said as calmly as I could:

"I'll leave you now."

I could hardly believe my own words. Did they represent an act of betrayal or an act of love and courage? I felt that the alien person had taken hold of my tongue and was controlling it against my will. The decision was made, and the words were out in the blink of an eye: *I shall leave you now*. I dimly recognised this line. Perhaps I had practised it in some forgotten dream, but the words forced me to screw up my eyes in protection from a screeching in my ears.

Something warm poured down my cheeks. I was about to turn my back on Barbara when I felt the softness of her hand stroking the tears from my face. And I saw, for the first time, the purple hollows under her eyes, and I heard a sharp intake of breath, which she held for several seconds while she suffocated in her own emotions.

We stared at each other for an eternity, and slowly her face engraved itself on my memory, and I knew that memory itself was now her tombstone.

Straightening up, I scanned the forest in front of me. I looked with hopeful eyes at the path that disappeared into a wall of trees and for some sign or footstep in the soft accumulation of seasons on the forest floor. I looked at the shapes and shades in front of me, but there was only an empty and rustling stillness, the occasional cry of warning from animals unseen, and the trees that bent, swayed and danced to the music of the wind. The wind carried with it the smell of the pines, and the sweet smell of generations of leaves in decay. So extensive was the brooding stillness that it was difficult to imagine a human foot had touched the forest leaves. But I knew there was someone there. There would always be someone there.

I set off in a rush. I did not know where the path would take me, and I was unsure as to what I would do or say when I got there. I was sure only of vagueness and uncertainty. We had arrived at the house at around twelve o'clock. If my grandfather had left one hour earlier, he might already be at the grave. I tried to convince myself that he had taken the gun to protect himself from the creatures of the forest. But somehow I knew he intended to end a life that had started at the grave. I hoped he would wait until dusk before pulling the trigger. This was my only hope, my chance to reach Eisenmann before he put a bullet in his head.

At first, the silence of nature rested me after the frantic drive up the Hildrizhausen road. Slanting streaks of sunlight revealed every wrinkle of the tree trunks and the green of the moss. It all flashed past as I took the forest at a run. I hoped to make good time in the cool of the winter afternoon. I estimated that if I hurried, it might take thirty minutes to arrive in Goldbachtal. As I slowed to a jog, I lost track of my surroundings. There was only the thumping of my heart, the pain in my calves, and the sound of Barbara's voice in my ear: *According to necessity, according to necessity.*

I realised that I was breathing in time to these words. They were set to a catchy tune that I sucked into my lungs and breathed out through my teeth: *Where things come, where things come, into being, into being.*

Stumbling to a halt, I rested my full weight against a tree and eased my straining body. At any time, I expected to hear a report. But the sound of a shot filled the forest by its very absence. I leaned forward and cocked my head. There was only the occasional and remotest whistling in the trees above, the rippling of water beside me, and the hollow and ghostly sound of a bird calling to its mate. I refocused my gaze on the track. It was clearly visible but I saw no sign, no footstep that suggested someone had recently passed. The forest was full of silent and solitary ghosts.

Setting off again, I breathed in time to Barbara's words. My breathing was like a train over the sleepers: *So they must also, so they must also, go to earth, go to earth.*

I decided to cut off a loop in the path and take a short cut through the trees. After a few minutes, I pulled up with a start. Something in front of me had moved. I tried to focus, but I was breathing hard, and my eyes were watering and distorting my vision. I looked long into that cold December afternoon, and the forest seemed to stir in its winter sleep. There in the trees and amongst the branches was a deer.

It was standing motionless, its head to one side as though it knew that somewhere there was danger. I slumped against a tree and watched the animal while I tried to regain my strength. Before long, the deer dashed off into the depths of the forest. I looked out for the nearest gap in the undergrowth and set off towards it. Soon, I was stumbling. My feet and ankles contorted on the uneven ground. I was close to exhaustion. No sooner had I emerged from one gap than I saw the next one in front of me. Like the runner in a nightmare, my body would not respond to my will.

I had forgotten about the hurricane. Not all the trees were standing. Sometimes I had to pick my way through a wall of two or three trees that had fallen one across the other. More than once, my foot slipped painfully between hidden roots, and when I broke through one wall, I was simply confronted with another.

Scratched and bleeding, I eventually emerged in a larger space. I fell to my knees and tried to catch my breath. In this desolation of fallen pines, I was on a low mound about five feet from the forest floor. From this vantage point I was able to see where the trees ended and the valley began. I knew this place. I had been here before.

From the corner of my eye, I saw a flash of light. It was the light of the sun, sinking through the distant trees but glinting off something metallic. I saw him then. My grandfather was standing to attention by the side of an upturned tree. At his feet was the turned earth of the soldier's grave. The sun had reflected off an object he had in his hand. I tried to shout but my mouth was so dry I simply let out a pathetic croak.

"No, please wait. No."

I jumped up and broke through the trees that stooped over me. The ground slid away, and I slipped. Catching my foot on a root, I fell headlong to earth. Grunting and spitting with frustration, I brought the flat of my hand down hard against the ground: *Where they begin, where they begin, so they go to earth, go to earth.*

I heard the words with every breath until I gasped like a helpless man drowning. I could strain every muscle, and stretch every sinew to breaking point. I could suck the oxygen from every beat of the heart, but I would never reach him in time. I cupped a hand over my mouth and attempted to cry out again.

"No. Wait for me. We have to talk. No, please no."

I shouted again and again until I fell to my knees. Choking for breath, I heard my cries echo and fade away in the late-afternoon light. Raising my head like a beaten dog, I saw the man move his arm upwards in a saluting gesture. He swayed beneath the upturned root rising massively over him. The sun hung in the trees, and silence hung in the forest. The world itself was holding its breath.

With one last effort I jumped forward and half-ran and half-stumbled across the grass.

"No," I cried. "Wait for me. There's still time ... a little longer … please wait for me …"

I was about five metres from him when he must have heard me. He hesitated and lowered his hand. He turned to me and our eyes met. I stopped, almost hypnotised by his stare. His eyes held a glimmer of recognition. I looked at him in astonishment. There was a peaceful, almost serene expression on his face. He raised one arm and held it towards me. For a moment, I obeyed. For just that moment,

I had no present and no future. My past rolled out before me, beyond my mother, beyond my conception and on to this man who stood in front of me and who linked me forever with this forest. My grandfather gave a veiled smile and a smothered chuckle.

"I almost forgot," he said "that everything must return from where it came."

I was still on my knees when he raised the gun to his temple. Then I sprang. My chest hit his with a force that locked us together. Our hearts beat one against the other, and in short and gasping whispers we breathed and lived as one. I caught a glimpse of light, the pale light of eternity slowly dying in his eyes, and something exploded against my head. Darkness closed in. I fell forward and as I dropped there was movement in the corner of my eye. I saw a large, black bird winging wildly out of the forest. Then I saw another, and then another, until the sky was alive with beating wings, and the squawking of birds in fear. Some animal, large and brown, ran into the trees. I opened my mouth to shout, but the air jolted from my chest as I struck the ground. The edges of darkness drew in. As I lost consciousness, I at first mistook the roar for a jet plane passing across the sky. It was an angry sound, monstrous and untamed. The sound rebounded around the valley, and I knew, as blackness finally closed in, that it was the echo of a pistol shot. I knew that the man who had pulled the trigger would be laid out beside me on the grave. Our blood was seeping into the earth. My blood, Barbara's blood and Eisenmann's blood, gone to earth together.

*

I had no idea how long I lay unconscious. He must have hit me hard for when I came to, I could do nothing except sit on my haunches, rest my hands on my knees and hang my head. I was unable to see my grandfather's body. I rose unsteadily to my feet and staggered backwards into the forest. I came to a shuddering halt as my head struck a tree. The earth seemed to stir under me again, and I fell on the pine needles, tearing my jacket as I did so. My thoughts were in turmoil. It was my fault. Here yesterday. Too late today. Too late for my mother. Too late for Joerg Eisenmann. Too late for Barbara and me. Now, too late to change anything.

I must have blacked out or nodded off. And as I lay unconscious, something or someone murmured to me from a faintly familiar but distant world. The words came soft, low and persistent: *What was it all for ... what was the point? If they forget us then why did we suffer? What then, was the point of it all ...?*

I awoke silently to half-consciousness. It was dark, and the sky was twinkling with stars, and the moon hung low. The chill evening breeze found the tear in the jacket. The breeze cut into my body like a knife. I was stiff with cold, and I drifted in and out of consciousness. From closer at hand, there was a sound of something ferocious. It was snarling, whining and slobbering in the blackness. I froze in terror. It was the monster from the forest. I had failed in my bid to save Joerg Eisenmann. If I had not come, he would still be alive. I was responsible for his death and now I was going to pay the ultimate penalty. I would finish in pieces like the women in the marketplace in Nüfringen. I kicked desperately at the ground. At any moment, I would feel the fangs in my thigh, the groin ripped apart. My heel had already made a deep furrow in the pine needles when torchlight swept over the ground in front of me.

I caught a brief vision of an animal straining at a leash. I saw gnashing teeth, a salivating mouth, and muscles rippling. Then, as quickly as it had appeared, the animal was swallowed up in the blackness. The light from blazing torches burned like monstrous eyes through the night. Horrified at this apparition, I was trying to scramble up, to give life to frozen and lifeless legs and to escape when I heard a voice.

"Keep back there," it shouted harshly. "Keep back."

A tall and dark figure moved forward through the trees. Behind this figure, babbling and mindless, was a group. The group huddled under an umbrella of lanterns, and whispered soft and low like the whispering of my dreams. As the dark figure neared, I saw it had a drooping walrus moustache and a peaked cap, and it was holding something in the hand. It was a pistol.

"Mr Slater," said a voice. "Mr Slater, you did not listen to us. You could be in serious trouble."

At first, I wanted to laugh and tell them I was all right. The crowd surged forward.

"Stand back there," shouted the policeman.

At once there was a burst of activity. Hands reached out to me. I dug my heels into the earth but I was soon floundering. Someone grabbed me from beneath the shoulders. I raised my arms and turned my head. It was too late. They had come. Those skeletal shapes in ragged clothes had found me. Groping hands hauled me to my feet.

"You were warned," the policeman said, "and you did not listen."

I staggered and nodded.

"Do not complain if these people punish you," the policeman said. "I have told you. We must not, we can not, interfere with their truth."

There was a sharp pain behind the knee and the earth came up to meet me. A brief vision of faces in the lantern light: the priest, the hotel keeper, Nadia.

"You must leave. Never interfere with their truth. If you do, you will be punished further."

Then there was the figure in jeans. Her hair stroked at her temples. The moonlight painted her face with calm so that it was beautiful. Now I would be all right. She could help me. I was struggling to my feet when I saw the man beside her. It was the priest. He had an arm draped over her shoulders. I fell back with a groan.

"Barbara," I said.

She backed away from me, muttering something in German.

I thought I saw her crying.

This time, she would not be back.

There was blackness.

Herrenberger Zeitung

31 December: English version

The town of Herrenberg was saddened by the death two days ago of Joerg Eisenmann. He was 73. It was well known that Eisenmann has been under intense pressure recently to step down from the company he set up more than fifty years ago. Eisenmann GmbH was the very reason for his existence. A proud man, it is thought that this pressure combined with old age and ill-health finally prompted him to take his own life while he was still on top. Franz Eisenmann, his son, stated that: "He would be unable to see his life's work taken from him and that taking his own life was entirely in keeping with his character."

Throughout his life, Mr Eisenmann has shown himself to be a great friend of Herrenberg and the surrounding villages. Numerous restorations have been funded by him including the churches in Herrenberg and Hildrizhausen, and the centre of the village of Nüfringen, which was destroyed in a bombing raid in 1945.

Franz Eisenmann said that as a child, he often heard his father quoting from the classics. There was one quote the elder Eisenmann was fond of making, and he put it on the memorial stone to the killed and missing of the war. The memorial, which stands in the main square of Nüfringen, was funded by him, and was to include all deaths and all nationalities. To make the point, Joerg Eisenmann had the inscription put in French, English and German.

233

"Ou les choses ont leur naissance, la aussi elles doivent sombrer, selon la necessite. Car elles doivent expier et etre jugees pour leur injustice, selon l'ordre du temps."

"According to necessity, where things come into being, so must they also go to earth, for they must die and be judged according to the order of time."

Such a tribute, says Franz Eisenmann, might also have been written about his father.

Joerg Eisenmann 1926 – 1999.

Epilogue

Stuttgart Airport. 2 January 2000. Afternoon

"Joerg Eisenmann had been under the microscope for some weeks," the Chief Inspector said. "Some people in his company were making allegations of a dubious wartime past. These allegations had to be examined. It is our duty, as good Germans, to root out and destroy the evils of our past."

We were sitting in a police car outside Stuttgart Airport's Terminal 1. Hart was leaning against the door in the front passenger seat, and half-turned towards me.

"We looked at the man's background. He arrived here in Herrenberg in 1945. In a sense, that is when his life began. There are no records before that."

He turned his head and looked through the windscreen at a jet plane taking off. The roar of the engines came from everywhere and nowhere at the same time as though it filled the air itself. Maximilian Hart patiently waited for the plane to disappear, but he allowed his head to remain angled towards the clouds.

"However, the lack of records is not unusual," he said. "In 1945, millions were uprooted and looking for a place to settle. Records had been destroyed during the war. Eisenmann claimed he came from the east part of Germany. Think of it Mr Slater. Even if you had managed to survive the bombing raid on, say, Dresden, for example, how could you prove or disprove an identity if all those pieces of paper - birth certificate, marriage certificate, school reports, and so on and so on, had been destroyed in the fire storm?"

I leaned against the door in the back seat, and kept my neck and shoulders still. My head throbbed painfully whenever I moved it, and the pain made me irritable.

"I've no idea," I said.

Chief Inspector Hart had retreated behind a speculative mask and stood on his distant pedestal.

"You would have no identity," he said. "In a sense, as one of millions, you were free to create your own."

Hart had not varied his tone. It was as though he had asserted his rights over the whole matter and would not accept any remarks or words of dissent. He said:

"And create his own identity was exactly what Eisenmann did."

This assumption of ownership and his detached speculation somehow trivialised my own involvement and my throbbing head. I was stung into action and lunged to take hold of what was mine.

"But how did you know," I said, "that Spohr and Eisenmann were the same person? And what are you going to do about it?"

At first, the policeman did not even lower his head. He appeared to give himself the time to reflect on what I had asked. When he was ready, he let his head fall forward and met my provocation with a defiance of his own.

"We do not know that," he said quietly. "Nobody knows this."

The temptation to sharply react was tempered only by the need not to aggravate an already aching head. I said:

"And how did Schneider die? Did Eisenmann kill him?"

Hart once again raised his eyes to the sky. He took a long breath and breathed slowly out again through his nose in a way that suggested a pained tolerance.

"Again, we do not know. All the evidence is circumstantial. We do know that Schneider made one telephone call while he was at your hotel. All external telephone calls are recorded on the hotel's computer system. For payment purposes, you understand. I checked the number, and we know that Schneider telephoned Eisenmann. Why did he do this?"

The police inspector shook his head and steepled his hands under his chin.

"We don't really know," he said with a shrug. "Perhaps he wanted to buy a car. Who knows? My guess is that Schneider thought he recognised Spohr and arranged to meet him. Perhaps Schneider tried to blackmail him. We simply do not know. The only people who could help us are now dead."

I looked down at my watch to remind the policeman that I had a plane to catch.

"Yes," he said, "just a minute."

He looked through the car window and reflected a moment. Lowering his hands from his chin, he let them hang at his sides almost in a gesture of defeat. Then he said:

"We should be thankful that death is the one event in our lives that we can not experience. I told you before that in a sense death really does not exist for us."

All this was just a preamble. I felt that Hart was about to attempt the difficult crossing of an obstacle. I decided to nudge him over.

"That does not help those who are left behind to mourn," I said.

The policeman's eyelids fluttered.

"Oh, you are wrong," he said. "It helps us very much indeed."

I looked again at my watch. Chief Inspector Hart leaned over the front seat and put his hand on my arm. He briefly closed his hunting-dog eyes. He seemed to be willing himself to talk.

"Listen," he said. "I spoke to Joerg Eisenmann four days ago. I told him what was going on. I explained to him that his life was under scrutiny. We both knew that any such investigation would finish him. DaimlerChrysler would have removed him without hesitation."

He took his hand from my arm, then changed his mind and put it back. He seemed to have made some kind of decision.

"I told him it was my duty," he said, "to follow my investigation to the bitter end."

He pulled at his moustache. His mouth twitched and revealed points of his upper teeth.

"We spoke it all through. We spoke through the next act, so to speak."

"And?"

A flicker of doubt passed over Hart's face.

"And, he took the only dignified exit he could."

I stared at him with growing resentment. I felt that in some way, this policeman had betrayed me.

"So now," I said, "things will stay as they were."

The ironic tone of my voice was lost on Maximilian Hart. He simply nodded at me.

"Correct," he said. "Joerg Eisenmann committed suicide. But he did so because his position in his own creation was now untenable. Schneider died of heart failure. And I shall put this in my report."

Hart's expression was proud and challenging. His moustache stood upright and bristling.

"And Martin Spohr," he said, "died in 1945. Ask those people in the forest, those villagers with me when I found you four days ago. You remember?"

I rubbed my bandaged head and nodded.

"Do you know what they were doing there? They had come to repair the grave. Today, in two hours time, they are to hold another service there. They intend to bless the spot again. You know, some things are bigger than us. Some things must not change. We do not have the right to tell people otherwise. And anyway, they would not believe us. Eisenmann knew this. I told you ..."

A deafening roar filled the air as another plane took to the sky. I was barely able to catch the policeman's final words.

"... death was the best thing ... only thing that could happen, really."

Hart stared at me. Was it my imagination or was there some hint of a deeper emotion reflected in his eyes? He said:

"And there are other things to think about."

"Like what?"

"Like the proposed second runway at this airport. It would bring untold misery to thousand of farmers. Not to mention the additional pollution and what that would mean for our children."

I opened the car door and got out. The driver was already standing by the boot. My bag was at his feet. I picked up the bag, and Hart's head appeared through the car window.

"One more question," he said. "Do you think your mother knew?"

"About what?" I said.

"About these bigger things. About the things that should be left alone."

I shrugged.

"I really can't say."

The Chief Inspector nodded.

"It just crossed my mind, Martin," he said. "After all, you and Martin Spohr share the same name."

"Coincidence," I said. "Anyway, it does not matter now."

The policeman raised his head and peered at the sky.

"Mr Slater," he said, "you have had a hard time of it in the last ten days or so. How do you feel now?"

"Remarkably well," I said. "But my head hurts."

A hand appeared through the car window.

"So good bye Mr Slater," the policeman said. "And when you arrive back in England, have a doctor examine your head."

I took his hand and something passed from his palm into mine. The car drove off and, looking down, I saw I was holding a piece of folded paper.

*

I surrendered my suitcases at check-in and made my way directly to the departure lounge. My flight was already boarding. I was left alone, holding my hand luggage. Through the huge, glass windows, I saw the moon, bending over the airport like a watchful mother. Was this the same moon that I had seen on the way up to the forest? Was this the moon that had cast its cold blue light over the rooftops of Herrenberg just days before?

At the gate, a woman in a blue uniform looked at me through lowered eyelids. Her head was slightly cocked to one side as if to say: *Do you not want to go home?*

I crossed the point of no return and, entering the bus, I was soon shuffling for space amongst the suits and newspapers. As I took the note from my pocket, I thought I heard the hours striking from some distant bell tower. I looked down and began to read.

Herrenberg, 01.01.2000

My dearest Martin

My head told me not to write this note but my heart has its way. After all that has happened, I want to say that one day, I hope we can be friends. I can not bear the thought that I shall never see you again. After all, we have a lot in common.

I am fine, and you must not worry about me. You might want to think about me as your plane flies over the Schönbuch Forest. On the second of January, at three o'clock, we shall hold a service at the soldier's grave in the forest. The villagers have repaired it and it is now as good as new.

Today I received two visits from our policeman. Of course he asked me whether father had left a suicide note. Unfortunately I had nothing to give him. But you should know that according to father's will, he is to be cremated, and that his ashes will be scattered in the Schönbuch Forest in the second week of the new millenium. This was his wish.

There is nothing we can do and nothing more to say. I hope and pray that God will always be there with you and that he will love and protect you wherever you go.

With all my love

Barbara.

Once on the plane, I shoved my coat into the overhead lockers and took my seat by the window. The increase in engine noise signalled take-off, and we took off eastwards and circled. I looked out through the window. In the distance I could see Stuttgart, its buildings cold and vague shapes in the wintry afternoon light. But far below and beneath the wings, quivering with unseen life, were the trees of the Schönbuch Forest. But it was the changing shapes and flashes of light in the spaces between the trees that held my gaze. There was sanctity about these spaces. They were bottomless hollows in which I saw the physical and the spiritual woven together, my past and my present existing side by side. The one could not be without the other.

My thoughts were interrupted by a sound at my shoulder. I felt suddenly suspended as if between two worlds. I held my breath, but I did not turn. I knew that if I did, I would see Barbara close beside me. She would always be there. I also knew that as my life went on, she would drop further and further away from me as others took her place. Then, I would have to turn round and peer into the distance, but I would always catch sight of her, of the hair threatening to fall over her forehead, of the slight arrogance of the uplifted chin. I knew that through the mist and the crowds of people that would push and pull in my memory, through all the sketches and all the outlines, Barbara would always shine through.

The light dimmed. Everything turned to grey and then the trees were gone, obscured by a great cloud. I closed my eyes and imagined that beneath me was the soldier's grave of the Schönbuch Forest. And beside it stood a group of people who had come to pay their respects to the dead. Amongst them was the girl who I had come to love and whose memory stood by me. Did she remember? Did she hear my plane flying overhead? Did she look up and offer one last wave or did she think that the noise was the sound of the wind blowing through the forest? But perhaps, just perhaps, and only for a second, she mistook the sound of the plane for a more distant sound, that animal roar from the heart of the forest, that echo of pain, resentment and sorrow from the darkness of a forgotten time.

Lightning Source UK Ltd.
Milton Keynes UK
UKOW05f1916290614

234256UK00001B/2/A

9 780755 210459